I0670759

Where Angels Sing

John Stamp

Dedication

This book is dedicated first to my mom. She has read every line of everything I've ever written, to include the sixty-five page "novel" I hand wrote instead of paying attention in sixth grade math class. She didn't have the heart to tell me how bad it was then and I still can't get any objective criticism from her now. Thanks Mom.

Chapter One

Six Months Following the Death of Poppy Montague

Detective Ben Wilke pulled off the access road adjacent to the Executive Terminal at the Charleston International Airport and turned off the engine. The atmosphere inside the cab of his 2008 Toyota Tacoma thickened immediately in the South Carolina morning sun. He slouched in the driver's seat and strained to see as his two targets pulled up to their awaiting Bombardier Global 700.

The jet was white with a general blue pin striping along its horizontal axis. Ben grabbed a monocular from his dashboard and peered at the tail number: AB-061279. He jotted the number on a dog-eared and abused notebook he balanced on his thigh. The main cabin door was open and a short stairway extended from the fuselage to the tarmac. At the top of the stairs, a blonde with thick-framed glasses dressed in a form-fitting, barely professional flight attendants' uniform awaited her passengers.

Wilke shifted his sights to the gleaming black Chevrolet Suburban that had thick tinted windows. The driver, whose face was familiar after so many hours of surveillance, was Charles Thispen, Congressman Andrew Tulley's full time driver/concierge. He was circling the rear of the vehicle to the passenger door. He held the door as Andrew Tulley Jr. slid from the vehicle and looked around the tarmac with a general aversion. His mouth was tight, his gaunt cheeks clenched, and his eyes were hidden behind a pair of dark Ray Ban sunglasses. His hair was askew, and the short sleeve button down Bermuda shirt he wore was rumpled. The man who he'd been following for a little over a month had been steadily losing weight. Wilke guessed it was the steady diet of booze and pills, and the fact that he had become a pariah of the Low country aristocracy that was slowly eating away at him.

Movement toward the hood of the Suburban drew Wilke's attention from what was left of the man, whose cornea he once dislocated with the muzzle of a Glock, to the elder Tulley. Congressman Andrew Tulley wore a dark blazer over a white collared shirt and khaki's. His silver hair was thinning and his countenance was brusque as he snapped an unheard complaint in the direction of Thispen who guided him by the elbow toward the plane. Tulley hobbled on an ebony cane, shuffling painfully, plagued by a back injury he sustained when a truck transporting illegal weapons was detonated at a transit yard near the Port of Charleston.

Tulley, who was the cover man in a conspiracy to sell the illegal assault weapons to Third World warlords, was under indictment for a slew of corruption and fraud charges stemming from the weapons investigation. To date, a team of lawyers had managed to slow the progress of his adjudication through various legal processes. The man batted at Thispen as he climbed the stairs toward his waiting host.

The sight of the Tulleys boarding the jet made Wilke's neck burn. The two men were his only link to a conspiracy that had resulted in the death of one of the members of his Narcotics Unit, the woman he was in love with. It had taken him almost four months to deal with the reality of Poppy Montague's death. Despite the medical facts surrounding her death, Ben Wilke was only moments away from her when she died, and he had not been able to save her. Though several of the people involved in her death had paid with their lives that day, there were more out there. The leaders of the conspiracy—Tulley among them— still roamed free, enjoying their lives while Poppy rested in a modest West Ashley cemetery. He had thought about killing the two men he watched boarding the private jet. Once he had managed to climb out of the bottle, that is. Revenge—or more precisely, justice—was all that he could think of. But he knew Poppy would never have forgiven him if he threw his life away in a fit of rage. So here Ben Wilke was, running an investigation. Like any other case, he was following one rung in the organizational ladder to lead him to the next. The only problem was that the rung he was chasing was about to board a private jet for parts unknown, leaving him in the dust.

***

Andrea Van Reimer, code named One, waited at the top of the stairs. A practiced smile trimmed her sharp features under a wig of platinum blonde and a pair of faux eyeglasses. She watched the old man shuffling up the stairs, cursing and grumbling accompanying each painful step. She enjoyed the view. Andrew Tulley was a piece of shit in the most efficient form of description. The man had been a congressman, an astoundingly greedy and entitled congressman, who was now facing, and literally fleeing, a looming indictment. One had pulled the short straw approximately six months ago when Central activated her and her partner, a cover man she knew only as 3-1, to play nursemaid to the broken old man and his drug-addled son.

She smiled broadly as the old man finally met her at the platform. She stepped back and welcomed him aboard.

"What is the big Goddamned rush?" he spat.

"The organization wanted to remove you from any undue strain brought on by the state of your current legal status. We believe it best for you to spend the next seven days in Aruba while certain negotiations are finalized."

The old man pursed his lips. His eyes studied her up and down slowly. He lingered as if trying to see through her form-fitting blazer and blouse. He raised an eyebrow and sneered with a lopsided twist of his mouth before moving to the spacious and expensively upholstered cabin. "SCOTCH!" he bellowed, "And let's go!"

"Right away, Congressman," One answered crisply. She watched Tulley Jr. slough his way to meet her inside the cabin door. He carried a leather shoulder bag which he held out only a second before letting go. She caught it by the strap before the bag hit the floor. Tulley Jr. didn't look at her. He simply turned toward the cabin and fell into a plush captain's chair on the opposite side of the plane from his father. She watched him for a moment to ensure they both were in their seats before taking a final look at the Tulleys' driver.

The driver tapped his chest once, then held three fingers over his left shoulder a moment before acting as if he were brushing away lint.

"3-1, did you copy that?" she asked. An inner ear transceiver transmitted her low tone to 3-1 who was readying the plane for takeoff.

"Copy. Vehicle matches the description of Subject Four. Too far away for positive ID."

One nodded to the driver who stood at the door of his Suburban before she closed the cabin door.

***

"Scotch?"

The jet was taxiing into position. One held a tray carrying two crystal tumblers, each containing two fingers of golden brown liquid which moved gently at the motion of the aircraft.

Tulley took one of the drinks and threw the expensive alcohol back, then grabbed the other as Tulley Jr. watched. The old man eyed his son as he sipped on the second drink that would have been offered to him. The younger Tulley did not try to hide a look of pure disgust. He watched the elderly man slurp and smack his lips as he reclined in the captain's chair and put his loafers up on a polished marble tabletop.

"What's the…"

"Enjoy, Congressman," One said, silencing him.

A moment later One offered the same selection of fine spirits to Tulley Jr. The man stared out the small cabin window. Dark eyes, shadowed and sunken, observed the marsh and trees that lined the asphalt runway. The greens and browns began to blur as the aircraft picked up speed.

"Scotch?" One offered Tulley Jr. a matching drink.

"Just set it down," he grumbled. "I don't get why I have to leave with him. I'm not under indictment." Tulley Jr. raised his voice to announce the last phrase. He was greeted by only heavy and slow breathing. The old bastard was already sleeping and the jet had yet to reach the air.

"The organization believes it best if you present a united front. We understand how difficult this has been for both of you. I have been assured that this will come to an end."

Tully Jr. did not react; he only stared out the window. He did not reach for his drink.

One moved to the small galley and held on as the jet achieved flight. She looked over her charges.

The old man was out, snoring as his fat body jiggled back and forth as the jet passed through turbulence. The younger Tulley stared into space.

An hour later, Tulley Jr. still gazed blankly out the window. The ocean below was streaked in sunlight and dappled in crests and troughs as the wind pushed waves to the East.

One was stationed at the tail end of the cabin where the small galley was blocked off by a heavy curtain. Through the break between the bulkhead and the fabric, she had watched Tulley Jr. for the last hour. The man, a shriveled and shrunken husk of the playboy his file described, only stared out the portal. He hadn't touched the drink. Senior, on the other hand, was deeply sedated. The old man hadn't so much as moved since giving himself a double dose of a sedative normally used to immobilize livestock. For a while Tulley Senior's snoring had stopped, and his breathing had slowed. One had wondered if he overdosed until the man groaned and coughed. He shifted his massive weight in the poor captain's chair before sliding back into a nasally rest.

The miniscule microphone in her ear clicked twice. The sound was so sudden in the quiet of the cabin that she jumped, causing Tulley Jr. to look her way. *Two minutes*, she told herself.

With a broad smile and another silver tray in hand, she approached Junior who was still watching her.

"I almost dropped the whole thing," she said playfully. "Spooked myself."

On the tray was an assortment of cheeses and breads.

Tulley looked to the tray dismissively. "Just refresh my drink."

"It's too late for drinks, Mr. Tulley." One's tone was matter of fact, her syllables clipped.

Tulley Jr. looked up at her, extending his head in question while perfectly exposing his carotid artery. With her free hand, One jabbed him in the neck with a gas propelled delivery system. Whereas with the spiked drinks, the transition to sedation would have been quieter and smoother while the sedative absorbed into the system through his blood stream. The direct delivery of horse tranquilizer into his blood stream limited Andrew Tulley Jr. to only a moment to grasp what was happening to him before his world started spinning. One watched as his eyes lolled and his muscles slackened. She pushed him to the portal he so enjoyed and was three steps toward the galley before she heard him vomit on himself.

She retrieved a compact parachute harness and dropped it to the deck from a small closet near the cockpit. She had already shed her heels. Next came the tight polyester skirt, her tightly muscled backside wriggling out of the horrible uniform and exposing white lace panties. The bra covering her proportional and firm breasts matched. She stood exposed to her two victims for barely a moment. Out of the closet, she retrieved a set of khaki pants and long sleeved shirt. Boots replaced her heels and the blonde wig and thick rimmed glasses completed the pile of accoutrements at her feet. She was just clipping the final straps of the harness to her when 3-1 emerged from the cockpit. He was similarly dressed, and likewise outfitted with a parachute.

"One minute," he said.

She nodded and braced herself against the bulkhead as she released the lock and opened the main cabin door. An incredible whoosh of wind filled the cabin. Anything not secured began flitting and dancing around the plane. After the atmosphere of the jet equalized, she pointed at 3-1 who nodded and slid past her into the sky. Before jumping herself, she checked the cabin one final time. She was surprised to find Tulley Jr. supine in the center of the cabin. Vomitus dribbled from his chin, one hand outstretched. He could barely lift his head.

"Why?" he cried.

One could hardly hear him over the scream of the wind whipping past the open cabin door. *All that effort for such a stupid question,* she thought. She looked him in the eye as she stepped to the door.

"Does it matter?" she asked. She stepped out of the vehicle into nothingness. The familiar twisting of her insides, and fluttering of her heart. The sensations that always accompanied free fall entertained her and she could not help but smile as she took in the world laid out before her.

***

The two operatives landed in the gently rolling Atlantic Ocean twenty meters off the stern of a sleek, gleaming white motor yacht. One was out of the water less than a minute before a crewman handed her an encrypted satellite phone. She studied the smoking contrail left by the Tulleys' jet, following the line of vapor from twenty thousand feet to where a small charge, set to a delayed timer, detonated in the turbine. It was not a large charge, but it was enough to incapacitate the aircraft leaving a trail of smoke from the sky to the water, just on the horizon from where she stood.

A feminine voice on the other end of the satellite connection spoke, stark and stiff, to the point of sounding unnatural. "Report."

"Success," she returned plainly, "However, we believe Subject Four had the targets under surveillance prior to departure."

There was a pause. One waited, outwardly casual, while inside she continuously asked herself if there was anything left undone, if she had missed some minor detail that was hampering the mission at hand. In her experience leaving something out when briefing central, even the minutest detail, was a virtual death sentence for an officer on field assignment; especially when it was some detail that Central was provided by another source. The voice disrupted her after a few moments.

"Surreptitious inquiry ordered for Subject Four, top priority."

"Understood," One responded.

The line went dead.

Chapter Two

3-1 was stationed a block down Water Street, to the south of the historic Charleston row house, where One stood poised to make entry. Finished in a brilliant white, the wood sided, narrow two-story home that was over a hundred years old stood dark and quiet. A tracker long ago placed on the frame of Detective Ben Wilke's vehicle showed him on Folly Beach. Prior research and surveillance logs suggested this activity, a relatively new development for the police officer, provided her approximately an hour to complete her inquiry into Ben Wilke, Subject Four.

One sat in the shadows, merging with a hedgerow in the adjoining space between the home Wilke rented from the retired widow of an intracranial surgeon whose permanent home was in Raleigh, North Carolina. One had gone through his and the rest of the named subject's records and found no signs of supplemental income that would support owning a home like this one. She took a tentative step forward and listened, extending her senses that they might alert her to an oncoming threat, but none greeted her. In less than a minute, she was across the driveway, up the brittle wood stairs, and in the front door. She was silent in her execution.

Subject Four had no security system, and no animals to impede her scouting mission. She moved quietly and efficiently from room to room studying the layout, the general state of disarray the home of a bachelor remained in, and other things left out or put on display that would assist in her assessment. There were very few pictures or art decorating the home. A heavy bag on a stand stood in the center of a room where a normal home would house a dinner table. The refrigerator held condiments, lunch meat, and a few Styrofoam take out containers. She swept the downstairs, and as she climbed the stairs the microphone in her ear chirped.

"Five minutes," 3-1 announced in a pre-planned communication.

She did not respond.

There were three bedrooms in the home. One was clearly where the subject slept. A queen-sized bed was in disarray, clothes were strewn everywhere. A single picture sat on the right-hand nightstand, the side of the bed closest to the door. One recognized the photo of Poppy Montague immediately. Having intimate knowledge of the events that led to her current mission, she knew Subject Four and Montague had shared a surreptitious romantic relationship, and that Subject Four was the person to find Montague's body during a disastrous failure of an operation almost a year ago.

The second bedroom was a clutter of boxes and bags One supposed were household materials Subject Four had not unpacked. According to her records, Subject Four had assumed residence in the home over two years ago. After a cursory look through a couple of the more obvious boxes, she noted nothing of value and moved on.

The third room on the second floor gave One pause. When she opened the door she at once stopped in her tracks, her face aglow with the soft blue light of a patiently waiting flat screen monitor. It wasn't the sudden light that had stopped the operative. It was the wall in front of the computer and modest foldout table that held the equipment. The room was stark, with no other furniture or decoration. A simple table, chair, and computer system in the center facing a wall littered with photos, reports, and a series of lines connecting one to the other. In the center of the wall were two photos, the Tulley's, both Senior and Junior. Lines ran between media and investigative reports, and some scribbles on notebook paper pinned to the wall. She followed the flow of connecting lines to other reports or photos. There were images she recognized, faces of deceased operatives from the previous operation. She studied those and found, with a degree of relief, that the Subject had only been identified by their clandestine identification. Subject Four had not been able to penetrate and find true names or associations that lead back to the agency, as far as she could tell anyway.

Subject Four had connected many dots between the recently deceased Tulley family and members associated with the organization. He was not far off from making some damaging connections. One wondered where Subject Four had come upon some of the information he received. Some of the more prominent names were associated with the arms smuggling operation, some ancillary connections to support personnel who had remained, to her knowledge, on the periphery of the failed Charleston operation. She had not made it from the obvious information covering the wall to the computer system before 3-1 made his next announcement.

"Ten minutes," he said.

That was her limit. She yearned to take the computer with her for further analysis but she had enough to report to Central without it. She left the room and started her exit. Putting an encrypted phone to her ear, she said, "Central." A few moments passed as she left the building before a reply came.

"Report," the cold female voice commanded.

"Probe of Subject Four complete. The Subject has compiled a detailed analysis of Subjects One and Two to include amassing potentially damaging leads to more compromising information."

The connection was quiet as the information was relayed to some unknown analyst or supervisor. When the voice came back there were only two words. Two words that would completely the change the dynamic of her current mission.

"Clean sweep," the voice ordered, and the line went dead.

Chapter Three

Eight Months Following the Death of Poppy Montague

The dead man didn't object to the flies crawling in and out of his mouth or over the hazy surface of his one remaining eye.

Tom Burgess knelt over the corpse, studying the dynamics of the wounds. In addition to the round he'd taken through the left eye, he was littered with defects to his abdomen. Burgess counted six wounds to the abdomen in addition to the one in the eye, and one more to the man's right knee. The man still clutched a lever action 30-30 in his right hand.

"How's your guy?" Burgess asked, rising to his feet.

Fred Young, Director of the South Carolina Department of Natural Resources, Law Enforcement Division, was standing over the body opposite Burgess. "He's holding up," Young drawled. "Life flight picked him up and got him to the trauma unit in Greenville."

Burgess nodded, "Did he say anything to you?"

"Nah," responded Young.

Not that you would tell me anyway, thought Burgess, without animosity. Whenever he caught a police shooting, things were awkward from the outset. *Half the time the cops think you're out to get them and the other half of the time the public thinks you're out to cover up a dirty shooting.*

Burgess's cell phone rang but he ignored it, again. Just as he had ignored the four previous phone calls from the South Carolina Law Enforcement Division (SLED) home office since arriving on scene a little more than a half hour ago. The drive alone to the remote point deep within the Sumter National Forest from his home outside Columbia had taken him three hours. Bureaucrats, admin folks who never carried a gun or worn a uniform, were in a panic. They wanted a statement from DNR Officer Aaron Krantz, age twenty-eight, who at 0630 this morning screamed for help over the DNR radio net. By the time the closest law enforcement units could reach him, the incident was long over. A deputy from Anderson County was the first to arrive and found Krantz huddled behind the rear bumper of his agency issued Ford F-150. He was using his belt as a tourniquet to staunch the flow of blood from a gunshot wound to his thigh.

"Body camera?" asked Burgess.

"Nope, we got his dash cam though."

Tom Burgess hated dash mounted camera video. He didn't know whether it was because almost every time he viewed one a police officer was getting killed, or if it was the fact that such surveillance gave him a big brother type chill. Someone was always watching over your shoulder to Monday morning quarterback an officer who had less than half a second to make the most important decision of his or her life. He saw the value in dash cams despite his personal dislike. More often than not, dash cams, and now body cameras, served as the silent witness that saved an officer's career from baseless claims of assault or some other wrongdoing. On the other hand, it was a sad state of affairs when society no longer trusted the word of the police.

Young opened a strong box mounted behind the rear seat of Krantz's F-150. Inside was nothing more than a sealed hard drive with two LED lights, one red and one green, and an SD slot in the center of its face. A small blue SD card was nestled in the slot. Young retrieved the card and handed it to Burgess. He attached a hub to an agency- issued tablet and inserted the SD card. The card had multiple files stored. Every time the police lights were activated on the F-150, the recording system activated and a record was kept of the police contact. Before playing the video, Burgess looked around the scene. The decedent's— Alan Wayne Moore—dilapidated old Chevrolet pickup was about twenty feet from the front bumper of the DNR vehicle. Moore's body was another fifty or so feet to the right of the truck.

"Not sure we're going to get much out of this," said Young.

Burgess didn't respond. He pressed play and stark shades of grey filled the screen. The tailgate of Moore's Chevy was plainly visible, but the background of trees and surrounding forest was ill-defined shadow. They heard Krantz report to Dispatch that he was in contact with a possible abandoned vehicle before he came into view, crossing slowly over the open ground between the two vehicles. The lights of the F-150 flashed in steady repetition and Krantz held his own flashlight in his left hand. He illuminated an empty cab and was just laying his right hand on the tailgate when the DNR officer jumped back.

"What the..." they heard him say.

A loud crack shattered the relative quiet of the forest and Krantz dropped to the ground with a scream. There was some unintelligible yelling that Burgess couldn't make out a split second before the muzzle flash of Krantz handgun ignited in rapid succession. Krantz's screams were drowned out as he fired from the ground, over and over. Burgess counted eight rounds fired in all. Then Krantz keyed his microphone and screamed for help. "Officer Down!" the young man screamed. "I've been shot!"

Burgess and Young watched in tense, helpless silence, while on the screen the DNR Officer experienced the worst moments of his life. The video stretched on for another ten minutes before Burgess pressed stop. He could finish viewing it back at the office where Krantz's peers wouldn't have to hear him crying and pleading, making deals with his creator if given the opportunity to live. He removed the SD card from the hub and secured it in a faraday bag he had retrieved from his evidence kit. Burgess slipped the evidence into the pocket of his blue jeans and looked again around the crime scene. Techs from SLED and a gathering of DNR officers milled about.

He stepped up to the rear of Moore's beat-up old pickup where one of his SLED agents was setting up a tripod to photo the contents of the truck bed. Careful to not disturb the crime scene investigator, who would be battling heat and bugs to document the scene for him long after he was gone. He studied the two female bodies in the rear.

The Pickens County units that had backed up Krantz identified the two women on sight. They were Moore's wife Tammy, and his mother-in-law Amber-Lynn. Seems the Moore's were well known in an area where only so many officers were available for a never-ending supply of dimwitted criminality. Burgess was able to gather that in the case of the Moore's, Alan was a fan of Wild Turkey, and once he was nice and lit, the only thing he liked better than more Wild Turkey was beating on his wife Tammy. The deputies told him that Tammy often gave as good as she got, and the whole family was on the sauce most of the time. "Guess old Alan wanted to play a little harder than she did last night," a deputy shrugged. Looking over the bodies, Amber-Lynn wore a night dress, while Tammy, who had carried a good hundred and eighty pounds on her five foot five-inch frame, had managed to find a pair of sorely stretched sweat pants with the word "Juicy" written across the ass. *What was it with giant rednecks using their asses as billboards?* he wondered. *Why did he kill Mom?* Burgess was not looking forward to interviewing the family and friends of Alan and Tammy Moore any more than he was looking forward to the forty-five minute drive further into the mountains of South Carolina. He'd been led to believe the Moore's lived like a clan in some backwoods trailer park. Tom Burgess's day had no end in sight, and it looked like every second would suck worse than the one before it.

"I gotta get going," he said to Young as he turned away from the dead women. He instinctively looked toward the corpse of Alan Moore, whose boots were just barely visible sticking out of the forest undergrowth, "I've got to get to the family so I can start some interviews."

The DNR Agent shook his hand. "Enjoy that. Anything comes up here, I'll give you a call."

"Thanks," said Burgess.

"Might not be a bad idea to take a deputy or two with you," Young added. "This family seems to take things kind of serious."

Chapter Four

The scenic, two-lane highway wound its way along the border of the Jocassee Gorge Wilderness Area. Any other time, Burgess would have enjoyed the view, happy to get a chance to come to the mountains and get away from the city. But today the views of the Appalachians held no appeal for him. He had to backtrack down Highway 178 toward Pickens, where he would pick up the first real road heading west. This would take him toward Six Mile, where the Moore clan lived. He was not looking forward to meeting them.

Traffic was relatively quiet for a Sunday afternoon. He was not overly familiar with this part of the state, but he did know that this stretch of road was popular with tourists and sightseers. He figured he could count it a win that he was not stuck behind some motor home doing twenty under the speed limit. The clock on his dash seemed to laugh at him as it clicked through the minutes, each incremental increase reminding him of the weekend slipping further and further away from him.

The miles clicked down and he rehearsed his death notification spiel in his head. *Sorry for your loss ma'am, or maybe sir.* He didn't know. *We don't have all the facts yet. Yes, we're doing everything we can to resolve this. No, I don't know what they're going to do with the truck.* It struck him as kind of funny that the hypothetical Moore relative was worried about getting the double murderer's truck back. Then it occurred to him—he needed a warrant.

Burgess was going to need to look over the Moore home. He retrieved his notebook from the seat next to him and flipped it open to the scratches he'd made with Moore's bio data. He got his cell phone off the center console and was happy to see he at least had a couple of bars. Reception was a bitch when you got up in these woods; he was almost in North Carolina. The crime scene was so remote they had needed a GPS fix to determine what state they were in. Looking out his windshield, he noticed that the highway was coming out of the dense forest and looked to be bordering a valley rich in trees, with rolling hills in the distance. He noted how sharply the land fell away from the road in places.

Tom Burgess knew what questions he was going to ask whatever kind of witnesses he might find at the Moore property. Despite the years he had working these kinds of cases and all the families he'd told that a loved one wasn't coming home, he still liked to write down a list of questions he planned to ask. It was both his ritual and battle plan. He never liked to go into an interview cold. Having that list in front of him, even though he could recite it from memory, put him in the mindset to work the case.

He scribbled with his right hand, notebook balanced on his knee, as he guided his dark blue Jeep Commander around a long, sweeping curve in the road. As the road once again straightened, he noticed a lone white BMW sedan sitting along the shoulder. A man dressed in khakis and a pastel lime green polo shirt leaned over the hood of the car. A map was stretched out over the white surface. Burgess checked his rearview mirror and noted the highway was devoid of other vehicles for as far as he could see. He slowed, pulling up parallel to the man, and rolled down the passenger side window.

"You OK?" he asked as the man turned.

He wore sunglasses, had short blonde hair, and was looking at a cell phone, "Yeah, just trying to get my bearings," the man said. "The service around here sucks." He tapped and swiped at his phone.

"The hills make it kind of touch and go," Burgess replied. "Where're you headed?"

"Trying to get to Clemson," he said. "I think I got a handle on it though. I found a map in the glove box."

"You'll keep heading down this highway til you get to Seneca. You might have to backtrack a little bit, but at least there you'll be able to get some service. Wish I could be more help, but I'm not from around here either."

"Thanks," the man said, slipping his phone into his pocket. "I'm good."

"All right," Burgess said. "Safe trip."

"You too."

He pulled off and saw the man gathering up his map. Burgess went back to his notes and watching the road. The terrain took him over hills and into valleys. At places the dips in the geography dropped like a cliff from the roadway. Five minutes after leaving the guy in the lime green polo, he noticed the white Beemer was behind him, so apparently the driver had taken his advice. The vehicle followed at a distance and they were the only two on the road.

Burgess had shifted his focus from the witness questions to logistics. Being a lone SLED agent meant he would need some resources from the local Sheriff's office when he got to town. He needed to see if he could get a deputy to join him at the Moore's place. For whatever reason, it put people at ease when a local uniform was with him. He also might need someone to do a crime scene. Waiting on the SLED crime scene unit on a Sunday was not much of an option. He hoped he could cover that with local assistance too.

RRRGH…

The engine surged, needle pinning the red line. The sudden shift in speed jostled him. He gripped the wheel with both hands, notebook and pen flying to the floorboard. *Shit.* Just what he needed, as the rpm's fell slowly back to cruise. He had visions of him sitting on the side of the road for hours while SLED tried to figure out how to get him roadside assistance on a Sunday. He looked over the dash. The instruments showed nothing. No check engine light, not overheating, not even the oil light. The Bluetooth symbol was flashing but he had long ago come to ignore the strange little blue light that was an utter mystery to him. Supposedly he could connect his phone to the SUV but he'd be damned if he knew how. With the manual in his lap he had tried to figure it out when he was first assigned the new ride and he still couldn't get it.

The Jeep lurched forward again, gaining speed as the rpm's rose at a clip. It wasn't a shocking acceleration this time but a steady charge.

"What the fuck?" Burgess breathed.

He let off the gas. Nothing. The vehicle crested eighty miles an hour.

He took his foot off the gas entirely and applied the brake. Depressing the brake pedal was like trying to crush a concrete block with his boot. A jolt of panic arced through him for just a minute but he suppressed it, mind racing. There was the parking brake, but he figured that might be disastrous at ninety-three miles an hour. Now the winding road was becoming a challenge for him. He guided the SUV around what normally would be a gentle sweeping bend. Now it was a hairpin turn at Watkins Glen. Burgess used up the entire two lanes, tires groaning against the load.

Taking the shift in hand, he braced himself and tried to slam it into neutral, but the electronic transmission did not engage.

105 miles an hour.

Reverse. Same result.

His breath was short and choppy as he tried the key, but the key would not disengage.

Then out of nowhere, the wheel leapt from his hands. It spun so fast that the faux leather burned the skin on his palms.

In his last moment, Tom Burgess watched helplessly as the road dropped away from his vehicle. He screamed as weightlessness and terror took him. His world spun as the machine barrel-rolled, sailing over the two hundred foot drop to the valley floor.

A few moments later, dust was still settling where Tom Burgess had flown off the road. The white BMW passed the dust cloud without even a tap of the brake lights.

A growing column of smoke climbed to the sky.

Chapter Five

Ten Months Following the Death of Poppy Montague

He still kept his curly black hair closely cropped to his head. But Max DeGuello had a beard now. He'd grown it out over time as a present to himself, after nearly a quarter century of service to the City of Charleston.

Though it wasn't completely his decision to hang it up, he couldn't say he was forced into retirement. During the shootout on John's Island the year before, he had suffered bullet wounds to his fibula, femur, and hip. His leg was now held together by a steel rod and an assortment of screws. The hip had been replaced. The department medical board had not believed him or his doctor, bribed with a case of Johnnie Walker Black to report to the board DeGuello was capable of full performance. Despite the fact that the doctor, the x-rays, and a persistent limp told another story, the board denied his request to return to duty.

A month after the ruling, Max DeGuello was a civilian for the first time in his adult life. A month after that, he was a full-time resident of the Conch Republic. He had a little house on Key West and a twenty-foot center console Boston Whaler he was still learning to pilot.

On most days, he was either haunting a downtown bar or cruising around the clear blue waters of Key West. Today, he slouched on the transom with a boonie cap over his eyes. A fishing pole dangled over the gunwale. Somewhere twenty or so feet below him, a mullet danced on the end of a hook. DeGuello was debating a nap in the mid-afternoon sun, but there was a little voice in the back of his head warning him he'd wash up in Haiti if he fell asleep on the water. Part of him didn't care. He had no place to be and no one to check in with. There was Carla, a vacationing teacher from Illinois who wanted to meet for drinks later, but even she was only a slight drawback toward shore.

The debate over to doze or not to doze was raging in his mind when the pole bounced in his hands. The sensation scared him from his daze and he jumped. "Shiiit," he yelped, grappling with the rod.

DeGuello was new to fishing, especially off-shore fishing. He felt something fighting at the other end of the line. He tucked the butt of the rod under his arm and started cranking on the reel. He'd had some luck with sea trout in the same area earlier in the week and he wondered if he'd stumbled onto another school. He struggled with the fish in a frantic give and take. One minute he'd be reeling for all his worth reclaiming line, and the next the fish would run. His reel would scream as the fish overcame the drag, putting distance between itself and the boat. Max had no idea how long the two fought, but eventually the fish tired and he could see his prize; a gunmetal grey torpedo of muscle. He hadn't been at it long enough to know what kind of shark he'd caught. The prehistoric fish was maybe four feet long and carried a black trim at the tips of its fins. The sea creature bucked and twisted ferociously, as it was hauled aboard in a net.

"Damn." He tried to catch his breath. With a pair of pliers, he wrestled the muscular fish to get the hook out of the side of its mouth. The shark's rough skin was like sandpaper in his hand and the thing bled profusely from its mouth. DeGuello's hands were shaking and were hard to control, but he finally managed to free the animal from the hook. He held it firm at the gills and the tail. He studied the predator for a moment.

"Beautiful fish," he said before dropping the shark over the side.

He scrubbed slime and blood from his hands, then turned to reach for a towel. When he did, an object in the distance caught his eye. A boat, one a little smaller than his, drifted in the water. Its occupants waved frantically in his direction. They were a good half mile away. Over the water he heard a faint, "Help!"

Max pulled anchor and fired the engine. The couple, a man with an open short sleeve button down shirt, Bermuda shorts and a pair of Costa Del Mar sunglasses, stopped waving as he approached. He was grinning kind of sheepishly. The female wore a cobalt blue string bikini. The material strained against her ample and firm chest. Max guessed her rack was fake, but he admired the work regardless. He was also thankful for the sunglasses he was wearing right then. He barely took his eyes off the woman as he greeted them. She had dark hair flowing over her tanned shoulders, which contrasted with her partner's tightly clipped blonde hair. She slithered languidly against the gunwale opposite him and rested her firm body on the side. She smiled at him as he cut the engine.

"You all need a hand?"

Max didn't catch the reply. A crisp pop and pinch preceded the twenty thousand volts that dropped him to the deck of his boat. Pressure, heat, and confusion was all he knew as the electricity flowed through him. He stared into the harsh sun through paralyzed and quivering eyes for what seemed an eternity. Finally, when the charge stopped, he lay curled up on the deck, gasping. He knew he had to move. He recognized he was under attack though his body would not respond.

Max DeGuello tried to take action but his deeply traumatized muscles only quivered. He fought to catch his breath. He felt rough hands cup his shoulders and drag him from the deck. He turned to kick and elbow at his adversary but was easily evaded. A jab of pain in the base of his neck felt like a bee sting. Almost instantly, what measly strength he did have in his limbs fell away. He felt himself losing consciousness as his knees banged the side of the boat and a rough shove sent him overboard into the cool blue water. The sedative injected into his carotid artery rendered Max DeGuello unconscious, floating face down in the sparkling southern edge of the Atlantic Ocean.

On the surface, a gasoline-soaked rag was twisted around the battery terminals and lit by a simple Bic lighter. The once-stranded couple held position twenty yards from the Boston Whaler until the fire melded the gas lines. After a brief time, the fuel tank ignited in a flash. The man pressed the throttle of his own launch, headed to the breakers. The little boat sped away, leaving a low column of smoke growing into the sky.

Chapter Six

Eleven Months Following the Death of Poppy Montague

Heiliea Williams sat on the stoop of the red brick row house of the St. Charles Place apartments. Her friends since before she could remember, Shela Adams and Luwanda Charles, were with her. Shela leaned against the crumbling stone slab to her left, and Luwanda sat beside her on the cracked stone, braiding Chevante's poofy black hair.

Chevante was Heiliea's three-year old daughter. Baby fat still clung to her small, button face cheeks. She was tired, Heiliea could tell. It was late, had to be about one, one-thirty, but Deshaun had wanted to see her, or so he said. Deshaun Cauldwell, Chevante's father, just got out of county jail two days before. He hadn't seen Chevante in more than a year, so Heiliea told him she would bring her out. He lived on the west side, out in Ardmore. She wasn't gonna go out there, but he was back around the block, hustling. She had brought Chevante out around nine when he texted her and said he was going to be out, so she came out on the steps. She and Chevante lived upstairs, two sections over in 619, but the second section was where everyone hung out. The Cherry Coke she bought her was almost gone. Chevante's eyes were soft; she was moving slow while Lulu tried to play with her. *Deshaun, come on*, Heiliea thought. But Deshaun was hustling, been at it all night. He told her when he rolled up he got fronted some crack-cocaine from Bax over on the west side. "Good shit," he told her. "Gonna get mine," he said. "Right," she had responded, like last time.

Last time, Deshaun got popped by the police for possession with three rocks. They tried to charge him with trafficking, but that didn't stick. It never stuck with Deshaun. He called himself Teflon, but nobody else did. He still caught a charge for distribution, but he only did eight months in county. The whole time Heiliea didn't see a dime either. She only brought Chevante out tonight so she could make sure she got some of his money. That fool didn't even deserve to see his daughter until he became a man and paid up. That government check only went so far. But it was getting late.

"Chevante baby, you getting tired," she cooed, scratching the little girl's back. She looked so cute in her little cutoffs, and pink tube top, little belly showing. Heiliea was dressed in a tube top too, although she was in a mini skirt and sported high heel chucks. After all, it was Thursday night; she and the girls were goin' out after Deshaun came up with her money.

"Yeahhh, she getting sleepy," Luwanda said, stroking her hair.

"Come on little girl." Heiliea stood, pulled her skirt back down around her thighs. As she smoothed out the strip of denim, she thought again about the panther tattoo she was gonna put on her thigh when she hit eighteen. Lulu lifted Chevante up into her arms.

"See if that skinny muthafucka got any smoke, if we're gonna be sittin here all night," Lulu told her as she handed off the child.

"He said he din't," Heiliea responded as she tip-toed down the granite slab stairs.

"Punk ass ain't good for shit," added Shela, not loud enough for Deshaun to hear.

Heiliea didn't respond as she stepped toward the broken strip of sidewalk leading to the corner of King and Romney Street. Deshaun and Willy were in the shadows under the tree just off the corner. She could only see him by the orange cherry at the end of his cigarette. "Deshaun!" she yelled, making the three-year old who'd already dropped to sleep on her shoulder jump.

***

Deshaun Cauldwell, puffing on a Newport, turned as he heard his name. Pulling the cigarette away from his lips, he rolled his eyes. "What chu want girl!" he barked. "Damn!"

Sucking his teeth, he turned away. *Fuck, this bitch getting on my nerves.* He texted her earlier asking about the kid, but really he was just hoping to get a piece of ass. That girl was always ready to fuck. But what he got instead was a thirty minute lecture about how he wasn't a man. How Chevante needed a Daddy, how she need money. "Fuck bitch, I just got outta jail," he told her. But then she just went on screaming, then her mom screamed more. *Gawdamn!* He left, and he and Willy rolled a blunt and baked in Willy's car. That was like three hours ago, and this bitch and her friends been hangin' over him. She wasn't screamin' now because she had the kid on her arm. *What the hell she doin' out with a kid at one in the morning anyway? Damn.*

"Don't come over," he warned her. Turning toward Willy, he said, "I'm a fuck this bitch up, she keep runnin' her mouth." Willy, stoned out of his mind, bleary eyed, hadn't moved from the wall all night, hadn't served a thing all night. He just stood there staring at him. "Dumb fuck," Cauldwell told him.

"Deshaun, you gonna spend time with your daughter or what? She been out here all night."

"That's not my kid! Damn! I told you to take yo ass to the house 'bout two hours ago, shit."

"You worthless mutha-!"

At that moment Deshaun caught headlights rolling slow down King Street. The car was headed his way. It was about two blocks out.

He turned and charged the bitch. Grabbing her by the arm, he swung her around and shoved her. She almost bit it, wearin' those fucked up sneakers. "I said get the fuck outta here, bitch!" The kid started screamin', the bitch started crying…and there was an old grey shitbox sittin' on his corner drawing too much attention.

Too much goin' on at once, killin' what was left of his buzz. Blocking out the noise, he turned to the car. It was dark, even under the street light. He couldn't see shit inside the ride. Looked like an old Monte Carlo, 'cept it looked like it'd been run through a fuckin' wall. Old school mag wheels made it look tough, fast but in a Mad Max sort of way. The passenger side window was down, or gone, so he went up to that. Leaning into the frame, he said, "What chu-"

POP! POP! TA-TA-TA-TA-TA-TA-TA-TA-TA-TA-TA-TA!

***

Heiliea was wiping snot from her nose when it started. She'd heard gunfire before. Anybody coming up in the Charles Apartments knew the sound of gunfire. But it was so loud, so close. Instinctively, uncontrollably, she froze, then jumped. Putting one high heel to the grass, she was about to bolt when a line of scorching fire blistered across her back. Heiliea smacked the ground full force, out of control.

Seemed like an eternity before the world re-set itself. It was dark and she couldn't see. Nothing hurt, but her mouth was full. She tried to scream but instead only coughed up a mouthful of tangy, metallic blood.

The adrenaline cleared her vision. She tried to move. Nothing. People were screaming now, as she choked and hacked. Eyes flicking rapidly, she could see her arm. Her bicep looked like it was turned inside out. But it didn't hurt...there was something though. She tried to breathe, hacking, struggling for one more breath. That's when it hit her, past her mangled arm, her hand limp and pointing in the wrong direction.

There it was, a little shoe. It was still...so still. People were screaming. Gurgling through a shredded lung, so was Heiliea.

"*Che...!*"

Chapter Seven

Ben Wilke ran. He was high on the beach, off the water. His calves burned as he churned through loose sand. The stars to the east dotted the sky over the ocean, a tapestry of vibrant constellations and a swath of shadowy clouds. The moon was full and bright, casting the world in a bluish hue that gave him comfort. He liked running in the dark.

His nightly run, or what had come to be a nightly run, started toward the north end of the island near the lonely Morris Island Lighthouse that stood against the waves and the strong currents off Folly Beach. The tall spire's light no longer served as a beacon for ships coming back to port, but it continued to stand, unrelenting, while the soft earth beneath it slowly washed away.

He had made his way south along the beach, sticking to the soft sand to make his body work harder to maintain his pace. Every two minutes he stopped and caused a flurry of silica particles to fly into the night as he ground out twelve burpies then continued.

Wilke had never considered himself much of a fitness guy. He'd always done what he needed to in order to maintain the physical fitness standards with the police department, but his early thirties metabolism, which seemed more in line with that of a jack rabbit than a human, kept him on the slim, lanky side of the fence. It was only in the last couple of months he'd added the nightly bout of torture to his lifestyle, and it saved his life.

In the distance, lights from the large hotel in the center of Folly Island grew to take over the night, drowning out the quiet beauty of the starscape to his east. A local band played on the sprawling patio near the pool. The bar was full of patrons, normally a solid balance of locals as well as the steady stream of tourists that kept the local economy humming. Wilke could almost smell the spilled booze, and cigarette smoke that mixed with the subtle chlorine fumes wafting off the spacious pool that took over the majority of the hotels' lower outdoor level. He could taste the bourbon flowing from the bartenders' steady hand, filling tumbler after tumbler as the night rolled on. The remembered sensations, scorched into his brain from long nights of doing his best to challenge the cadre of barkeeps to keep up with him, left him with a thirst deep in his throat, even as he ran. He came to within a couple hundred yards of the resort before stopping to stretch against an abandoned lifeguard station just inside the shadows. From the darkness, he could hear the raucous laughing and chipper giggles as the nightlife raged just inside the gates of the hotel. He watched for a moment as he pulled his ankle up to his hip, trying to stretch a kink out of his quadriceps.

He stopped at the same place every night and continued his surveillance every night. Watching and listening, feeling the thirst that had almost overtaken him. The call of the thirst was palpable despite the exertion and dehydration his workout caused. He wanted it so bad; to feel that bit and the warmth that the harsh liquid would provide. The smooth descent into numbness that he craved.

He watched for a few minutes more, feeling that pull. Then the equivocations began; those little voices in the back of his mind that tried to plead with him. Just one drink, they would say. Just one, then straight out the back gate. One drink would not kill a man. What harm could it really do?

Wilke finished stretching his legs and turned away from the lights, back to the darkness. There was no place in his life for indulgence. It had taken too much from him. He found hope in preparing himself for the day that he would get his chance to do right by fallen friends. He did not know where to find the people he sought, or who they were. But he knew they were there. When they showed themselves again, they would be his.

Time to run. Breaking from his perch at the lifeguard station, he ran toward the incoming waves lapping at the very edge of the continent, only to turn at the last moment before touching the water. He picked up the pace on the hard-packed sand and traced the curving line of water as it rushed in and out with the tide.

He'd made it a quarter of a mile before the phone clipped to his waistband chirped. He ignored the call for just a moment before stopping. It had been so long since he was the one to get a call on a

Saturday night that he'd almost forgotten what it meant. It was Banks, now Captain Peter Banks, calling him at almost three o'clock in the morning.

"Captain," he answered, trying not to sound out of breath.

The Captain spoke plainly, giving him his marching orders. Wilke felt his heart flutter in his chest, battling with the butterflies in his stomach. The Captain's orders were followed by one simple question.

"Yes sir," Wilke answered. "I'm good to go."

Chapter Eight

She stood, hip cocked, just inside the tree line. She was just off the rutted path that stretched from the barn near the main tasting room, down a gradual decline that lead to the clear waters of Cayuga Lake. She was out of eye shot of a dozen or so milling tourists taking in the view and sipping wine on the deck attached to the tasting room of the boutique winery.

"You have been cleared," a cold crisp voice told her through the phone. The phone was encrypted, and worked via the backbone architecture of what was once the APRANET rather than normal cell signal.

"Copy. Orders?" she asked.

"Stand by," said the voice, "Further instruction will be forthcoming."

Biannca grimaced. She had been on the bench for almost a year since the operation in South Carolina tanked. Now that she was finally cleared, they still wanted her off the board. "Understood," she responded. The line went dead.

Biannca rolled her eyes, then fluffed her dark auburn hair, checking her make-up in her mirrored face of her phone. She still wasn't a fan of being a brunette. She had found in the last year taking graduate classes at Cornell University in Ithaca, New York and working as a sommelier at the Goose Watch

Winery, that blondes really do have more fun. She had a pert, twenty-two year old, golden haired co-worker who consistently got more tips, and she got hit on more than Biannca did. Biannca also had noted that when she was out at the bars, the blondes were bought drinks more too. One last look in the mirror and Biannca was comfortable with the state of her hair. Her makeup was holding up in the growing heat of the early summer day. Back to work, she told herself.

The tasting room, a wide, oak-trimmed space littered with displays of various red and white wines as well as local arts and crafts, was full. Locals and tourists ranging from undergrads from the colleges around Ithaca, to retirees, and even a bridal shower, filled the room. It was Sunday in June and the weather around the lakes had finally turned consistently warm. During the spring, summer, and fall, the wineries sprinkled around the Finger Lakes were a high draw for tourism. The wines, even in Biannca's opinion, were stellar. She wandered toward one of the tasting stations, where a thirty-something white female with stringy 'she-dreds' and the earthy scent of patchouli oil was stocking the bar with a fresh batch of clean wine glasses.

"Hey, Shell, everything ok?" Her name was Belinda, manager of the tasting room. Very crunchy, very idealistic, not very well travelled, but she meant well, so Biannca was nice to her. Her co-workers at Goose Watch knew her, and Michelle "Shelly" Bonevant, a lower New York refugee who wanted out of the stinking, crowded, funk that was New York City. "Shell," as Belinda, and now the rest of the staff at the winery liked to call Biannca, came around the bar and helped her boss load the shelves with glassware.

"My dad," Biannca/Shell complained, "He wanted to know how the quarter was going, or so he said. He really wanted to try and pry out of me how I'm living. Is my research coming along? Am I out partying too much? Blah, blah. If he would just come up here for a weekend, he would never worry again. Where the hell am I going to party up here, a corn field? He lives five hours away and it might as well be on another planet."

Belinda was grinning in that way that said, "Been there girl," trying to nurture the old soul and spinning around what New Age hippy buzzwords she was going use to counsel Biannca's fake life. Biannca enjoyed it when she did this. She had realized that Belinda could actually be a threat to her cover if she wasn't careful. Every weekend she found herself coming to the winery for the distinct purpose of spinning another fake drama for Belinda to guide her through. Biannca had caught herself after her third month at the winery letting her stories get wilder and wilder until she had to cut herself off. Her cover was pretty general, as it was each time she switched personalities, three times in the past year, while waiting to be cleared for duty. Salzburg, Vancouver, and now here in the very quiet rolling hills and long lakes of upstate New York. She had to keep backgrounds vague and she had found herself, like some rookie, adding details to her fake life that she herself was having trouble keeping straight just to entertain herself at the expense of this woman. She knew Belinda was married or engaged to some farm to table, vegan, farmer/hipster near Taughannock falls and couldn't help but wonder how much 'advice' that man actually absorbed on a daily basis.

"It's all energy, bro," said Belinda. She liked to call everybody bro because she didn't believe in gender specific labels. "You couldn't spell men without women," was one of Belinda's favorite sayings while enjoying a glass of wine on the deck with the staff after hours. To Shell, it was funny every time.

"The energy," echoed Shell. "If he could only feel it," she said, nodding her head in agreement.

"All in good time," Belinda smiled. She looked up as the doors to the tasting opened and a giggling, red-faced group of fifteen or so Canadians stumbled in. "Ooo," Belinda said, stepping from around the bar, "Drunk Canadians, enjoy," then disappeared into the crowd as the group of sloshed wine tasters closed in on Shell.

***

The decision to go underground in upstate New York was not Biannca's. She had decided when she first realized the world of fake identities and covert operations would be her life, that she did not want some analyst to be able to locate her using some behavioral profile. Biannca's answer to that issue was random chance. Biannca compiled a collection of geo-coordinates, around three hundred locations around the world where she could blend as a Caucasian female. The locations were stored in a small program linked to a random number generator. When she was notified after the shit show in South Carolina that she would be under review and was ordered to stand down, she activated the program. By the time the company cruiser docked in the Caribbean, she had already established her identity and travel plans for Salzburg, Austria.

She set herself up in a modest flat in Salzburg, just outside the old town, and took work in a coffee shop. She had tried being a redhead then, but found that being a ginger engendered an air of suspicion almost everywhere she went, so that style choice was nixed just as soon as her ninety days as a barista came to an end. The second hit on her random generator was Vancouver and she was impressed with her luck. Around five years before her current exile she was ordered to stand down, and her options were Huntsville, Alabama and Pittsburg, Pennsylvania; the stop in Pittsburg came during February. She thought she had done well in catching Salzburg on her first round, and Vancouver turned out to be a dream.

Given that the players in Hollywood were tiring of paying union wages and struggling under contract regulations, the film industry had invaded British Columbia. Biannca found that she could not help herself. Despite her mission to lay low, she took work as an extra in four different movies during her

BC tenure. She kept herself from returning to her natural blonde status and settled for brown hair with gold highlights.

When upstate New York was selected for her, she had sighed and almost come off her regimen. How do you give up the fringe of movie making to hide out in a place where there were more livestock than people? She'd struggled with the decision, but ultimately had disappeared from Canada one night in early April. She appeared six days later, after a quick stop in Vegas, as Michelle Bonevant, graduate student at Cornell.

Now, the long Saturday nights of slinging drinks behind her, "Shelly" sipped a 2009 Cabernet Sauvignon from Lamoreaux Landing Winery while sitting on her deck overlooking the gently lapping waves of Seneca Lake. Taking in the view night after night, she decided that now, after all the trepidation, upstate New York was not all that bad.

Biannca rented the small lakeside cabin for a couple of reasons. The first was that there was a dock she could sit on and enjoy the quiet star-filled nights while she waited out her current state of exile. The dock held a small, twelve foot Jon boat. The owner left the boat for renters use and for the fact that he didn't have any place else to keep it. The boat was old but the ancient twenty-five horse Evinrude attached to its aluminum hull was strong and dependable. The second feature that drew her attention to the location was seclusion. While it was true that Biannca in her true form was a social butterfly, that sort of thing lent itself to straining her back story and could let her indulge, much like her fascination with her twine-haired manager at the winery. Her nearest neighbors were the owners of the rental and they were almost a half mile away down a winding dirt road. Gullies, long ago carved by water draining from the hills and old forest somehow preserved from farming, and vineyards, surrounded the little cabin. It was a mile hike through thick growth to get to a main road and long forgotten trails snaked with no apparent plan or direction between the lake and civilization, providing Biannca with strenuous running grounds and isolation while she kept in shape.

She worked at the winery on the weekends because it gave her something to do and afforded her the opportunity to gauge the general nature of the people in the area. More specifically, working in the modest tourism industry of the Finger Lakes gave her the ability to observe what the average visitor to the area looked like and acted like. The clientele varied widely, from locals on motorcycles, to those fleeing the congestion and human clutter of New York City, to busloads of Canadians coming down from Ontario and Quebec on a weekend getaway. She had spotted three different individuals she was sure were intelligence officers, two Chinese and one Russian, who were up from the city. The level of alertness that comes as a side effect of working in the intelligence world was hard to hide when someone knew what they were looking for. Biannca was reminded not to get complacent, even in the relative beauty and peace the lakes provided.

It was going on eleven o'clock on a Sunday night, which meant she would be sitting in an advanced Organic Chemistry class come morning. With one final sip, Biannca paused to note the lack of singing frogs and other night creatures that normally serenaded her at night. Then she rose and retreated to her bungalow. The structure was simple. One main living room adjoined on an open floor plan with a small kitchen, the two separated by a four-foot island and prep station. A full bathroom sat adjacent the kitchen and on the side of the room, a rough staircase ran up the outer wall to a small loft where the bedroom overlooked the rest of the space. Biannca shut off the kitchen light as she passed the main door and the cabin went dark. She flattened herself against the old timber floor. Sliding doors leading to the deck and the window on the opposite wall of the main door evaporated as a storm of suppressed, machine gun fire, turning the small domicile into a slaughterhouse.

Biannca crouched beside the sixty-year old wood stove. She gathered a set of keys from a prepared spot on the counter, then opened all the burners to full. She counted in her head, one-one thousand, two-one thousand... while duck walking into the bathroom. The cabin was pitch black, save for lithe streams of moonlight catching the dust and powdered glass filling the cabin. She waited for another volley, but there was only silence.

Chapter Nine

Julian Marson, team leader, call sign 2-2 watched the attack on the secluded lakeside cabin with a clinician's interest. 1-8 had confirmed the target at the subject location moments before. As luck would have it, the target had been sitting in the open on the back deck, sipping wine without a care in the world while his spotters, 1-8 and 1-6, had gotten into position. The shot would have been simple enough as would be clean up, but 2-2 had told them to hold while the rest of the team got into position. They had a plan and 2-2 never deviated from a plan. He'd seen paydays turn to shit when some asshole started changing shit at the last minute. The target wasn't going anywhere. His two spotters, 1-8 and 1-6 had the shoreline North and South buttoned up. His raiders, 2-4, 2-7, and 2-9 were preparing to make entry at two points on either side of the small structure, and he had over watch in a gulley just east. He let the operation proceed once he received a confirmation that the raid team was in place. The suppressors on their FN-F2000 rifles did not dampen the report of the weapons completely, but he doubted the old couple further down the lake would make any note of the sound.

The fusillade lasted almost a full minute before the empty stillness of the woods returned.

"Breaching," he heard the growl of 2-4 say in his earpiece.

The splintering of the front door shattered the stillness and the crunching of shattered glass under boot crackled across the water, but that could not be helped. If the target had not been dropped during the opening salvo, a quiet, slow entry would open the team up to casualties, and that was unacceptable. He could hear them moving through the small room in a methodical, orchestrated movement. Fifteen seconds passed, then twenty. 2-2 felt a stirring in his spine, right in between the shoulder blades. A nervous twitching that a leader without a real time view of what was happening urged him to call for report. This was an important contract for 2-2, one that had to come to fruition. It was his reputation and record for handling the most delicate of operations that had caused their overseer 'One' to ring his mobile and not another's. 2-2 held off on calling for status. He had professionals sweeping the kill zone below him. If there was a problem they knew how to handle it. Thirty seconds passed.

Whirrrr....

The lake. 2-2's view of the dock directly behind the cabin was partially occluded, but the sound of a small boat launching was unmistakable.

"Movement on the boat, heading into the lake," called 1-6. The staccato cough of 1-6 and 1-8 firing on the fleeing vehicle floated to 2-2's position.

In the darkness the small aluminum craft arced away from the dock, leaving a mild wake in the moon streaked water. It was too dark to see the target in the boat. 2-2 could see the angry sparks of rounds shredding through the thin metal hull and the engine cover.

The raid team exited the house and joined the spotters on the smooth pebbled beach and the five mercenaries' small boat.

2-2 remained on over watch. He couldn't see his personnel but he could see the small craft struggling toward the deeper water. The engine was smoking and choking. Central was going to need verification of the kill. That was going to mean diving for a body in a very public setting. It was going to mean digging into his bottom line. 2-2 had plans for this pay day. Wasting his own funds to go find a target was nowhere in his plans.

"Hold fire," he ordered.

Flames were licking out from under the engine cover and he sighed. He was about to watch what should have been a simple termination devolve into a shit sandwich and it would be all for a confirmation. He didn't see any movement inside the boat, though that did not surprise him. The target was diminutive and her file was impressive. That bothered him. He squinted when flames met the gas supply and the small Jon boat went up in a *whoosh* which billowed across the lake. The cool pale streaks of moonlight on the water were replaced by glowing orange as an aluminum and gas funeral pyre lit the night. The boat was a bad idea, he told himself, just poor tactics. It was too slow. And if she was alert enough to survive the opening salvo, how could she think that was an option when she knew we were packed with weapons that boat couldn't out run? 2-2 watched the flames start to die. He grimaced, setting his anvil-like jaw.

People panic when they're boxed in, he told himself. He'd seen even the hardest men fall apart under even the first whiff of combat. Watched a fellow operator come apart at altitude, freezing up and forgetting how to operate his parachute. He had watched another step out of a helicopter while forgetting to grab the rope during a fast rope insertion. Stress did weird things to people. 2-2 sighed and rose from his position in the shadow of an old pine tree. He felt like there were a hundred sets of eyes from all over the lake looking his way.

"All units—" he stopped when a flash skirted his peripheral vision. Before he could react, he felt the impact to the side of his head and another to his knee. The first registered as a deep thud, the second he heard and felt a sharp crack. Then he was falling, rolling, and tumbling down the steep shale wall of the gulley adjacent the cabin. The trip was a short one, as he smashed into a protruding rock the size of a grizzly bear.

Chapter Ten

The ten-month old slept on her back, arms lopped haphazardly over her head. Muffled wisps of her breathing were the only sound pulsing slowly through the room. She was in her crib, a white cage of plastic and wood. A miniature solar system drifted counter clockwise over her head. The tiny room was purple and plush with a zoo full of stuffed animals of various shapes, sizes, and colors. The rainbow hued spectrum of critters lined the walls like goofy eyed sentinels. A changing table, dresser, and rocking chair were the only breaks in the chain around the room; even the closet was guarded by the motley crew of plush guardsmen.

He watched the solar system drift slowly in circles around his daughter's head. Her mom had insisted on it, determined her little girl would grow up to be a scientist, not be some starry-eyed celebrity chaser. It made him chuckle, the thing was so out of place. But whatever, with his genes the kid needed all the help in math and science as she could get. He couldn't deny the fact that but for eager science geeks, hoping to party with the soccer players on the weekends, there is no way he would be a high school, much less college, graduate.

She stirred ever so slightly, little fat legs bouncing like she was running a sprint. He imagined the pudgy infant leaping hurdles, a trailing smear of drool and slick of pureed carrots trailing in her wake. Though it had been almost a year he'd tried to be around as much as possible, fatherhood never ceased to amaze him. The sheer amount of slime and drool, and snot, and crap that little body could produce blew his mind. And despite the fact he was a veteran cop, there was no end of bodily functions that child could do to make his stomach do back flips. Blood and guts—not a problem, but baby snot, ugh. Just the thought made him squirm. Zoe snorted in response—or was that a fart—either way it was impeccable timing. Maybe she'll be a comedian. From out in the living room where Marla was snoozing on the couch he heard the tell-tale "chirp...chirp," and he cringed. Viejo knew immediately his perfect night was ruined, shot through by either some over-eager patrolman, or an overly eager dealer. This Saturday night was drawing to a close. He looked at his watch—going on one-thirty. His eyebrow arched. *How long was I in here?*

Rising from his position, leaning over the crib, he creaked in places no thirty-three-year old should creak and groan. Leaning over the crib, he kissed his fingers and placed them to the little one's cheek.

"Gotta go to work, kid," he whispered.

In the living room Marla was draped across the couch, a book lying across her breasts. She wasn't quite snoring, wasn't quite-not snoring. She snorted and rolled to her side, book tumbling to the floor, when the phone chirped again. "What is it?" she asked, not giving a damn.

"Work," he answered, "I gotta go. Thanks for letting me come over again tonight," he said softly.

"You come over every night," she groaned, her almond shaped deep brown eyes snapping open. Her mocha flavored skin tone seemed to glow in the low light, jet black hair a rat's nest propped on the side of her head. She looked great, as she sat up like a zombie climbing from the grave. Her face was crinkled in a frustrated pout.

The phone chirped again.

"I know. I'd like to talk about that some time if we could?"

Marla was hoarse from sleep. "We have talked about it, we tried it, things just don't work for us."

Viejo clipped his badge to his belt, slipped the paddle holster inside his jeans, dropped a faded green polo shirt over both and looked at his feet. He opened the front door as gingerly as he could, then looked back. Her eyes were closed; she leaned back on the sofa, heel of her palm rubbing her head. "I'm thinking of changing things up, wanted to get your take on it. Dinner, maybe next week?"

"Like a date?" Her eyes were still closed, voice not so hoarse.

"Yeah."

"K, call me."

"Thanks again," he said, snuck one last look at Zoe's room, and slipped the door closed behind him.

Chapter Eleven

Biannca ran.

Guided by minimal moonlight that managed to streak through the thick canopy of trees. Night vision goggles had already saved her life. She had spotted the darkly clad merc. She could tell he was a mercenary the second she had crept out of the narrow crawl space between the foundation and the bathroom where she had burrowed a small escape hatch through the floorboards in the bathroom closet. He had been in her direct line of flight.

The plan had always been that the remotely activated boat would draw whoever came after her away and then keep them occupied after the explosion. Biannca had seen enough work done over her time with the agency to know that there needed to be confirmation of any kill. The small boat exploding two hundred yards off shore would have required a search by whatever team came hunting. She'd planned to use that search requirement as a way to gain distance on her attackers. When the figure on over watch had shifted his balance and caught her eye, all that time she had planned on evaporated. She had used the cover and her advantage of seeing in the dark to close on the man as he watched the boat do its work. Using an asp baton she had kept in her go bag stashed in the bathroom closet, she stunned him with a strike to the back of the head, then hopefully injured his knee with another strike. Before fleeing, she used the geography to send him sprawling down the steep shale-encrusted gully. With any luck, his team would believe he had simply fallen; that might buy her some time. Biannca had purposefully refrained from killing him because an injured man took at least one more man out of the fight. Given that the team hunting her were mercenaries, that might not hold true. However, if she had killed the man, the mercs would definitely have left him to rot in the woods. At least keeping him alive might have extended her chances of escape a little.

Biannca followed a game trail. The night vision illuminated her tiny flight path which led her uphill toward the highway. A half mile from the cabin, she came to an old rutted dirt road. There she broke from the trail and turned left. The forgotten road, not more than a pair of worn tractor tracks cutting through the trees, led her back down toward the water for another half mile. There in the darkness, a Y junction in the path offered two directions, one north, following the lake, and another west, heading for the shore. The road was a misty soft green framed by black and green flecks of undergrowth and trees. Just to the north of the Y intersection, Biannca reached into the darkness and pulled a raggedy brush-covered tarp away from an all-wheel drive Jeep Wrangler.

Without pause, she tossed her pack to the passenger seat and leapt inside. As she landed in the driver seat, a boiling fire in her left side doubled her over. She stifled a cry and with a gentle hand probed a wet wound on her side. She hissed as her fingers explored the insult. She had no time for that. Gently putting pressure to the wound, she tried the key. The meticulously maintained vehicle purred to life and she crept away from the hiding spot with her lights off, night vision leading the way.

***

2-2 struggled to regain his senses as 2-4, and 2-7 dragged him to his feet. He felt his boots under him, scraping at the dirt and rocks of the gulley floor but they didn't seem to want to support him. He felt his toes dragging against the ground as his knees buckled, as he tried to gain his balance. Coming around, he batted away the support of his two operatives. 2-2 slouched against a large boulder and tried to flex his right knee. Pain arced under his knee cap and up his thigh, but it worked.

"Shit," he breathed.

"You good to go, sir?" 2-4 asked. "We probably gotta exfil, people are gonna come snooping round here pretty soon."

"That was a nasty fall," said 2-7, staring up the steep face of the ravine. She spoke more out of an academic observation than concern for her team leader.

2-2 noted the comment but was not surprised.

"You slip or something?" she asked.

"I didn't slip," 2-2 responded sourly. He put a fingerless glove to the back of his head and felt a growing lump behind his ear.

"We got prints up here," 1-6 announced.

All heads snapped toward 2-2. He couldn't gauge how many of the operators for hire were judging him for letting the target get away or for letting the target get the jump on him. He felt his age as he studied the four much younger faces around him.

"She had night vision," was all he said. "1-8, fall out," he transmitted over the radio, "We're moving. 1-6, lead the way."

For a moment, no one stirred.

"Move!" he ordered.

Chapter Twelve

Twenty minutes later Viejo rolled his black Toyota Camry into the lot on the back side of the Falsom Arms Apartments. The Camry was old, had some dings and scratches, but it also had opaque tinted windows all around. It was the perfect dope car. Just crappy enough to blend in anywhere in the city.

Blue lights and portable halogens cast strobes and stark shadows throughout the project. He locked the vehicle and walked calmly across the patchy grass that made up a quad of sorts between the buildings. As he approached the crime scene tape that was stretched between the buildings, he saw the patrolman manning the entry log stiffen. Viejo didn't recognize him but where he was once one of those vaguely recognizable detectives from the Special Operations Command. Thanks to the events surrounding the Congressman Tulley investigation, everyone from the freshest intern to the cranky old Supply Sergeant knew who Esteban Viejo was.

"Viejo. Narcotics," he said without breaking stride. The patrolman had already held up the tape for him.

"Yes sir," the kid responded.

Katherine Fenner was standing over the still form of a white t-shirt, black jeans clad black male whose one remaining eye was fixed on the oak tree blocking what would have been his view of the night sky. The rest of his head, brain included, was in fragments littered around a larger chunk of gray matter next to his pristine Nike low tops. Two crime scene techs methodically took measurements from the corner of the red-bricked row house twenty feet away to various points around the body and the rest of the evidence on the scene. An ever-present note pad was in her left hand, a pen in her right, the butt of which was slowly being whittled down by two rows of immaculate white teeth while she studied the scene. On the opposite side of the scene, her partner Bob Martin was strolling down the crowded crime scene tape asking if anyone saw anything. Of course they didn't. They both knew the answers they would get before even starting the canvas. For an area that was basically a block party every night, its inhabitants had very poor vision, and even poorer memories. Fenner didn't pin her hopes on solving this case on the canvas her partner was attempting. As she turned back to the body of Deshaun Cauldwell, she noted a lone Hispanic male wearing jeans and a polo shirt, hands in his pockets, slowly approaching the crime scene from the rear of the complex. She sighed.

"What are you doing here, Viejo? This is a homicide, not a dope bust."

***

Without a word, Viejo stopped and looked around the dark nook surrounding the crime scene. Scanning the surrounding brick, tree trunk, and other assorted junk strewn about the taped off scene, he stopped and focused on a metal junction box affixed to the brick wall. Pointing at it, he smiled and strolled to the box. Tapping the top hinge with the heel of his palm, the lid swung down in a whiny *clang!* Fetching a small surefire from his belt, he shined the beam inside to reveal a crumpled mass of cellophane. He retrieved a set of latex gloves from another pocket and fished out the clear plastic. Inside was an off-white crumbling disk of crack cocaine. Revealing his find with a flourish from his free hand, he set the bag gingerly back inside the junction box.

"Now it's both," he said. He dropped the gloves to the ground and nodded to the techs, "Grab that too ladies, and mind the prints on the bag, thanks." He noted the scowl plastered across Fenner's strikingly attractive, coffee hued features and felt a twinge. He only had a couple of years on the job over her. They ran the streets together for a while when they were both in patrol. Had some good times, made some good arrests together. They went their separate ways when he went to Narcotics and she went to the Domestic Violence Squad in the Central Detectives Bureau. He stopped on the other side of Deshaun Cauldwell's cooling corpse and said, "I'm not here to mess with you, Kat. Captain Banks ordered me and Wilke to come down. What's the big deal here anyway?"

Fenner held up a long, slender index finger and pointed to a dark canvas tarp covering two lumps. He'd walked right past it; the light from the streetlight didn't make it that far past the huge oak tree dominating the little patch of dirt, and the halogen lights cast stark shadows that hid the object on his approach. He turned toward the tarp. From behind him, Kat said in a low tone, "Brooks wanted them covered until the crime scene guys are ready to process them. He wanted the halogens left off until then also to keep the bodies off social media and the news,"

Viejo felt a weight dragging his heart to his guts. "Aw damn," he breathed. He went to the smaller of the two bumps in the tarp and knelt near the edge. After putting on another set of gloves, he grabbed the edge and gingerly pulled the tarp back.

She was small, a tiny little girl lying on her stomach as if she'd fallen asleep on her father's shoulder. She looked peaceful, quiet, had a couple little specks of dirt dotting her chunky cheeks, but don't all kids at that age? Her eyes were closed, one tiny little fist curled up under her chin, as if gripping her favorite blanket. Viejo felt like he'd been sucker punched. The reaction shocked him.

***

Fenner kept an eye on Viejo as he checked out the little girl. She could see the recognition on his face as soon as she pointed out the tarp to him. As far as she knew, Viejo had a daughter of his own. They hadn't talked in years. Once he went to the dark side, they were kind of on opposite sides of the moon. Fenner heard the stories, couldn't get away from the stories. The exploits of Bank's narcotics unit, every rookie cops wet dream. Running and gunning, t-shirts, jeans, and fast cars, the department sledge hammer when the streets got too hot. Some of the things she'd heard, and some of the ways the prosecutors downtown talked about Viejo and that other goon Wilke, how they kept the streets in check, sounded more to her like the wild bunch than twenty-first century police work. She couldn't be a part of that. She knew him, had seen him in action. He got the job done, like a wrecking ball, and she'd fielded enough questions from Internal Affairs on his account when they were in the bag, to know she'd never see lieutenants' bars if she was associated with him or the goon squad. Upon reflection, she wondered if that belief was blown since Peter Banks was now a Captain. She saw Viejo's head drop as he pulled the tarp further back to reveal the gaping hole in the toddlers back. His blood would be at a raging boil when he came back. She knew this because hers was up too. Hazard of the job. It was good to see though, she thought, that he still cared. Being a badge carrying thug hadn't stripped him of his humanity. Maybe there was hope for him yet. She turned away when he dropped the tarp back over the child. "Son of a bitch," she heard him curse.

***

Viejo stifled a growl in his throat as he rose. Looking off across the project, dark, gloomy, absolutely no place for a baby girl. He took a deep breath, the stench of stale beer, cigarettes, and closely packed humanity filling his nostrils. He closed his eyes for a moment, and the little girl's face flashed across the back of his eyelids. He knew he'd be seeing her over and over again in the near future, his memory unable to escape the trauma of what he'd just seen. Putting it away, he concentrated on his breathing. Let it go slowly. As it went, he felt the flush fall from his cheeks, felt his heart rate fall ever so slightly. There was no room for that sort of thing in his line of work—at least that's what he kept telling himself. As he returned to the corpse of Deshaun Cauldwell, he noticed Kat turn away. "So what happened? Collateral damage?"

Fenner was still eyeing the ground around the body, "Looks like it," she responded, "Martin is trying to canvas...you know how that goes."

Viejo shined his light across the roadway adjacent to the body. Sweeping the light back and forth, he moved closer to the street and stretched the beam further around the intersection. Turning back to the body, he followed the line of fire from Deshaun to the little girl and mother. He clicked the light off when Kat broke his train of thought.

"You know him?" she asked.

Viejo knelt in front of what was left of Deshaun's face. "Deshaun Cauldwell," he said, "just got out a couple of weeks ago. We put him in last winter. This isn't gonna help the recidivism rate any. Willy Thompkins with him?"

Kat shook her head, "Nobody else here when units responded. Who's he?"

Viejo got back to his feet, scanning the crowd, "Running buddy, pot-head."

Viejo and Kat Fenner turned as Detective Bob Martin strolled up the sidewalk. To Viejo Martin, he was the quintessential detective. The man had been a detective since before Viejo was born. Still had the bushy salt and pepper seventies' mustache, matching seventies' hair helmet. He still sported the khaki trench coat, and a tie that clashed tragically with the patterned shirt. He was a throwback, but the man had put away more homicides than he could remember. Viejo had fought to work crowd control when he was a rookie just on the off chance he'd be able to work with Bob Martin. If there was such a thing as master at police work, it was him, not that you'd ever know it from talking to him.

"Who called the Goon Squad?" He grumbled in a thick, rusty tone, "Fuckin' world must be comin to an end. How are ya, Este?" The old man asked with a smile and offered his hand.

Viejo took it with enthusiasm and a matching grin. "How you doing, Bob? Not trying to cramp you and Kat here but Banks called me. Guess he's taking this one kind of serious."

Martin threw his hands up, "Aww bullshit, only thing that fucker's worried about is explaining to the Chief why there's a dead three-year old on his lawn. Just another suit," grumbled the old man.

Viejo grinned at the cranky old copper. Martin had been on the 'kiss my ass' program, having locked up his pension years ago. He didn't hold his tongue for anyone.

"What'd you get, Bob?"

Martin swung around, canvas belt on his trench coat swinging around him like a ribbon around a drunken gymnast during a floor routine. He waved a dismissive paw at the assembled crowd, "Jack shit! None a those dumb bastards saw nothin', just out to see the show. Only thing I got was boxy old piece of shit. No one saw a tag, no one got a look at the driver. People around here perfectly content to let these animals kill each other, even when their kids get caught in the cross fire." Viejo couldn't help but cringe. Martin might have well been on a soapbox preaching over Cauldwell's smoking corpse while referring to the dead man as an animal. Not that it was far from the truth, but the newspapers and the Chief especially didn't share his opinion. Martin quieted down and continued, "Only thing remotely interesting I got here is that the ride came to a stop before the shootin' started. Don't seem like the regular M.O."

Viejo nodded, "I didn't notice any tire marks in the street, seems off. Usually these jackoffs tear through spitting bullets all over the place."

"Yup," Martin agreed.

"From the look of these trajectories, Deshaun was in the center of the window frame when he took it in the face."

"So he didn't recognize the car for sure, or at least if he did know it he didn't see it as a threat, the driver we don't know about. Little more forethought from the shooter than we're used to," Martin summarized.

Before they could continue their confab, an ear-rattling wail bellowed from the crowd across the street and was abruptly joined by screams, and cries of "Chevante! Baby! My baby!" Viejo looked up to see a three hundred pound black woman faint as four more women tried to catch her. They were all howling and crying now.

"Christ!" Martin hissed.

"Right on cue," Fenner said dryly, nodding toward the news van parked across the street. "The real mourning can begin now that the cameras are here. Councilman Candor's gonna have a field day with that kind of footage." Just as a Scarface poster hanging in a thug's apartment points to there being dope in the house, the howling and wailing and screaming for change is the loudest only when the news cameras are rolling. They would be more than happy to talk to the cameras and cry for everyone to do more for the community. *But to help a cop, not in a million years*, Fenner told herself. At some point you start to wonder if it's just easier to be a victim, always complaining, always expecting someone else to save the world around you, and you never have to put yourself at risk. At least as long as you can duck a stray round every now and then you don't.

Fenner knew she was stereotyping but she couldn't help it. The real problem in the inner city was maybe five to ten percent of the population, but the remaining ninety or so were either too complacent or too scared to help. At some point you start to wonder how you can help people who won't help themselves. It made her sick that such a small percentage could make life so hard on everyone else. They were animals. Running wild over the backs of good people. She broke from her melancholy and looked over at the still form of Chevante Williams. Sometimes the innocent got caught in the frenzy when they started eating each other.

"What've you got?" The bark came from a short, skinny, bald, beady-eyed fifty-year old Lieutenant named Adam Brooks. Gold bars and gold badge gleaming, Viejo noted he was wearing parade shoes as he stomped into the scene.

"Lieutenant," Kat and Viejo said. Martin smirked.

***

Brooks, Patrol Watch Commander, closed on them like a frail, bald version of Hitler while he tried to imitate Patton's swagger. Viejo couldn't figure out why he put Brooks and Hitler together—maybe it was the overly manicured mustache. Viejo also noted that Brooks' intro coincided with the arrival of the news van, "I said, what have we got?" Brooks over-enunciated every word.

Martin jumped on the grenade. "Deshaun Cauldwell, crack dealer, age twenty-four, Heiliea Williams, baby's momma, age seventeen, Chevante Williams, age three and change, baby."

Brooks visibly bristled at Martin's approach, but they all knew he didn't have the balls to reprimand the veteran detective. Viejo had seen Martin flat throw brass out of his crime scenes in the past. It was amazing to watch. Brooks didn't want it to happen to him in front of the news.

"That's it?"

"So far," Martin responded dryly.

Brooks straightened, extended his lower jaw and somehow managed to squint his beady eyes up even more, "Well, you better get something, Goddamnit!" he bellowed, just loud enough for the onlookers to hear, "I've fielded calls from Councilman Candor, the Mayor. And the Chief is already asking for updates on this, so whatever you don't have, you better find right quick, or I'll be damned if you two won't be on the bricks quicker than you can spit."

That doesn't even make sense, Viejo thought. He saw Martin balling up like he was getting ready to strike. He jumped in. "Cauldwell had a partner he rolled with, Lieutenant. He must have seen something. I know where to find him, won't be long til we do." *Had to say something, right?*

Brooks squared up on him. "The Captain wanted you here, Viejo, not me. Far as I'm concerned, you and you knuckle draggers are detectives in name only. You fuck up one little bit," he pinched his needle-like fingers together, "and I will personally see you walking a beat out on John's Island. Remember that."

Viejo didn't respond, didn't look away from the prick, just stared back into those tiny little eyes. Both men knew a tool like Brooks didn't have the juice to force transfer a locker room trashcan. It wasn't more than a second before Brooks turned away. Viejo grinned imperceptibly. *You lose,* he thought.

Brooks stomped off toward the cameras, fists bunched, shoulders curled, trying his damnedest to look like a battlefield leader. Viejo couldn't help but watch.

Martin watched him, a blank unenthused look on his face.

"What? I figured if we gave him something it would be the quickest way to get him to go away."

"There's hope for you yet," Martin responded with a pat on the shoulder. As they turned back to the scene, the three of them stopped as if they had seen a ghost.

Walking through the shadows came Detective Ben Wilke. Fenner and Martin were quiet. Viejo smiled broadly.

"They finally let you out?" he asked.

Wilke's hands were deep in the pockets of his jeans. A dark, long sleeve Henley made him almost a shadow in the darkness. He shrugged.

"Banks called me, wanted me in on this."

"Awesome," said Viejo. To Fenner and Martin he said, "We're gonna go find Willy Thompkins. It'll give us some place to start." He started for the Camry. "I'm driving," he said to Wilke, who shrugged.

Kat acknowledged him with a weak nod, Martin said, "Sure thing, just be gentle, knuckle draggers. We want him to talk to us."

Viejo tossed him the finger, and he and his partner disappeared into the shadows.

Chapter Thirteen

Joseph Broadstreet stood at the East corner of King and Romney Street, just outside the crime scene tape. Dressed in a black hoodie and dark blue jeans, he was a hulking shadow amongst the throng of onlookers who had come to watch the spectacle unfold within the bright yellow ribbon. He was still, rigid as a board, eyes staring blankly across the street at the small bundle lying motionless under a gray tarp. People all around him saying, "Lord Jesus," "Poor child," and so on. Jesus had nothing to do with this, he wanted to tell them.

The crime scene techs and detectives swarming the scene took pictures, scribbled notes, and measured the body lying just off the sidewalk. The flash of the cameras, the staccato bursts of light blazing in the dark, lit the scene for split seconds at random intervals, as if shining light on the remnants of the three lives that were extinguished so quickly, literally in the blink of an eye. He'd seen the whole thing.

Walking up King Street only an hour ago, his cheeks and eyes still burned with the tears that had been flowing; shame scorching a path down his features, draining his hope with every drop that fell from his chin. He'd tried, tried for an eternity tightly packaged into a chaotic and crushing four weeks.

Do good deeds.

That was what he promised himself when he got out: do good, help others. Barely a month ago now that had been his mantra, and tonight he was on his way to smoke it all away with a crack rock that probably would have come from the dead asshole growing cold on the other side of the street.

He hated him, hated them. He hated himself because he was one of them. A living plague causing misery in an already struggling neighborhood. He had tried and failed only to be saved by the untimely and needless death of a little girl and her mother. Broadstreet felt a rage boiling in his dark soul. The lights, the wailing mothers, and the crowd were too much for him. His stomach knotted and his throat was tight. He was too ashamed to be among real people. He turned and pushed his way through the crowd. He had to get away. He didn't deserve to be there.

Chapter Fourteen

Like all half-assed Scarface wannabe's, Willy Thompkins lived with his grandmother and two sisters in the Henemore Central Projects. A cluster of eight-story, concrete block walk-ups set up on the north side of the Charleston peninsula. It was going on three thirty in the morning when Viejo and Wilke made the long trudge up a cement stairwell that smelled like piss, stale beer, and body odor. Gang tags and other spray-painted nonsense polluted the walls. The fourth floor was dank and humid—the air conditioning, built by the lowest bidder barely made a flutter up this high. Wilke banged on the steel door loud enough to ensure that anyone in the apartment knew the police were there. Good thing for them, the windows to these apartments didn't open so if Willy was in there, he wasn't getting far.

Wilke banged again and got a cranky, high pitched,

"Wha'chu want!" for his troubles.

"Police! Open up!" was his response.

"William ain't heeah!" An old woman was right up on the other side of the door now, "Ain been heeah all night."

Wilke mouthed to Viejo, "'William?'" Then he said in a slightly empathetic tone, "We know ma'am, that's why we're here."

They jumped back as the heavy steel door popped open like it was on a spring, "Oh Lord Jesus, William?" the wide-eyed, heavyset, middle-aged black woman was on the verge of tears.

Wilke and Viejo filled her doorway. Wilke ignored the woman's panicked features and turned to Viejo. "Guess he's not here."

Viejo gagged on his tongue trying not to laugh. His partner's observation had caught him off guard. He tried to recover some semblance of professionalism. "Is Willy around, ma'am?" he coughed.

The fact she'd been played had yet to be realized. "Is he okay, Lord Jesus?"

"Ma'am, we're looking for Willy. Does he stay here?" Viejo asked.

"Yes, where is he? Is he hurt?"

"We don't know, we're looking for him," Wilke added, raising his voice and over enunciating every word.

Viejo held out a card with a single ten-digit phone number on it. Unlike most business cards, it didn't pay for his clients to get caught with a policeman's business card in their pocket. "Will you have him call us when you see him?"

It was dawning on her now. But she still took the card. The old woman's brow creased, her lips bunched up and her cheeks puffed out, "You only said dat stuff so I would open da door!" she yelled as Viejo and Wilke turned and began walking away. When they hit the stairwell, she was strutting out into the hall. "You mutha-f..." the steel fire door cut her off.

The two detectives made it down two flights of stairs before Viejo burst out laughing. "I know ma'am, that's what we're here about?" Viejo mimicked him as they made their way. "Sick, dude."

"Yeah, she was pissed."

Chapter Fifteen

Biannca grimaced and swore under her breath. She held an old towel to her side where she had taken what she guessed was shrapnel from the cabin when it was shredded by automatic weapons fire. Most people in Biannca's position would need to be held together with duct tape and massive quantities of whiskey. Surviving a coordinated attack in the middle of the night by a group of well-trained mercenaries was A: not a probable outcome, and B: not something you shake off. Inside the Jeep, Biannca flipped through radio stations as she drove down winding back country roads at a casual pace. She settled on a talk show after the host, whose voice reminded her of a warm grandfather seated in a rocking chair reading a bedtime story, introduced his next guest as the foremost expert on the shadow government bent on dominating the world through global government. "Huh," she said to herself.

The talk radio quickly turned to background chatter as she calmly contemplated what was happening. Earlier in the day she had received a call from Central advising her she had been cleared for duty. Not ten hours later, she was evading gunfire. The call had come over her encrypted phone, a phone that now sat in pieces inside the tire tread impression she left with the Jeep. Was the agency trying to clear her from the board? If so, why had they waited so long? Central had her location as part of her check-in procedure, even during exile as she called it. Maybe they wanted her on domestic soil so as not to raise questions? That wasn't it, at least not in her experience. She had mitigated threats for the agency on four separate continents.

Revenge? She mentally tried to recall the profiles of her targets in the past. There were seven who were actual targets of her assignments. Another fifteen kills had been collateral, usually bodyguards, or associates who had happened to be standing on the 'X' when she chose to act. One was a Russian oil magnate who had been well connected, but she dismissed him because she had managed, in her estimation, a masterful assassination by lacing the lingerie of his favorite whore with a toxin tailored to his genetic profile. It had looked like a massive stroke when the old bastard kicked. Another was a scientist from North Korea. Nowhere near as smooth an operation as the Russian scientist, though very connected within the bat shit country of his birth didn't have the juice to open a yellow rice Chinese takeout anywhere else in the world.

She wondered for a moment about the wildfire protocol, but dismissed it immediately since she tied up the loose ends on that disaster herself, and she had just been cleared. A wave of pain radiated across her abdomen. Biannca shook her head, trying to clear her mind and focus.

She had a plan, she always had a plan, and contingency plans for those plans. She stuck to the rutted and narrow back roads that stretched and wound over and around the rolling hills and barrows that made up the geography of the Finger Lakes. Deep gouges torn out of the earth as glaciers receded at the end of the last ice age left a number of deep lakes stretching north to south. The most prominent among them resembled the five fingers of a hand, hence the Finger Lakes.

Surrounding the lakes were a number of small towns sprinkled in between miles of rich farmland, which, over a couple centuries of cultivation, left a spider web of overgrown trails just wide enough for her Jeep to make it through. She kept the lights off and drove by the ambient light enhanced by the NVG's as long as she was away from civilization. When she did run into small hamlets between her and the first stop on her evasion, she did so with a fearful eye to the sky. She had to fight to keep her pace casual when she was out in the open. Her heart pounded in her chest and her breath caught in her throat as her mind went wild with all the different ways they could be hunting her. Chief among their arsenal were the satellites that littered the skies around the globe.

Whoever it was who came after her, their attack had been well planned. Her ploy with the remote starter she jerry-rigged into the boat had saved her but the asshole who had blocked her path probably ruined all that. She was pretty sure she didn't kill him, though not for lack of trying. The guy was pretty stout and just by gauging how the impact felt when she landed the expandable baton across his head, she didn't think it had killed him. If she was lucky, shoving him down the ravine finished him, but she doubted it.

That meant the time she had been hoping to gain by using the boat was gone. She was being tracked and she had no idea what kind of resources the assholes hunting her had. If she was lucky, this was just some repercussion of an old mission and not an official sanction. Until she knew otherwise she had to run with the idea she was being tracked by satellite, that the whole world was coming to get her. If that was the case, her whole plan was for shit if they got a lock on her. There was nowhere to hide anymore when you had a high-resolution camera watching you from space twenty-four hours a day. And she didn't have the firepower to take that group on head to head, even when she wasn't wounded.

She tried to staunch the blood with gauze she dug out of her go bag but she felt wetness seeping through the cotton. Biannca felt fear and she hated herself for it. She realized she was on her own and she had only one option.

Run.

Chapter Sixteen

Cortland, New York is a small college town east of the lakes. It being early summer meant the small town was relatively quiet on Monday mornings. The lull between classes left only a sprinkling of college students meandering around campus.

Before committing to her stop, Biannca circled the campus twice, doubling back and cutting through a couple of sides streets littered with fraternity and student housing. Confident she was clean, she pulled the Jeep into a long-term storage facility just to the south of campus. She chose the self-storage facility because it was not staffed daily by the old couple who had converted part of their farm land to the four rows of squat corrugated metal buildings. She entered her code and drove to her space in the rearmost corner, where an eight-foot chain link fence was her only impediment to escape into a large stand of trees.

She groaned and felt her sticky, blood-soaked sweatshirt clinging to the driver's seat as she gingerly stepped out of the Jeep. She hadn't seen anyone on her approach. She stepped casually to the orange roll-up door and struggled mightily, her wound complaining, to get into her unit. Her oblique muscles screamed. It felt like her body was being ripped apart by the shrapnel embedded in her side. The walk to the rear of her rental took her breath away. She hissed as she stripped from her bloody clothes.

Her storage space was paid for using a credit card and ID from one of her collection of personas. In the center of the area, a charcoal-grey Volkswagen bug was squeezed in the room. Behind the vehicle was a bench which held a light purple backpack and a plastic storage tub.

Inside the tub was a medical kit and a couple of sets of clothes. One for cold weather and another for warm. She opened the medical kit with a groan and retrieved a bottle of alcohol and a handful of gauze. She shivered against the burning while she washed her side with the stinging ethyl alcohol. She dabbed the alcohol away from her side, then flipped on a small desk light that stood on the bench. She looked herself over and grimaced at a deep furrow left in her side where a bullet had grazed her. Just above the wound, a piece of wood about the circumference of her finger had buried in her side at an oblique angle.

"Shit," she breathed as she probed along the length of the craggy shard buried in her flesh. It wasn't overly deep, but the shard stretched another three or so inches under her skin. With one hand full of gauze, she gripped the shard with the pliers from a utility tool that accompanied her clothes. She ripped the wood out with a cry she could not hold in. The field-expedient surgery took her breath away and she dropped to her knees gasping for air in the stuffy, enclosed space. After a moment, she held the shard up and through the bloody coating recognized the dark-brown layer of paint on one side. She guessed it was part of a door frame, then threw the wood away in disgust. Denying herself the rest her body yearned for, she injected herself with an antibiotic from the med kit and bandaged herself up.

Ten minutes later, dressed in mid-thigh length khaki shorts, a purple tank top, and a pair of matching purple Chucks, she pulled the VW from the unit. Covering the bloody front seat with a towel from the back seat so as not to transfer blood to her new clothes, she quickly backed the Jeep into the space vacated by the little car. She took the backpacks from both the Jeep and the bench, and a fleece jacket from the plastic bin. She tossed it all in the front passenger seat of the Volkswagen. Going back inside, she reached under the bench and retrieved a black duffel bag. Unzipping the canvas, she set a digital kitchen time for two hours, disengaged a safety, then slid the bag under the rear of the Jeep.

A minute later, Biannca was pulling out of the sliding gate and heading north out of town.

Thirty feet away, peering out between the blinds covering the office window, Doris Goodwin held an ancient wall phone to her ear. She tried to see the license plate on the purple car but wasn't fast enough. Her hand shook as she wondered about the strange, bleeding woman she'd seen on her morning patrol around her buildings. Every morning for twenty years, Doris had walked down the hill from the house to make sure no vandals had broken in during the night. In twenty years she had never seen anything like this. Sure, every now and then a unit got broken into, but there had never been so much blood. It had taken Doris a good while to get back to the office. The phone rang and rang as she tried to get a hold of her husband Jerry.

Chapter Seventeen

Charles McKetrick dropped his satchel in a chair next to his desk and hung his suit coat over the same. He paused to look out his polarized window across the Washington DC Mall and the Smithsonian Museum of Natural History behind that. It was quiet — a couple of joggers warmed up at a bench along the well-manicured paths stretching in a long rectangle between the Capital Building on one end and the Lincoln Memorial on the other. Over the monuments, he could make out a network of contrails crisscrossing in the early morning sky. It was barely six a.m. in DC and the ants were on the march.

On a squat bureau under the window, a French press coffee carafe sat on a knitted potholder which bore the stars and bars. He took up the carafe, realizing he had left it half full last night when he finally called it quits. He couldn't quite recall when that had been. Last night had been a study in patience. A lesson McKetrick had yet to master even after almost thirty years in government service. As Assistant Director over the Office of Logistics and Special Projects, he had a staff of people. Someone of whom would already have a steaming pot of coffee waiting for their boss in any other senior level office inside the Capital beltway, but that wasn't how things worked in McKetrick's little slice of government. He had fetched coffee for several executives in his day.

That experience, normally while undercover on a surreptitious mission against said executive, and the blowhard bureaucrats he had served under, had made coffee a barometer of sorts in McKetrick's world paradigm. A man should be able to fetch his own coffee. No one was so important they could not cover their own basic needs.

Walking to a small kitchenette within his executive suite, McKetrick started the process of cleaning out the carafe, and set a kettle on. Steam was barely visible oozing from the spout of the blue kettle when there was a knock on the door. Before he could answer, the heavy wood door swung open and a twenty-five year old, rail thin, spectacled analyst wearing a rumpled suit coat entered and jetted toward the expansive desk in the center of the suite. The young man strode right past his boss while trying to wrangle a tablet in his hands like it had been dipped in grease. The man stopped in front of the desk, confused for a moment before McKetrick made him jump.

"Did you go home last night, Gerald?"

The former Navy analyst skipped a step almost leaping in a one-eighty to face the AD. McKetrick took in his employee and raised his eyebrows.

"Gerald, you look like you just emptied the nation of Columbia of one of its top exports. And I'll be pissed to find out you are doing coke at work."

Whatever Gerald had on his mind short circuited as the analyst tried to digest his boss's attempt at a joke. He stood with his face screwed in confusion for a moment before getting himself back on track. With an unconscious shake of his head, the young man breathed a single word. "Rhino."

"Where they going?" asked McKetrick.

"Looks like upstate New York."

"You able to piggyback?"

There was a little bit of a delay. McKetrick could almost feel his assistant's panic rising as he waited for the connection to go through.

Gerald sighed before saying, "I got it."

McKetrick rose from his desk and walked to a wall safe hidden behind a portrait he kept of Teddy Roosevelt. Inside were a group of files stored in a leather valise. Next to the valise was an encrypted phone and a Heckler and Koch 9mm compact handgun. McKetrick grabbed the phone and the gun.

Chapter Eighteen

The sun was rising by the time 1-8 managed to meet them at the targeted point.

"Wide base, off road tires, SUV or a truck," said 2-4.

"I got blood here," commented 2-7.

2-2 adjusted his compact M4 in the front of the Range Rover's passenger seat beside him and cringed.

"Let's go." He wasn't losing this job, and his timeline for scheduled check-in with Central was quickly approaching. If the bitch had found transport, this mission was going to stretch. One did not like extending what should have been a simple, direct action. They needed to lock this down quick and move on. He tried to tell himself he was a professional, that contingencies were part of the job. Take her scalp, get the confirmation, and move on, he told himself. He was in a business that held little patience for failure, or deviation from an ops plan. 2-2 felt a throbbing in the back of his head. If he had any opportunity in the future, that bitch was going to die badly.

They travelled with 2-2, 1-6, and 1-8, in a black Range Rover that struggled to manage the dense trees and narrow lane, as they followed the tracks that wound through the woods east of the lake. The going was slow and most of the time 1-8 was out on foot jogging to ensure they could follow the tracks of their fleeing prey. The sun was up now and 2-2 was dreading a call that he knew was soon to come.

He twisted and flipped the encrypted phone over and over in his hand as if the device was an electronic worry bead. He thought of the contract and he thought of his share that could very easily be in jeopardy. His plans, everything his future meant hinged on this final play. The phone vibrated and the sudden movement made him jump in his seat.

2-2 looked at the phone. There were no lights, no screen. It looked like a relic with only a keypad, microphone, and speaker. It vibrated for a second time, then a third before he answered.

"Status," the caller stated. The voice was female and seemed like it might be computer-generated.

"No resolution. Target is evading," 2-2 answered.

There was a long silence, then, "Estimated completion."

"Unable to speculate."

Another long silence, "Understood, communication to follow." The call ended.

"Fuck," uttered 2-2.

1-6 was staring at him as the Range Rover rolled slowly around a corner.

"We're good," was all 2-2 said.

When the Range Rover pulled around the bend, they were greeted by a twin to their vehicle parked on the side of a two-lane highway. 2-4 leaned on one arm out the driver's side window. 1-8 stood at the front window.

2-2 suddenly realized he might have spoken too soon. The encrypted phone vibrated again.

"Yes," said 2-2.

"Assets are being calibrated to assist. Historical data analysis of her comm's device indicates potential search grid at two viable locations. Data is being transmitted now."

2-2 looked to 1-6 who retrieved a small tablet from the rear seat. 2-2 activated the device and a notification of data transfer lit up the screen. 2-2 tapped the notification and an aerial view of the area with two pinging dots filled the screen. Cortland and Ithaca.

"Thank you, One," 2-2 said, feeling the need for the nicety.

The connection went dead.

Chapter Nineteen

2-2 was itchy. With 2-4 and 1-8 patrolling the west side of the little college town he, 1-6, and 2-7 had taken up post on Highway 41 leading out of Cortland. The tablet displaying a satellite map of the area sat on his lap. Despite the fact it did not yield any more clues no matter how many times he zoomed in or out on the OLED screen, he couldn't help but return to the map every couple of minutes.

The wait was maddening. The clock on this fucked up operation had stretched two hours, then three. Now it was almost six hours since they lost contact with their target. She was making them, him look like a fool. Added to that was the naturally impatient disposition of his shooters. Men and women who needed to work, needed to do. His people didn't like sitting static in some town in the middle of nowhere. Especially one where the locals took notice of strangers driving aimlessly around. Patience was needed in their chosen line of work, but so was efficiency and quick, quiet execution. This job was proving to possess none of those traits and his people were getting jumpy.

He looked out over a farmer's field. A lone bull stood watch over a cluster of black and white milk cows that lay in the tall green grass chewing incessantly on the sweet vegetation. A hill covered in lush greenery provided the backdrop for the scene.

The mere fact that he'd been staring at that goddamned bull for almost an hour infuriated him.

"This stretches on much longer they'll call it and pull the contract,' said 1-6 from the driver's seat.

2-2 didn't answer. The idea of losing the payday was not something he could face. He wanted out. He'd been renting himself out to the highest bidder, sludging through godforsaken shit holes fighting other people's wars for too long. He was tired; he had scars that bore no meaning. He'd told himself this was it and every second the timetable grew he felt his freedom slipping away.

"I didn't come to East fucking nowhere just to stare at fuckin cows," 1-6 said.

No shit, thought 2-2, but was in no mood to discuss the obvious.

Silence returned to the Range Rover cabin and like clockwork, 2-2 looked back to the digital map in search of inspiration. A notification popped up on the screen. He tapped the notification and a transcript filled a window. A call to the local Sheriff's department.

Female, bleeding, leaving in grey sedan, caller stated there was no crime committed, no destruction to their business at a local self-storage facility. No car had been dispatched. The operator had told the caller they would keep an eye out.

A quick search and 2-2 found the units on the map. Not more than a mile away from where he sat. He looked in the direction of the business. His brow creased as he noticed a thick column of black smoke rising toward the sky.

Chapter Twenty

Nothing blows a weekend like a three-year old getting dropped in the Projects. Willy Thompkins hadn't showed all weekend despite Viejo and Wilke putting word out to their sources they were looking for him. If the little shit was still alive, he was holed up under a rock somewhere.

That led Charleston PD Chief of Police Andrew Vaden to order Captain Peter Banks to take control of the investigation. An investigation like this demanded action and Banks unleashed Special Operations Command on the East Side of Charleston. They needed buys out of the main drug houses on the peninsula. Snitches, one after another, full-time losers, crack heads, and heroin zombies were conscripted, with possession charges hanging over their heads to repay society. The Narcotics Unit stuck to the lower tier low-life's for the weekend operation due to the real object of the operation being entries into the various gang hangouts to A: look for evidence leading back to Chevante's murder; and B: put enough of a beating on the local thugs to keep anyone else from getting whacked through reprisal hits. They didn't want to use any of their higher end sources, dealers who'd bargained to go after their suppliers and higher rungs of the food chain to keep their self-serving asses out of jail. Despite the fact they usually came through with good intel, and got them good busts, those jackasses always played both sides so at least half of what you told them, if not all, made it back to the very people they were helping to take down. With the pressure coming down from the Chief's office via Captain Banks, and the public via Councilman Demario Candor, a convicted drug dealer in his own right, the Unit was on the spot. They needed to get this tied up and tied up quickly.

By 0300 Monday morning, Viejo was seeing triple as he typed the affidavits for search warrants on five houses they were able to buy from. All five were tied to violent gangs who'd shot up the projects and each other in the past. He and Wilke finished the last of them by 0400, and the Unit hit Bennies Diner downtown for breakfast and coffee while they waited for the judge to wake up. Judge Gadlaw was their go-to guy. Come 0500, Viejo knew he could find him at the Rod & Gun Club on the Upper Peninsula; he had a thing for shooting skeet at dawn. Another great thing about Gadlaw that Viejo and Wilke found particularly useful was that when they met him at the range, arms loaded with paper, Judge Gadlaw only read far enough down the first page to make sure the formatting was right.

He hated losing his time on the firing range. The judge didn't even flip through it before asking, "These good?"

"Yes Judge," Wilke said as he raised his right hand.

"Good enough for me, boys," he said, and signed each one.

Chapter Twenty-One

Treat Moncrief was slow to exit the matte black Toyota Range Rover which was parked behind the rear entrance of the Eversuds coin laundry on Highway 17 in West Ashley. He noted a non-descript dark tan Volvo parked in the small lot, and a beat up old Ford pickup truck that made him want to laugh out loud. He sighed as he pulled open the old metal door which groaned on its hinges and slipped inside.

The rear of the Eversuds was as unremarkable as any given hallway could be. There was a constant drone of washer and dryer units humming in the background. The hallway was painted in white primer so tinged by decades in the humid Lowcountry environment that the walls almost seemed to ooze their own brand of grime. The linoleum floor was off-white, not due to color choice from years past, but simply due to the traffic tracing the same worn path repetitively back and forth. Moncrief followed the worn black trail down until the hallway bore right and the structure opened up into a large workshop. Washer and dryer units of varying age and in varying states of disrepair were scattered throughout the open space in what was actually a very methodical manner, though to look at the scattering of machines, one would never know. The only reason Moncrief understood the arrangement was that he had stacked and restacked, then disassembled and reassembled the units over and over since he was thirteen years old and the old man had put him to work. The old man had caught Moncrief trying to wrench his way into the coin bin of a washing machine chasing quarters, and instead of breaking his hand, he had put Moncrief to work.

The residual smells of detergents, aromatics, and softeners caught in Moncrief's throat each time he entered the building. He felt stifled by the scents, felt like they clung to him like death clings to a morgue. He heard a clang on the opposite side of a rack of tools and paused. Peeking around the rack of shelves, he saw the two men he had been summoned to meet. One encouraged a rage that Moncrief could barely control to boil within him, and the other triggered a mix of disappointment and gut-melting fear. Stepping out from behind the shelving, he approached them.

Carter Blanding, the soft, doughy bastard, took an involuntary step backward, and Moncrief took pleasure in the slight gasp that escaped the weakling in the suit as he appeared. Blanding was light-skinned and balding, his hair close cropped to his scalp. Wire rimmed glasses trimmed vacant eyes that darted from Moncrief to the old man and back again.

The old man was on his knees, scrubbing carbon off the filament of a gas dryer. He didn't look up as he addressed Moncrief.

"You don't make life easy on anybody, do you?" he wheezed, speaking from an awkward angle.

Moncrief shrugged, but before he could respond, Washington was on his feet and the wire brush he had been tending the dryer with flashed before Moncrief's eyes. Tiny wire bristles tore into his cheek.

The impact and the fire tearing through his nerves in response to the hundreds of small wounds dotting his face made Moncrief stumble backward with a grunt. "Take your medicine, boy," Washington's voice was cool. He followed with another bristled combination to Moncrief's shoulder and the side of his head.

Moncrief could barely get his hands up in front of him as he fell to his knees.

"No, you don't," Washington said, swatting the bones on the back of his hand.

The wire brush carried with it subtle but enormous effectiveness in the hands of the powerful man. Moncrief was twenty years the junior of Harold Washington and could not defend himself. His hand was numb and would not respond after one strike. He fell to his back, and Washington battered him again and again until he thought he might pass out. Each impact carried with it a torrent of pain as a swarm of metal stingers attacked his flesh, only to be torn out. It seemed like an eternity before Moncrief realized the assault had ended, and that he was whimpering. When he finally built up the courage to crack an eye, he saw Washington holding out a hand to him.

"Get up, son," the old man said plainly. "Lesson's over."

Moncrief gasped in an attempt to regain his composure and reached out greedily for the man's hand so as not to reignite his wrath.

"I'm docking you twenty-five K for the intolerable actions you saw fit to carry out last night. That money goes to Carter."

Moncrief was still trying to comprehend what had happened to him. He held a hand to his cheek, trying to keep an amassing flow of bloody pinpricks from draining down his neck.

"But..."

Washington cocked his head, and Moncrief shut up.

"But?" Washington asked.

Moncrief dropped his eyes to the grimy concrete floor of the workroom.

Washington faced him. "You, me and Carter have an arrangement, young man. He hides our money, *our* money." Washington stabbed Moncrief in the chest with the butt of the wire brush to drive home his point. "You distribute our product on the streets, I bring in that product, and keep the supply lines moving. We have a system here that has worked for decades, before you were even sweeping floors in this place, learning how to be a man. Before your momma shit you out, this system was here. You jeopardized all of that because what?" Washington pointed at Blanding, who visibly shriveled away. The chubby man refused to look in Moncrief's direction. If no one else were in that room at that moment, Moncrief would have torn the weak bitch apart. He looked back toward Washington who continued, "You think he's got it too easy, 'don't never get his hands dirty,' I think are the words you used, at least that's how Carter put it."

Moncrief could not be sure if he should speak or not.

Washington tossed the bloody wire brush to the floor and turned his back on Moncrief. "Any other day you'd be dead for what you pulled last night. Lucky for you, I have something in the offing and I can't afford a personnel change at the moment." Washington stressed that final point, "I have tried for years, boy, to get your head right. Time's coming where you're gonna run out of chances to fuck up. Get out of my sight."

Moncrief, holding a hand to his swelling and bleeding cheek, looked at Carter Blanding. The man was visibly shaking and refused to look at him. He looked one last time at Washington. Their eyes met and Moncrief held the man's stare for a moment. He had no doubt the old man would kill him without a second thought. Moncrief made up his mind about something he'd been considering for a long time right there in that moment. He turned slowly and left the laundromat.

Chapter Twenty-Two

The trouble with spying on a spy agency was that everybody knew the game. Everybody was suspicious to the point of paranoia, and everybody watched everybody else. The only thing working for Gerald was that his quarry, a faction within the CIA, was trying to run under the radar. That meant normal security protocols that would be followed, such as tracking computer use and reviewing communications logs, were skirted due to a lack of resources. This left the door open for him to be able to hack into their illegitimate operations that were run using the same agency resources and networks.

On the one hand, tasking a satellite under the guise of a legitimate operation was relatively easy. On the other, increasing personnel within an illegal conspiracy just to run log checks was not only a risk of one more potential leak, but the whole point of a machine within a machine was to get a job done and move on. Extra layers of bureaucracy, even in the name of operational security, would only slow things down.

From his office inside the red castle of the Smithsonian, Gerald could sniff around the scant files his targets kept. He'd been networked into one of the most protected agencies for almost a year. McKetrick had been suspicious that something was wrong inside the agency but it wasn't until the debacle in

Charleston that he was unleashed to focus his trusted few on a conspiracy hunt.

Things were now starting to come together. Gerald didn't know whether to be excited or horrified. Given some of the names he'd been able to connect to a growing list of suspects and the types of things they were allegedly doing, he felt fear gnaw at his insides. He felt like he was perched in the middle of an open field at Gettysburg, moments before each side opened fire.

Chapter Twenty-Three

Viejo and Wilke pulled to the corner of Luciente and Vernon streets and waited. It was relatively quiet on the streets at just past seven in the morning on a Tuesday. A couple of people ambled here and there, actually going to work, while others migrated toward a point a block away and began congregating as if waiting on a bus. Trouble was that there was no bus stop where the assorted group of skinny, gaunt-faced mass was forming.

"Like clockwork," said Viejo.

"Yup," was Wilke's quiet reply.

Viejo took his eyes from the street where he was scanning the growing crowd of heroin addicts and studied his friend. Wilke had lost weight over the last few months, almost a year now since Poppy died. Not that there was excess before the incident last year, but Wilke seemed to Viejo somehow harder now than he was. There was a tightness to his partner's jaw line that was not there before, and a darkness to his eyes; a focused intensity that had at some point replaced the cocky casualness that Viejo had always associated with his friend. He wondered how that change had managed to sneak up on him.

After the Tulley incident, the entire unit had been placed on administrative leave while the department and the state completed their respective investigations. The team had kept together during their time off, mostly thanks to Banks who quietly insisted they got together every couple of days if for no other reason than to keep an eye on each other. As the investigation cleared each one of them, they began to filter back to work, or in the case of Max DeGuello, retire. The rounds DeGuello had taken to his leg had all but shattered his femur. He walked with a permanent limp and from what Viejo had last heard was spending his days fishing offshore with a couple of other retired detectives. Viejo had a hard time comprehending a man like Max DeGuello with his feet up soaking a line.

Wilke was the last to return to the office. The department psychologist would not clear him. There wasn't much a cop could not learn through the grapevine, but in the case of police psychologist's notes and reports, that realm might as well be Fort Knox. Not even Banks could break through that barrier. He and Banks had become Wilkes' pseudo-minders during his forced banishment from police work. They made sure he was not alone as much as they could and tried to keep him in the loop as to what was going on when he wasn't there.

Finally, after a couple of months, Wilke was allowed back on light duty. It made Viejo cringe every time the unit had an ops brief, then left the office. Wilke usually slouched against a wall or rocked back and forth in his desk chair, watching them go. Being forced to stay home was bad enough for a cop who was at his best running the streets. It was even worse having to stay behind to mind paperwork while your friends ran off into the urban wild without you. Viejo didn't know what had transpired to allow Wilke his return to police work, but he was glad for it. The Narcotics Unit had gone through a complete turnover after what had happened a year back. Viejo was glad to have a part of the original band back together. Though he still hadn't heard how it was Wilke had been cleared for active duty.

"There he is," Wilke stated.

Viejo looked out the windshield, tracking where Wilke was looking and found the swaggering, loose, ambling form of the particular street creature they were looking for.

Thomas Wrightsell, aka Crackle on the street and to almost every uniform, dope, and burglary detective prowling the Charleston peninsula, was a long-term heroin addict and petty criminal. The name Crackle was a moniker handed him by a quick-witted patrol Sergeant a little less than a decade ago when he had answered a suspicious person call behind an East Side grocery. The Sergeant had spotted a smoldering pile of ragged clothes and twitching tennis shoes lying on the pavement just below a damaged length of copper conduit. Crackle had been trying to steal copper for scrap, a quick way to get easy cash in his attempt to chase the dragon. On that particular night, Crackle had grabbed hold of a piece of metal that happened to carry a main electrical line to the building's environmental system. When the patrol Sergeant approached the spasming lump on the pavement, he noted that Crackle had been fried to the point that the ends of his hair were crackling and popping from all the juice that had flowed through him. From then on, Thomas Wrightsell would forever be known as Crackle to his friends in the Charleston Police.

Today Crackle was looking a little less ragged than usual. He walked with a shuffling limp. He was missing the ring and little fingers of his right hand as a result of the electrocution that gave him his name. Today however, his clothes seemed a little cleaner. He wore dark jeans and a baggy, grey-blue flannel shirt. Viejo put their unmarked Toyota Camry in gear and slowly approached where Crackle was about to cross the street. They stopped in front of the skinny black man who flinched and hopped back awkwardly. Wilke rolled down his window.

"Get in," he said.

The apprehensiveness, dominating Crackles features faded and he smiled wide, "Damn Wilke, you scared the shit out of me," he said while jumping in the back seat.

Viejo put his window down to match Wilke's as he immediately recognized the smell of a man whose last shower happened at an indeterminate date in the past.

"What's goin' on fellas, I ain't seen you guys in a little bit. 'Specially you Wilke, where you been man?"

"I thought for folks like you not seeing the police was a good thing?" Viejo said, looking at his confidential informant through the rear-view mirror as he guided the unmarked police unit around the block.

"I don't mind seein y'all. Shit, I'm clean anyway," Crackle responded with a sniff as he cleared his nose.

Wilke and Viejo paused and Viejo thought for a moment that Wilke would grab that softball line of bullshit served to him by their source and run with it. He didn't. Wilke's quick-witted humor that was as much a part of his friend as was breathing didn't show itself. Wilke didn't even acknowledge the lie. Instead, he turned in his seat and studied the CI as Viejo crossed the peninsula toward a set of abandoned lots where they would be able to talk in peace. If Wilke wasn't going to speak up, Viejo couldn't let the words of his CI go.

"You're clean?"

Crackle looked at him through the rear-view mirror for a second before his eyes, glossy and dull, flickered away. "Yeah."

"How long?"

"Uh," Crackle stuttered. "Been a little while."

"Uh-huh, so you just happened to be on that corner at feedin' time with the rest of the walking dead. Why?"

"I wasn't goin' to get anything."

"Bullshit."

"Na man."

"Bullshit." Viejo repeated himself flatly.

Crackle sucked his teeth and flopped back in the seat, looking put out. Wilke tossed him a McDonald's bag and a napkin, and the faux hurt hanging on the drug addict's features faded. "There you go," he said as Crackle attacked the breakfast burrito inside.

"What happened to that little girl?" Wilke asked him.

"Yeah, that's messed up right there," said Crackle, his mouth full of eggs and sausage.

"What's the word? Who did it?" Viejo asks.

"Dunno."

They both turned around in their seats to look at their source. Crackle looked back at them with a blank look on his face.

"What?"

"You forget how this works, Crack?" asked Wilke with an edge to his voice.

Crackle stopped chewing.

"You work or you go up to county for that bindle we've still got sitting in Evidence. There's a warrant with your name on it. How you gonna be feelin' in three days if we take you in?"

"Come on, man," Crackle pleaded. "That happened a long time back."

"Think the judge is gonna care about that?" added Viejo with one eye on his partner.

Crackle sighed. "Look man, all I know is that Deshaun jus' got out like a minute before they shot him. Don't know who did it. Whoever shot that little girl got bigger problems than you. Whole neighborhood wants to kill 'em, everybody from the civilians to the boys runnin' these streets. Killin's one thing." Crackle clicked his tongue. "Man they got no place to hide anybody finds out who did it."

Streets have a heart, that's good to know, thought Viejo.

"You ever buy from Deshaun before?" asked Wilke.

"Nah man, he into that crack game, I don't mess with that stuff."

"Yeah, best to stick to the horse. That crack'll kill ya," replied Wilke with a tone Viejo knew. His partner was losing patience.

"Come on Crackle, Deshaun have a beef with anybody? The streets talk man."

"I know," answered Crackle through the last bite of his burrito. He went to licking remnants of cheese from the wrapper and said, "Only thing I heard was that he had a problem when he got out with some North Charleston motherfucker. Bainert or some shit like that. Over some girl or somethin like that."

"Bainert, that's all you got?" Wilke pressed.

"He drive some fast an' furious rig, like a Honda or something, all lit up and bright orange. I seen it around a couple of times but I don't know him."

Viejo threw the car in gear and pulled away from the empty park.

The return to the corner brought a sigh from Crackle and a wheezing, "Shiiit," when he saw that the crowd waiting for their morning fix had grown to almost twenty loafing addicts, each trying to seem less suspicious than the next. The car pulled to a stop a block down from the gathering and Crackle got out. He was shuffling off when Wilke called out to him.

"Crackle."

Crackle turned his way and rolled his eyes.

"This is a two-way street man. Don't fuck up. You work or you go in. Don't waste my time again."

"Man, Wilke?"

Viejo pulled off, leaving their CI and his excuses behind them.

"Crackle's not a bad guy, man," Viejo said.

"He's a fuckin' junkie. He fucks up, we drop him and get a new one, fuck him."

Viejo didn't respond.

Chapter Twenty-Four

"Oh thank God, we're saved!" announced Doug Martin, peeking up over his computer monitor as Viejo and Wilke wandered into the Central Detectives Bureau at 180 Lockwood Drive.

"That happy to see us?" Viejo responded. "We're happy to help you tie-wearing bureaucrats out."

Martin scoffed, "Grab a notebook and a pen, sonny. If you plan on following us around for the day, you just signed up to learn something."

"Uh-huh."

Viejo and Wilke made a beeline for that substance that is more necessary to a cop's day to day than the badge or the gun—coffee. They had just made it when Captain Banks entered at speed. He stopped inside the doorway and surveyed the dozen or so detectives milling around the wide-open office that made up the Central Detectives bull pen. He found his detectives.

"You four, conference room, now."

Five minutes later the two detectives from homicide, Martin and Fenner, and the Narcotics Detectives, Viejo and Wilke, were seated on opposite sides of the long, pressed laminate table, looking to the Captain in dress uniform who was seated at the head.

"Where are we?" was all Banks asked.

"Got word on a street of a beef Cauldwell had with a North Charleston thug over some girl, but so far no one is talking. Whoever shot Chevante won't find any comfort on the East Side of Charleston. At least that's what we got from Crackle."

"Crackle's still alive?" blurted Martin. "Jesus, that junkie must have the genes of a cockroach."

No one responded and Banks ignored the old detective.

"Where are you two?" Banks asked the homicide contingent.

"Deshaun just got out of County, served a little less than a year on a possession with intent to distribute charge. We're still waiting on most of the records from the jail. Talked to a couple of the corrections officers who ran the pod Cauldwell was housed in. Nothing big coming out of there other than some chatter about him living well. Apparently he had quite a stout account balance at the canteen, if you can call that living large. We'll know more on that when we get his records and phone recordings from the jail."

"Anything else?"

Viejo spoke up, "We're pretty sure the car fire Thompson processed the other night was the shooter vehicle. It was burnt to shit, but Thompson and the rest of the Crime Scene guys had it towed to their garage. They're going to see what they can get, but I wouldn't put much stock in something turning up."

"So we've got shit then," stated Banks flatly.

The statement alone, notwithstanding the gruff manner it was delivered in, made the four detectives squirm just a little. Everyone at the table, even the cranky Martin, who was a decade Banks' senior by department time, was suddenly studying his hands rather than keeping eye contact with the command officer.

"Guys, and lady," said Banks, nodding to Fenner, "We have all been through this before. Whoever shot that little girl has the entire city at a standstill. You four are the people the Chief and I want solving this. Forget the media, forget the Mayor, and get me something to feed the beasts by this afternoon. Press release has to be ready by five. You're on the clock. Viejo, you've got PC on dealers in the area that might have had a competition issue with Cauldwell working that particular corner?"

"Yes sir," Viejo nodded.

"Martin and Fenner, you've got an angle with the jail records?"

"Yes sir."

"Go knock on some doors then," Banks said, rising from his seat.

As the detectives filed out of the conference room, Banks studied Wilke, who was last in line. As they reached the threshold, Banks noted Wilke looked at him briefly and offered a weak smile. Banks gestured for him to hang back.

Wilke stopped and looked as if he were standing for inspection at roll call. Banks sat on the conference table and looked to make sure the rest of the meeting had filtered down the hallway.

"Sir?" Wilke asked.

"How you doing, Ben?"

He watched Wilke's features intently, knowing that his only real answers would come from the miniscule tells that a person can't hide. A facial twitch, a body movement that would either confirm or refute whatever words were given up by that person being questioned.

"I'm good sir," he answered, still slowly shifting, almost imperceptibly, from side to side, "Just glad to be out of the office."

"I want you to know there's nothing wrong if you need more time. This case is going to carry with it a lot of extra political and bureaucratic bullshit. Stuff that we don't always react that well to. There's nothing wrong with sitting this one out."

Wilke let slip a wry grin and briefly looked away from him toward the hallway. It was that small indicator he was uncomfortable. As if the doorway was an escape route. Banks had seen it a hundred times—on the street when a subject unintentionally took a stutter step away, or in an interrogation room when they leaned away from him as if trying to create distance between themselves and the questions they know they can't answer.

"I'm good sir," he said, looking him fractionally in the eye. "I like being able to contribute again."

Banks studied him in silence for a long moment and he watched his detective protégé squirm. The kid was tough and instinctively one of the best cops he'd ever worked with. Ben Wilke had a feel for police work that is a rare trait. He knew people, he had a barometer for when things were going bad, and he had a poise that kept him in control when everything and everyone else on scene started falling apart.

But everyone had a breaking point. Banks had feared from the first moment he saw Wilke after the death of Poppy Montague that her death was Wilke's breaking point. Banks had been confined to a hospital bed recovering from shrapnel wounds sustained when an unknown subject had dropped a pair of grenades on him. Banks recalled the vacant look on Wilke's face, the shallow bags around his eyes, deflation in his shoulders. As if he had been drained of life. He hadn't been able to say anything to help the young detective then with the rest of the squad, or what was left of the squad, all huddling around each other. Banks felt a pang of guilt, almost a painful stab in his stomach. Seeing Ben Wilke today and every day reminded him that he had ordered Wilke to hold off on attacking the location where Montague had been held so that he could get his people in position for their raid at a storage facility in downtown Charleston. He had held Wilke and the others back — what? Maybe a series of minutes, five, ten minutes? Banks could not help but ask himself every time he saw Poppy's face flash through his mind. Her subtle, devious grin that was her hallmark. Like a spring wound under a cannonball just waiting to be pointed in the direction of the enemy. Banks could not help but wonder if that fateful order had been the difference between life and death of one of his own. Never mind what the autopsy showed, never mind what the medical examiners told him. That she suffered massive cerebral trauma, that there was no way she could have survived whatever unknown assault had been perpetrated against her. The doctors guessed some kind of poison but there was no reference for what they discovered during their examination. None of the expert opinion or analysis mattered to Peter Banks. Bottom line was that he had taken precious seconds away from the rescue of one of his own, and he saw that every time he looked Ben Wilke in the eye.

"Ok," Banks finally told him, "Go knock on some doors then."

Wilke all but scrambled for the door. Before he was able to flee, Banks stopped him once more.

"Ben," he said.

Wilke stiffened and stopped just barely past the threshold of the room.

"Anything changes you step back, got it?"

Wilke looked at him meekly and nodded before escaping into the hallway.

Banks let him go and stayed propped on the conference room table staring into the hallway. He had a brief moment of silence to try to wrangle in the demons that had been stirred by the encounter with his detective. A stern clacking of sharp heels on tile followed ominously by a wraith-like shadow brought him out of his stupor.

"What the hell do you think you are doing?"

Banks stepped back inside the conference room and held the door for a green-eyed, pantsuited brunette standing in the hallway.

"Good morning, Doctor," Banks said.

"You released him for full duty." It wasn't a question.

"I did," Banks acknowledged.

Doctor Phyllis Cannor froze and stared at him for a moment, arms crossed. She was leaning back on one spiked heel, "You obviously haven't been reading my updates then."

"I've read each one intently. It's my job to know the status of my personnel."

The doctor's eyes flared and Banks had to remind himself not to stoke the flames any higher. He and the department's staff shrink did not have the greatest of relationships.

After the events that occurred near the port of Charleston and the shootout on John's Island, he and his unit had all been required to meet with Cannor for evaluation and debriefing. The meetings went better for some than others. Cannor suspiciously got along fabulously with DeGuello. He even remembered walking into the office for a session and seeing DeGuello and the doc leaning against opposite sides of a door jamb as if the two were flirting in the hallway during high school class change. DeGuello of course had nothing to say about the matter, and when he pressed Cannor, which he could not help but do, he and the psychologist had ended up with the status they currently found themselves in.

Every contact with the woman seemed to either begin with her cross with him or ending with her furious with him. Banks understood and empathized. He had gone through two marriages that had ended up with the exact same reactions from both wives, so he had allowed it might be him. After a softening of tactics had no effect on the working relationship between the two of them, he'd even tried to get DeGuello to give him a hand, but his old friend was so mired in bureaucratic nonsense surrounding his medical retirement that it was almost impossible to get a hold of the guy. Then DeGuello finally got approval for retirement and left a smoking trail of rubber down I-26 enroute, code three for Key West. As far as Banks had been able to tell so far, DeGuello was one of the most prominent stool pigeons in the historic district of the Conche Republic and getting a hold of the guy at this point was an exercise in randomness. If Max DeGuello wanted to be found, he could be, but most of the time he was either haunting Old Town or chasing red fish on his boat and not open to communications.

Regardless, Banks for whatever reason was on the wrong side of Doctor Phyllis Cannor and today was no different. She was all but tapping her toe while she stared at him, plumes of pure disgust radiating from her as she waited for him to explain himself. Pride told him he couldn't give into her so easily.

"So," Banks said, leaning on the conference table, "What can I help you with today, Doctor?" he asked.

"Don't give me that, you know exactly what I'm here for. I just saw you send him out. Wilke is not ready to be back on the street."

"I disagree," Banks said flatly.

"You're not a doctor!" Cannor bellowed.

Banks kept his inflections in check. "You're not a cop," he told her. His volume even may have dropped a level.

Cannor stepped back, bracing herself as if she had been struck, then shifted position to be more head-on with him. "Benjamin Wilke is a patient in my care. I decide what he is ready for and what he is not."

"Ben Wilke is a detective under my command. You are a psychologist holding an advisory position. I have received your advice regarding my cop. If he says he's ready, then he's ready." With that, Banks rose and calmly exited the conference room.

"The Chief will hear about this," Cannor called behind him.

"Might want to try the mayor," Banks replied over his shoulder. "He's got more juice."

Chapter Twenty-Five

Biannca was violating almost every tactic she'd ever been taught about escape and evasion. She blew her lead on the off chance her pursuers responded to her distraction. She had planted herself on the far side of a gas station a few hundred yards down the road from her storage unit. She was on the opposite side of the pumps and the store front. The VW was positioned caddy corner to the building, partially hiding the bug from the road. She had wanted so badly to close her eyes while sitting in the confines of the driver seat, her side burning.

Through the windshield she watched a thick smoke fill the sky. A haze covered the storage units and four red fire trucks, two tankers, and a ladder truck crowded a field adjacent to the facility. A red and white Sheriff's cruiser sat to one side of the highway, a grey, uniformed deputy kept traffic flowing past the scene. Cars slowly streamed past the burning business. Biannca studied each vehicle as it went by. Several had stopped along the side of the highway and a crowd was building on the shoulder a little way down the road. Everyone in town seemed to want to come out and see the spectacle.

The fire was only intended to cover her tracks. Biannca found that cleaning up evidence when clearing an operation was almost impossible. There was always something left behind, and with modern techniques, something could be microscopic and still compromise her mission. Fire wasn't one hundred percent effective and it created quite a scene; something in her line of work it was best to avoid. But it was a proven method and a lot less time consuming way of cleaning a location than most. She'd only had to cover herself in this manner once before, and that was at the end of an assignment in Venezuela. She had perfected her technique since then. A little more accident and a little less evidence. She still remembered the news reports of the fire she'd set in South America. It resulted in a square mile of ghetto outside of Caracas reduced to scorched tin and ash. A fire like that brings way too much attention, so it was good she was cruising thirty miles off the coast by the time it set off. In hindsight, as much as she hated to admit it, Biannca could relate to fire bugs. *Setting fires was pretty cool*, she thought, as she watched streams of water try to stanch the creep of heat and flame as the fire swept from one storage unit to the next.

Biannca kept an eye on the crowd, using the onlookers for cover and on the road looking for...them? She'd know them if she saw them. As it was, she wondered how long she could hang there herself. This was a small town and sooner or later somebody was going to notice a stranger in a strange car sitting among them. She decided if she started getting looks from the locals, she was going to have to bail.

It occurred to her this surveillance might come up with nothing. What would it mean if she didn't mark anyone suspicious? Had they been called off? Not a chance. If it was the agency trying to take her off the board, she would have to run far and long before she would be rid of them. The idea of the chase ahead of her made a deep, locked away part of her want to fold up and cry. There was a real hopelessness in facing an officially sanctioned execution. Hopeless, if she decided it was. She crushed the whining little girl inside with a sledge hammer and decided she didn't do hopeless. There was a reason she was sitting in that parking lot. She needed to know who and how many people she needed to kill.

The first responders had the blaze down to a roiling smolder of smoke and steam before she saw them. In a town of college kids and academics, they stood out. Cars varied from Fiat's, Mini's, and Volkswagens to Ford F-150's. Range Rovers, especially ones with generous doses of mud caked along the lower fenders were something of note. Two men inside, both erect in the front seats, the passenger leaning toward the fire scene while the driver navigated the stream of rubberneckers. She was curious but not sold, until a twin of the first Toyota SUV rolled slowly by, three men in this vehicle, with short cropped hair and dark clothes, an observation facilitated by the fact the driver had the window down. A telltale sleeve of black arm tattoos wound around the bicep and forearm perched on the window frame. Those guys screamed military and they were the best option so far. They headed back toward town.

Her instinct was to hunt. To stalk them, more intelligence meant a possible advantage. If she counted both Range Rovers as adversaries, then at the base she was outnumbered five to one. On the other hand, she knew what they looked like, and if they had migrated to Cortland then they had support. Biannca didn't want to admit it, but the term Central was poking at the back of her mind. If Central was assisting, then her adversaries not only had her history but eventually they would have a satellite guiding them, if they didn't already. Real fear nibbled at Biannca's spine. That was worst case, and it was all she had to go on. It meant running, and running forever. She put the Bug in gear and turned out of the gas station, away from the small college town, away from her quarry. She felt like she was in a boxing ring and had just turned her back to her opponent, but now she had to run. Her only option was to run.

The drive from Cortland to Syracuse takes the average traveler around forty-five minutes. Biannca took six hours to get from one town to the other. The winding back roads of upstate New York did not offer much in the way of cover from possible satellite surveillance, given that most of the region was cultivated farm land but the seldom travelled, and open geography gave her a great field of view in the event her pursuers began catching up. Instead of travelling due northeast to reach her destination, Biannca had started out northwest, travelling through the tiny upstate towns, past the lone interstate US 90 that cut across the state. She headed north, almost to Lake Ontario, where she hitched right and made her way to Sodus Bay, then backtracked to Hancock International Airport in Syracuse.

She guided the little Volkswagen to the long-term parking garage and in less than a minute swapped the VW for a deep blue Ford Escape. She knew she risked showing up on CCTV surveillance while she swapped out vehicles, but the long-term parking seemed the best bet for stashing a car without having someone come along and tow the damn thing. She paid the fee and slowly left the airport without noticing any potential tail.

Biannca had set up a protocol for herself that periodically she would 'clean' herself as best she could. Instead of continuing on to the next stop on her itinerary, she went to an expansive mall that sat on the shores of Onondaga Lake. Destiny USA was a massive facility which housed everything from go-cart tracks to comic book shops. It was going on seven o'clock when she arrived at the mall. She parked the Escape in a spot near Macy's and went inside.

Her side was screaming as she started her casual patrol of the shopping center. After being cooped up in the car for so long, she started to realize how exhausted she was. She did the math in her head and realized she hadn't slept in over thirty hours. She circled the lower floor of Macy's once, before heading into the mall, then found the nearest coffee shop. The mall closed at nine, and she had planned to roam around mingling with the shrinking crowds until there would be nowhere for anyone tracking her to hide.

She grabbed a cup of coffee and sought out the first restaurant to offer a steak dinner. She insisted on a seat overlooking the thoroughfare and without a glance at the menu ordered a Filet mignon, rare to the point of bloody. She could've gone for about a gallon of pinot noir also but knew the alcohol would only blunt her edge. She was already weak enough from the lack of sleep.

The steak was passable, the people-watching was uneventful. After the meal, she paid using a forged credit card and made her way to the upper floor, so as to have a greater view of the wanderers below. Biannca made one lap around and then another, taking note of possible escape routes in the form of maintenance hallways and one abandoned storefront covered in black plastic.

It was a half hour from closing and she was leaning on the railing, looking over the last remaining stragglers roaming the mall. She was feeling pretty good about herself, and looking forward to finding someplace to sleep, when a dark figure rose on an escalator in front of the Lord & Taylor department store.

It wasn't so much that her adversary had caught up to her. It was the fact that they could not have done it without some means of support from Central. Biannca had the heart wrenching realization right then and there that her life would never be the same. The man with dark close- cropped hair and goatee turned in profile as he walked off the escalator and headed her way. She didn't move. It wasn't that she was frozen, like a rabbit hoping a passing fox doesn't realize she's there. Biannca was making a decision. Run or fight. She knew she couldn't run forever. She also knew that these guys did not move without contingency. If this merc was roaming at her front, there was another one who had come up the opposing side of the upper gallery. That way they could watch each other while at the same time flank her if they made an identification. She had to fight with every fiber in her soul to keep from scanning the rest of the upper floor. There was a stairwell and a maintenance hall to her right. The mercenary at her front was closing on her but hadn't spotted her yet. She put a smartphone she had picked up but not activated to her ear and looked down at the lower level turning her head just so as he passed.

She felt the man's eyes on her but didn't feel that he'd made a connection. He passed within twenty feet of her, and she slid along the railing toward the opposite walkway. Still keeping the phone to her ear, she moved from her position and headed in the opposite direction from the man. She had made her decision—at least part of a decision. If this was her new life, she would make the most of it. She was going to kill every one of the sons of bitches tracking her, then she was going to make her way to the beltway. Her rational mind told her with no equivocation that she was going to lose. At the same time however, she knew deep down that she had already lost; she just wanted to take as many of the assholes who had stolen her life with her as she could when they finally dropped her.

The merc didn't appear to give her any further attention and she slipped inside the large department store at the end of the thoroughfare. Inside, she wound her way toward the center of the store where assorted appliances and kitchen furnishings were on display. The store was almost empty save for employees. She found a blender sitting on a stand. She leaned over to study the device, eyeing the buttons, and informative stickers affixed to the large mixing reservoir while she cut through the power cord and shoved it in her pocket. Next she moved to a display covered in fine china and silverware. She pulled a boxed set of knives from the stand and continued through the store.

She moved toward the Women's Petites section where she found a padded vest made of nylon with a relatively hard stuffing. She slipped a size extra small over her petite frame, then ducked behind the circular clothing rack where she freed three of the longer knives from their box.

"What are you doing?"

The question startled her.

Biannca rose to face a girl, maybe eighteen years old. Her name tag read *Cindi*. "I'm trying on a vest and perusing a set of knives," she answered casually, "Cindi with an I, huh?" she asked. "You're from the country, aren't you?"

Cindi's candy red lips pursed and she cocked a hip to the side. She pointed a glossy index finger in her direction. Biannca took the offered digit and snapped the finger back until her immaculately polished nail met her wrist. Cindi's eyes bulged and her mouth dropped open in a gasp. Before she was able to scream, Biannca pivoted inward and drove her elbow through the base of Cindi's skull. The girl folded in a daze at Biannca's feet. She kicked the girl in the face, then tossed her into the hollow within the clothes rack. She took three knives and secured them in her vest.

"Cindi with an I," she scoffed.

Chapter Twenty-Six

The target who had previously passed her by was surveying the upper gallery when she walked out the front door of the Lord & Taylor. She stood in the empty floor, staring at him for almost a full minute before his eyes found hers. She saw him jump before he was able to gain his composure.

The two predators watched each other for a moment. She could see that behind the tightly cropped beard and dark eyes, the man was playing through his options. Biannca reveled in the game. She had unsettled him, putting him in a reactionary mode, leaving her with the initiative. Entertainment was not the only reason she watched him however. She waited, and waited. The mercenary pulled out a cell phone and put it to his ear, his focus on her never wavering. There it was. Whoever was after her didn't have direct real time comms. That meant there was a lag in communication. That was an advantage. Biannca was all about finding an advantage.

She started walking then. Purposely taking her eyes off him, she scanned the lower level of the mall, then the upper. Two men in addition to her mark were coming from the upper level. Further down, she saw movement on her level though the targets were halfway down the almost quarter mile distance, trying to close in. The bearded merc on the upper level was tracking her as she walked toward her battle ground. At least four enemies were closing on her position. She found the abandoned store front she had been looking for, and defeated the lock on the door in a matter of seconds. She opened the metal framed door a crack and looked back at her pursuer. They met eyes once more. He was like the scout in a pack of wolves who had stumbled upon a lone elk. He wasn't about to initiate an attack on his own, but instead paced back and forth burning nervous energy as he waited for the rest of the pack. She slipped inside and shut the door.

The store was dark and open. Empty racks, bits of scaffolding, and assorted tools were scattered around the floor. She picked a screwdriver up from an open tool box as she made her way toward the back of the open space. A couple of mannequins stood in silent conversation to the left of her. Another group lay in a jumbled pile of torsos and detached limbs to the right. She heard movement outside the door as the team assembled outside and tried to figure out what to do.

***

2-2 gathered 2-4, 1-6, and 1-8 outside the storefront. Plastic tarps were hung behind the glass wall to protect shoppers from the eyesore of an ongoing project or dead space in the mall. The mercenaries lined up in twos to either side of the glass door. 2-2 tried to push on the handle. It gave, opening easily. The long experienced solider eyeballed the frame and the space around the entryway as he pushed. Their quarry was well trained and had a record of achievement that made him at once appreciative and respectful of her. Though they had never worked together, they had run in the same circles. He knew who she was and what she could do.

2-2 sensed nothing and entered the dark open space. His pistol, a suppressed Beretta nine millimeter held close in but at the ready. He swept the room to his left and felt 1-6 slide past him to cover the right. The four mercenaries formed a sort of phalanx as they entered the space. The men moved slowly, fanning out as they spread across the room. 2-2 was on the outer perimeter of the room. He searched for other exits and ancillary rooms that might afford the target cover and points of ambush.

He also could not help but notice the support columns standing in the empty space. Each one was mirrored and had not been covered up, so even in the dim light the space seemed larger and more open. Different mannequins either standing or lying around the space in full or disarticulated parts were another distraction. The eye was drawn to the human forms disrupting his focus while he moved. While scanning right, he noticed 1-6 skirting around one of the columns, his gun low, his manner casual.

"Six," 2-2 hissed.

The mercenary bearing the call sign looked in his direction with all the military bearing of a man being asked to pass the salt at the breakfast table.

"Tighten up!" 2-2 hissed.

1-6's face screwed, eyebrows furrowed. He nodded in 2-2's direction and continued around the column.

**

Old Fuck, 1-6, otherwise known as Jacob Brindle, age thirty-five, former Army Infantry, former Blackwater, former State Department contractor. He had been around the world. He had kicked in doors and smoked assholes in four different countries. And this fucker thinks he can put a boot in his ass, trying to teach him tactics mid-op. Who's the asshole who blew a simple ambush in the first place? On some girl spook too. Brindle felt his neck growing red as he stepped around a mirrored column and poked the bulbous suppressor attached to his handgun around the corner to clear it.

Brindle saw the target's face in his mind. He remembered the rest of the photos in the file too. She was smokin' hot, like stop traffic on I-95 hot. Brindle scanned his area as he moved. The place was empty, which told him that this superhero they were contracted to take out wasn't very smart or just another empty legend of the intelligence world. He'd seen it before. On deployment while he and the rest of the grunts were sleeping in the dirt, living like animals, the intel types lived in air conditioning eating fucking steak and lobster. Then when the time came to actually hit the field and do some work, they were nowhere to be found. And worse yet, he remembered distinctly almost getting vaporized on missions those kinds of assholes set up, and for nothing. Brindle caught sight to the old man, 2-2, and smirked. *Fuck that guy.*

A gaggle of mannequins stood to his right, his eye drawn to the anatomically correct nipples. He veered a little closer. Nipples on a mannequin? Sure enough, the dudes had them too. He peered through the silent group standing in a crowd, staring into the middle distance. He didn't see anything human.

***

Biannca let the sloppy bastard get a step past her before sinking one of her knives into his carotid artery. The man jumped at the shock of the impact, but she already had relieved him of his sidearm in a single chopping motion, breaking his grip against her forearm. She grabbed the handle of the knife and steered him like a puppet toward the direction of the gunfire, already coming in from her right. They were flanking her on both sides so she kept moving firing in a circle while using her victim as a shield. It was dark, but the space was open. She fired over and over, felt the bullets coming in her direction popping in the air. The mercenaries held true to their occupation. Her human shield absorbed a dozen impacts as she backed him in a spiraling motion toward her egress point. She was close to her fallback point when the man's strength faded, but not close enough. She had seen at least two of her attackers drop, one to her left and one to her right. If her count was accurate that meant one target was loose in the vacant store with her. The dying merc's weight became too much to bear and she pulled the knife free with a yank. Blood shot from the wound like crimson silly string from a can.

Biannca somersaulted and came up in a crouch behind one of the mirrored columns at the feet of another man with a gun. She moved on autopilot, reacting to the threat of the gun rather than the fear of her position. Driving forward, she closed the ground between the two of them and used her forearm to block his gun hand while catching her opponent under the chin with her own firearm. She squeezed the trigger with the muzzle of the suppressor buried in the flesh under his mandible. She watched as smoke billowed from his mouth and his eyes suddenly went from intense to languidly turning in different directions.

She was past him and through an access door at the rear of the store before a half dozen more rounds splintered the weak, wood door and puffs of white gypsum coughed from the surrounding walls. She made two more blind turns and kicked through another door before stopping. She froze in a dark hallway, a red emergency exit sign her only light. Controlling her breathing, she listened for her pursuers.

***

2-2 groaned and coughed which made his sternum feel as though it were splintering under his level IIIa ballistic vest. He reached inside his vest to probe the injury. She had clipped him just to the left of his sternum. It wasn't 2-2's first time suffering a gunshot wound, but the injury had left him stunned. Body armor was designed to stop the body from suffering penetration by projectiles, but very often did little to assuage the accompanying blunt force injury caused by the force of the impact. There was no wetness or holes in his chest, and he could feel the bullet inside the layers of Kevlar with the back of his hand. He rose to his feet and noticed what other damage their target had wrought.

A swath of blood pools and smears cut across the concrete floor where the petite woman had manhandled six-feet two-inch Jacob Brindle. Blood pooled around the still corpse of 1-6. 2-2 felt nothing—cost of doing business. Likewise, he felt nothing more than frustration when he looked at the misshapen head and bulging eyes of 1-8. A body count was not something Central would react well to. There was nothing on the bodies to lead back to the contractor, but the fact that he had suffered not one, but multiple losses at the hands of the target was an embarrassment and was something Central could use to re-issue the contract, in which case he would get zero. He studied his one remaining man. 2-4 was holding his left side after likewise suffering a shot to the vest.

"Get their gear, make sure they're clean," 2-2 growled as he switched out magazines on his nine millimeter.

2-4 nodded and limped toward 1-8 while 2-2 looked to the front of the empty store. The sounds of activity grew. He wondered how far the sounds of suppressed weapons fire had carried. Though the tools are known as silencers, firing a suppressed weapon was far from silent. Would some rent-a-cops dare come in on their own? Or was some SWAT team being called in? His eyes followed the target's path. He could see her face in his mind as he rejoined the hunt. She had gotten the jump on him twice now. 2-2's professionalism, much less his patience, was running thin. He helped 2-4 by stripping 1-6 of his vest, weapons, phone, and patted his blood-soaked clothing down for anything else that might be used to identify him or put the contract in jeopardy. He couldn't believe it when he found a wallet in the dead man's back pocket.

He held it up for 2-4 to see before stuffing it and the rest of the gear in his pockets. 2-4 shook his head wearily. The sounds outside the store grew louder as the two mercenaries abandoned their associates to what they hoped was an obscure and unexplained death by local officials.

***

Biannca crept and jogged through the maintenance halls around the perimeter of the mall until she saw placards bearing the names of stores she had recognized as being near where she had entered from the parking garage. She stopped at a double entrance door and listened. She heard the sound of footfall rushing by outside. As they receded, she slipped slowly out of the maintenance hall into an alcove off the main thoroughfare of the main gallery. Store security gates were closed or half-closed, and many of the storefronts were dark, their teenaged clerks slipping out as early as possible once their customers cleared out.

Biannca quickly scanned the area and the rails along the upper and lower levels. She was on the opposite side of the hall from the exit to the parking garage. She sensed no danger and casually tread across the walkway to a spur that would take her to her car. As she gained the spur, she noticed herself in the mirrored window of a closed store. Her eyes widened at the flecks of blood scattered around her cheek like dark crimson freckles.

Then she noticed the figure rounding the corner behind her. He wore a dark, waist-length jacket and a dark ball cap, turned backward, with a small, subdued American flag embroidered on it. He was reaching in his jacket. She pivoted and dropped to a crouch as she flung the smaller of her blades in a backhanded throw. The man groaned and dropped back to crash against a metal trashcan with a clang. The blade handle stood out from his diaphragm like a mast without a sail. She pivoted again and ran for the door.

She tried to count how many enemy she had encountered, and guessed at five or six. She had no idea how many were chasing her. She felt a true dread in her gut as she slammed through the exit and charged for her car. They were after her. Not just some rent-a-goons settling an old score, but an officially sanctioned execution. The only way they could have tracked her was with support from Central. The agency itself was hunting her. The fact that she had just survived a hit meant little to her in the way of solace. She knew from being on the other side of the coin that this was just the beginning of her new life, always on the run, always looking over her shoulder.

She found her vehicle. She sat down in the driver's seat and immediately started scanning the mirrors she had pre-positioned before she left for her reconnaissance. Turning the key in the ignition she heard an almost imperceptible hiss, then the faint whiff. She knew that scent.

Biannca's faculties only lasted long enough for a single thought to race through her synapses. *Not like this.*

Chapter Twenty-Seven

Joseph Broadstreet sat on the ancient, stained, and frayed twin bed. He had no idea how long he'd been sitting there—five minutes, three hours, he couldn't be sure. When he had paid for the room, he had just reached into the still damp duffle bag he'd taken from America Street and counted out the fifty bucks required by the old Indian man behind the desk. He had snatched the key from the old man without saying a word and the old man hadn't requested any kind of dialogue, didn't even require a name for the room as long as Broadstreet had the cash up front.

The flop house was an old apartment building that had long ago been forgotten or ignored by city regulators. Broadstreet had heard sounds ranging from moans and slamming furniture to yelling and crying as he'd ascended the three floors to his room on the far east end of the building. When he'd finally gained entry through the rusted, screeching lock on the cardboard thin door he had thrown down the bag and run for the shower. The shower had decades of growth around and inside its once white porcelain tub. Thick lines of black highlighted various cracks and crevasses where the fixture was slowly falling apart due to age and disrepair. But after the water flowing from the lime-encrusted showerhead had lost its orangish tinge, the shower had been hot. That was all Broadstreet cared about. A hot shower to scrub away the remnants of the destruction he'd wrought on the East side drug trade. He had scrubbed, trying to grind away the sticky, flaking blood and matter from his hands and face, the stuff that he'd not been able to free himself of by wiping at his face and eyes with the sleeve of his sweatshirt. Rivulets of red mixed with the water that coursed away from his body, past the lines of mildew and mold into the slowly flowing drain.

The heat of the shower and the cleansed feel of his skin after drying with a towel that held the same consistency of sandpaper had sapped his strength. Still moist from the shower, he'd collapsed on the twin bed, falling against springs that fought his weight with pokes and prods and passed out, not even noticing the smell of the bedding or the dilapidated apartment.

He wasn't sure how long he'd slept but he woke with a start, and when he did, the sun was just starting to fall to the west. Now, as night set in, he found himself staring at the money. Fifteen hundred dollars stared at him from the floor of the dingy apartment and he stared back. A little voice in his head was whispering of the opportunities that money presented him: a nicer hotel, a legendary night at a strip club. That little prospect almost got him. It had been almost fifteen years since Joe Broadstreet had felt the heat of a woman. When he'd first gotten out he had ventured around the East Side searching out a prostitute, but when he found a street littered with slowly shuffling women with vacant eyes, he'd felt ashamed and retreated. Another voice called out to him from deep in his mind. This is it, the little voice said, the calling toward the swift release into bliss that he knew a quick inhalation of smoke from a crack pipe would give him was right there, urging him from a place deep in his soul.

Something was different now. Now Broadstreet heard a different voice pecking at his mind. It was the opposite of the release dope could bring. This was control. The ability to determine his own actions. To control the fate of others. What happened the other night charged him like a battery. He needed more to fuel that power, to seek that control. He found his coat. A dirty old field jacket in black that he'd found at a thrift store. It carried streaks and dots of flaky crimson now, in accompaniment to the dust and dirt it had accumulated in his time on the street scrounging to find real work. He reached slowly inside the breast pocket and found a single item. Just touching the photo made his insides squirm, caused a flurry of pain, shame, and sadness to swirl and crash around inside him. He looked on the photo for a long moment and decided.

It was a deadly game he was taking on, one that he'd seen others play and knew that it seldom if ever ended happily. For a moment, his mind drifted back to the pile of money, then his vision took in the stained, rusty length of rebar laying on the floor beside the money. He thought about what he'd done the night before and remembered the faces of the men whose lives he'd ended. Then he realized how calm he felt, how satisfied he was. He knew he had found his place, his role in the outside world.

Chapter Twenty-Eight

The detectives at the narcotics unit drafted search warrants for known drug houses around the East Side of Charleston by the handful. Banks gave the unit until noon to have a plan in place and a list of targets to hit. In the meantime, Viejo and Wilke stopped at the Crime Scene office to see what Eric Thompson had come up with on the burnt-out wreck of a car that might be related to the William's killing.

The Admin Assistant allowed the two detectives to badge their way into the secure facility and as they made their way back into the lab area, they found the muscular form of Eric Thompson wearing a lab coat and glasses. He was huddling over a mangled piece of charred rubble, shining a flashlight at oblique angles, studying the piece with a magnifying glass. The big man jumped when he heard Viejo scoffing.

"Fuck you, Este," Thompson said, "You scared the shit out of me."

"Sorry man," Viejo faux-apoligized, "but you in a lab coat and glasses." Viejo mocked like he was looking for witnesses. "You're just doing that shit to make it look like you know what you're doing, right? You're sellin' it pretty good."

Thompson looked past Viejo like he was ignoring a bug flying around his head to shake

Wilke's hand, "How in the hell did Banks let this asshole on a murder case?"

Wilke shrugged. "Wanted someone in the lead he could control, I guess."

"Uh-huh," said Viejo.

"How you feeling, Thompson?" Wilke asked.

Thompson absently put a nitrile-gloved hand to the left side of his abdomen. "Good and bad. I feel fine," he said, "I just can't run for shit anymore."

"Never ran in the first place," Viejo sputtered.

Thompson paused to look at his friend, "Is there a reason you're here? Or did you just have fuckin' up Eric's day on your schedule for this morning?" After a brief pause, he waved them to follow him, "Come on, your stinking pile of shit is back here."

Wilke and Viejo followed Thompson through the lab, past a row of drying hoods and work benches to a garage. The burned-out car they located on the night of the shooting was not there. Instead, a scattering of blackened or in some cases pristine objects, perfectly untouched by fire, were laid out on a tarp on the floor.

"We shot photos of the car and left it at Leary's tow yard. We collected some pieces we thought might have preserved prints or DNA, but so far we haven't found much. The only thing I can really show you on this thing is a little bit of possible blood spatter over here." "Wait," Viejo stopped him. "Splatter?"

"Spatter," corrected Thompson.

"Splatter?"

"Spatter, lose the 'L,'" Thompson sighed.

"Spatter?"

"Yes." Thompson drew out the word.

"What the hell is spatter?" injected Wilke.

Thompson pointed to a few dark specks on an unburned portion of sheet metal on the passenger side door. "Spatter is what happens when blood hits something, you Neanderthals."

They looked at the specks.

"What a horrible word," Viejo commented.

Wilke nodded, "Like moist or phlegm."

"Ugh," replied Viejo.

Thompson interrupted them. "We took some samples for the lab. The direction of the spatter goes primarily down at a pretty steep angle, and it's pretty small. Best guess around here is that it will end up being back spatter from the rounds Cauldwell took to the face."

Viejo and Wilke studied the blood for a moment then looked over the—for lack of a better term—junk, spread out on a tarp on the floor of the garage. There was a rear-view mirror partially melted with the glass intact. Documentation, an owner's manual for a ninety-three Chevrolet which Viejo was surprised to see. *How could paper like that survive a fire?* he wondered, while scanning the rest of the items. He noted a plate containing the vehicle identification number, one that he figured they found on the dash or something. Being honest with himself, Viejo realized this was pretty much the only piece out of the collection he had any idea how to use.

"What's up with the VIN?" he asked.

"Last registered owner in the database let the car go to repo in 2001. After that, nothing. That car was a throw away," Thompson responded. "Whoever torched it did a decent job—we've got a couple of partials from the door handles that weren't engulfed, but our guys here didn't get any hits in AFIS so we sent the handles up to the lab to see if they would have any better luck than we did. Sorry fellas, like I said there wasn't much left to go on here."

"It's cool," Viejo said, turning away from the tarp to look over the rest of the garage. The space was huge compared to the little refrigerator box that someone called a garage at his townhouse.

"Thompson, how you like this side of things?" Viejo heard Wilke ask as the three started to return to the lab.

Thompson stopped to look at Wilke and matched eyes with Viejo at the same time. Este noted a hint of suspicion from his friend but also a flash in Thompson's eye that he hadn't seen before.

"Honestly, I love this crap," Thompson answered in a somewhat hushed voice, "I never had any idea what these guys did on scene. You know, in patrol we'd call them to a burglary or a car break in and they would show up and toss some powder around some poor bastard's car and that was it. But now that I'm here, Damn. We got lasers and crap. I'm not kicking in doors or running the street, but dude, this is like a freakin' playground for adults in here."

Viejo couldn't believe how animated an answer the Thompson had given them. He was like a five-year old playing with a new puppy.

"And besides I'm not stuck sitting in a car for hours on end, sifting through shit with you ugly bastards anymore. I'm good."

Chapter Twenty-Nine

Joe Broadstreet wandered at a shuffling pace down the cracked and broken sidewalk. His head was down and his shoulders were hunched. A hood from the interior of the black field jacket covered his face as he approached the leaning row house with peeling pastel-blue paint and uneven steps.

Raising his eyes ever so slightly to look at the house, it pained him to see its state. This was the third time in the last hour he had walked past. Each time he desperately hoped for a look at its occupants, while at the same time being deathly afraid of what he might find. It had been almost twelve years since he had seen the residents of the decaying home.

The woman and child who lived at the home were the reason his life had led him to where he stood. Why he hid in plain sight as a vagrant in his own neighborhood. Part of him wondered briefly what might have been, how things might have worked out, but he shut that down. There was no point. That life was long gone.

A twinge in his shoulder caught him unawares and he had an instant of difficulty breathing as he stopped two doors from the location. It was almost as if he were back in that night that ended his life. He stood slumped against a telephone pole, watching the house, and could almost feel the rain from that night. He felt the fetid water from the street seeping through his clothes to mix with the blood streaming from his chest and shoulder.

He had been out. She hadn't even had to ask him. When she told him he would be a father, a previously undiscovered switch had struck in his soul. When he had told Zim that he wanted out, Zim seemed to take it better than he figured he would have. His partner told him he understood, but he also told him he was out of his mind. "What kind of Dad would he be swinging a hammer or mopping floors when he could own the streets with him and give the kid whatever she wanted?" Joe hadn't tried to explain, didn't have the energy or feel the need to make his uncle, his own family, a man who had never known a father and never seen three of his five kids, much less tried to make a life for them, why he wanted to go straight. He and Zim had left things in balance. He was out, gave up his stake and made right on the buy money he'd had outstanding. A clean break.

Then three of their mid-level guys were taken off in separate raids by the police two days after he quit the life. Joe had nothing to do with it, but none of that had mattered. Fact was, if he'd have been in Uncle Zim's place, he would have thought he had sold him out too.

The night it happened. Right after he put the little girl that had taken over his life down to sleep, he caught a glimpse of something out her window. He heard movement outside and he knew. He had heard on the street, you can't help but hear from the street after ruling a neighborhood for so long, but he hadn't thought to follow up with Zim. He was only a couple of days into his new life but the life felt good. She was with him every night, they both were.

He stepped out the front door and walked down the steps to find Zim and two others waiting for him. He saw disgust, even under the weak yellow street lights. They hated him. Guys he had fought with and won the side streets and back alleys of the Charleston Peninsula with suddenly hated him. His own family, Zim, was standing there with them.

"Sup Zim?" he'd said.

"We got some real trouble last couple a days, B. Some real trouble you suddenly ain't a part of no more."

"Wasn't me, man," was all he could say. Not that it mattered.

"Bullshit!" spat Peep, a wiry thin 'friend' he'd been running with since the two of them were thirteen years old, holding dope for Zim. Joe had saved Peep's life twice when bangers from North Charleston tried to rob him for his stash. Peep was always the guy to catch heat, smaller, skinnier than the rest. He was the first option any predator took when trying to attack their herd. Now, years later with a gun in his hand, all was forgotten.

Peep raised the gun but Joe was faster. Peep's two rounds flew wide while Joe's took him in the chest and the groin. Peep screamed as he fell.

Zim and Mo—who was another of Joe's lifelong friends—were firing when Joe started moving laterally into the street. Their first string of rounds missed as did Joe's own. The three men danced a skittering circle around the street as they fired nine millimeter and .38 caliber bullets at each other. Joe took a round to the left leg just above the knee from Zim, but was still able to put Mo down with a round through the sternum. He was hobbling toward a Buick parked across the street to find cover when Zim shot him in the side.

The impact dropped him across the hood of the car, and he slid down between the Buick and a Honda sedan. He couldn't breathe, choked on copper-tasting blood flowing into his throat and mouth. Joe Broadstreet felt a fear at that moment he had never known. Strangely he didn't fear for himself. He feared for his daughter Ren. How would she grow up without him? Joe could not allow that. But it was over, he knew it. Sizzling pain raged with every attempted breath. The gut wrenching question of what Zim would do to Mara and his daughter lingered despite the pain.

"No!" he tried to scream, though it came out as a gurgling choke. Zim had stopped firing, but he could hear his Nike's tapping on the wet street as he approached him. The older man's shadow crossed his vision, then a silhouette in Zim's outline stood over him, "No," Broadstreet choked, then fired blindly in a panic at the darkness hovering over him.

There was a yelp in the distance and one more stinging bite to his abdomen. Then darkness took him.

When Joe woke up, his first sensations were the restraints binding him to his hospital bed. The smell of bleach, and the sight of the concrete walls surrounding him told him he was in jail. He knew the place far too well to mistake the familiar mix of cleaning agents and body odor.

The night when he tucked his daughter into bed was the last he'd ever get to touch her. To run his hand across her face or to kiss her fat little cheeks. When he was ambulatory, Mara brought Ren to see him through the thick glass of the visitor's room but that hurt more than being shot. The little girl wanted her daddy and she cried, not understanding why Daddy couldn't hold her.

They charged him with murder but it was dropped to manslaughter when his lawyer, a public defender—they couldn't afford any better—talked Broadstreet into taking a plea. No one cared when he and Mara argued self-defense. To the criminal justice system, he was just another number. Another East Side drug dealer caught up in a misdemeanor homicide, which is what they called it when drug dealers killed each other. He was sentenced to twenty-five years.

For the first couple of years, Mara was pretty good about bringing Ren to see him. Though it felt like a dagger being twisted in his heart whenever he saw the little girl. His little girl who he was forced to watch grow up on the other side of partitioned glass, talking to her through a phone line. He put on his best performance each time. Eventually however, the visits became more and more drawn out. Mara met someone on the outside, and after about five years of dedicated visits, they just stopped coming.

He didn't blame them. The visitor's center at Lieber State Correctional was no place for a little girl. Joe hated the fact that his little girl had to know a place like a prison before she was even able to say the word. He hated the fact that the only thing she knew about her daddy was that he was in prison. It was a relief when they abandoned him. It hurt but at least she didn't have to see her old man as a convict. He was never going to be a father for Ren, and would never be a husband for Mara. They both deserved better.

As time went on Joe fought for his place in prison. Fought to be left alone. Fought because people remembered him from the streets. In prison, that brief span when he was just a dad, just another blue collar shlub punching a clock, didn't matter. In prison, he was still Broadstreet, was still a heavy hitter from the East Side of Charleston. Perceived enemies that he and Zim had messed with over the years were waiting for him when he first entered the prison system, and they were still showing up years later, still with an axe to grind over some historic slight whether real or perceived.

Joe accepted who he was. It was easier once Mara and Ren were out of the picture. He was able to revert to the base creature he was before Mara came into his life. Just another street warrior—no more, no less, no future. When someone came for him, he welcomed the fight. Welcomed the opportunity to hone himself, to sharpen that primal predatory lust for violence that most men are able to ignore, and some never realize. In the years before Mara stopped coming to see him, he suffered seven attacks just because of the name that followed him into prison. Through all of those attacks he left his assailant alive and without any lasting injuries. Once Mara gave up on him, once that anchor of humanity was shed, he was the subject of seven more attacks in the years following. Of the nine men who made attempts on his life, six of the nine could never walk again without some form of assistance, Joe learned that if you shatter a knee or an ankle to the point of permanent damage, a man will shrivel inside a prison. Like a wounded gazelle on the African plain, they are a constant target of opportunity for predators and unable to mount revenge. Two of the men who attacked him never walked again, having suffered severe spinal trauma after Broadstreet stomped on the base of their skulls, and one man walked away suffering only broken ribs. He was rescued by prison officers, who Broadstreet never disrespected or fought with, before he could permanently ensure no threat from the man would ever resurface.

Despite the injuries Broadstreet inflicted, he was never charged with a crime that would add to his existing sentence. In the twelfth year of his sentence, he was contacted by a state attorney and told he would be assessed for a parole hearing. Broadstreet took the news in stride. He'd become accustomed to life behind prison walls. He had no idea what he could possibly do in the outside world. Of course, he thought of his family. Ren would be driving a car soon, not the little baby he once rocked to sleep but a young woman entering high school. He hoped Ren grew up well—he believed in Mara. Despite where they had both come from, Mara had a character and a strength he himself never knew before he met her. Mara was the one factor in his life that changed him from a street predator to a man, someone who could value human life. Broadstreet had to wonder when he realized the state wanted to release him back into the world if he still held that value Mara was so able to cultivate in him.

The realization and fear of who he was in terms of society brought him pause. He stayed up long nights lying quietly in his cell, staring at the flat ceiling, wondering who he was. All the years of violence and fighting had made him numb to the pain of others. He wondered if he had reverted fully back to being that street creature Mara had once saved. The knowledge that her grace, her balance, and love of life and others in it would not be there for him when he walked free scared him. It was there in that dark prison cell that he had made his choice. He made a deal with himself. He would not be the animal he was in prison when he re-entered the world. Nor would he turn a blind eye to the evil on the streets. He would make the world a better place for his daughter, even though he would never meet her.

That resolution was easier to dream of than accomplish. The parole board granted him release on a cool spring day and he was assigned to a halfway house in Charleston. He had a plan for getting out. He would get a straight job, whatever it was, and build from there. He would go to church, not because he felt any true calling but because there would be a chance for service there. He remembered being a kid and hearing through closed ears as various churchmen tried to talk to him and others like them. It didn't work then, but maybe with his life to share, Broadstreet could make a dent.

When he checked into the halfway house, he was in the door a total of three minutes before he realized society and the system did not believe in an ex-con nearly as much as he believed in himself. The rules of the house were simple and meant for the lowest common denominator.

Don't miss curfew.
The homeless shelter feedings are at 7am, noon, and from 5 to 7pm.
No drugs in the house, though no drug tests will be administered.
Try and find a job.
If you get locked up you will probably go back up to the state.

Broadstreet listened to the orders handed down by a bored and dispassionate, state-assigned home supervisor. The man, a middle-aged black man, did not even bother to shake his hand or converse other than to establish his identity. Jim Matson showed him his living quarters, and told him the rules. Broadstreet didn't let that get to him. He expected them to look on him with no less disdain than that which he felt for himself. It was outside that house where he would make his climb to respectability anyway.

Then he tried to get work. Turned out there were no real options for an ex-con except bussing tables, washing cars, or getting back in the drug trade. Broadstreet wasn't proud—he jumped in, first taking temporary work with a staffing agency that had an agreement with the halfway house. He carried rubbish at a commercial remodel for a day. Then the site foreman overheard a couple of guys from his halfway house talking about how Broadstreet was a killer and went up for murder, and the staffing agency cut him a check for forty dollars and cut him loose at the end of his first day. It was a liability issue they had said, nothing he did, though when the guy signing the check said it, he wouldn't look him in the eye.

Broadstreet didn't give up. He went to the next place on the list posted in the hall at the halfway house. A restaurant where he could wash dishes. He was there ten minutes early and spent the entire morning washing grease and grime in cloudy water while servers and managers spun around him like a well-oiled machine. He made it a couple of days at that job. It was good for him too. He didn't have to talk to anyone, there was music on in the kitchen, and the manager seemed to let him work without hawking over him like he expected him to steal everything he came into contact with. Then during a break between breakfast and brunch, he declined to smoke a blunt with the manager and two servers. The servers were fine young coeds with bleary eyes and flat expressions that declined to register his existence. The manager did not take the news well when Broadstreet opted out of getting high. Maybe it was being snubbed by an ex-con or perhaps the manager thought maybe he couldn't trust Broadstreet not to rat him out. Whatever the case, he was cut loose from that job at the end of the shift.

He had a total of a hundred dollars cash on him and no prospects at the end of the dishwasher job. The boss, as he liked to be called, at the halfway house questioned why he couldn't hold a job and was quick to make the veiled threat by reminding him that keeping a job was a requirement if he wanted to stay out in the world and not go back to Lieber.

Broadstreet felt the pressure but still kept the goal in focus. He was going to be a productive member of society for once in his life no matter what. Then a week without work stretched to two, and the line at the shelter feedings started to feel like home. He felt desperation turn to fear, then fear creep toward disgust. Disgust turned to despair, and he was about to throw it all away from the business end of a crack pipe. Then he saw that little girl shot down in the street. Dumped by a group of animals acting out some feud over drug money or some shit. He was one of them, an animal, and he hated it, hated them, all of them who make the world a place where a toddler can be shot while in her mother's arms.

Broadstreet shook himself out, feeling rage building in his chest. He noticed his breathing intensifying as he thought about that little girl and it scared him. Not so much the biological effects, but the simple fact that he was excited because he recalled how it had felt the other night. That had been a spur of the moment, self-defensive even. He had yet to actually plan something out. He looked at the old house once more. Part of him prayed for a glimpse, even fleeting, of a girl who may be his child while at the same time feeling his soul quake at the thought. Slowly, Joseph Broadstreet turned and walked away.

He rounded the corner keeping his head low. The pain and embarrassment of what he was and what he should have been tormented him. He thought about his little girl and her mother going it alone in a neighborhood like this. He should have been there—he wanted to be there. What kind of man allowed his family to fend for themselves? He hated himself, he hated his previous life and all the people who had been a part of it, the people who were animals, predators just like him. At the corner of the next block he saw a lone figure. The kid, maybe sixteen or seventeen, thin and wiry even under a bulky hoodie and dark jeans. He looked up and down the street trying to seem chill but there was the slightest hint of hop in his step. He was holding,

Broadstreet told himself. The darkness that was eating at him suddenly eased. He made eye contact with the dealer who nodded in his direction, then slowly turned toward an alley adjacent to the intersection. Broadstreet felt a warmth spread over him. Felt a respite from his self-loathing. He followed the kid into the alley.

Chapter Thirty

Everything gets real quiet right before a raid. Wilke felt it, that split second as the van rolled up to the target, all his senses suddenly expanded. The rough texture of the forty-five caliber Glock scraping against his gloves, a trickle of sweat luging down the center of his back. The van jolted to a halt.

The doors flew open and seven cops dressed in tactical vests, three brandishing M-4 assault rifles, one carrying a ram, charged the front door. Four uniforms bolted around the side of the house to cover the back. The entry team formed in a stack, the rear officer Trisha Ray, facing away from the door, covered two curtained windows. Viejo, third in line, carried an M-4. Wilke was poised on the opposite side of the door, ram high and ready. Trisha tapped Detective Pat Billings on the ass of his blue jeans, Pat in turn hit Danny Thomas on the shoulder with his free hand, Danny, Viejo on the shoulder, who in turn signaled the guy in front of him. Everyone was ready. Wilke focused on Viejo's free hand as his fingers counted down, three-two-one.

Wilke's ram shattered the door frame, knocking the doorknob clear across the room. It bounced and skittered among wood splinters across a scratched and warped hardwood floor. The brass fixture came to a rest at the toe of Tommy Wright. Tommy, wearing white and grey striped boxers and a stained wife-beater was holding a white mug in his right hand, a pop tart in his left. Tommy's eyes were wide, his mouth hanging open. He and Wilke looked at each other for the briefest of seconds before Wilke retreated a step. In his wake the entry team, led by Sasquatch-sized Detective Brian Smith, flooded the room.

"Police! Get Down!" Smith bellowed.

Smith approached Wright. The Eotech holographic sight affixed to his M-4 never wavered from the skinny drug dealer's forehead. The team fanned out around the debris-strewn living room, then moved two by two through the rest of the dilapidated single story ranch. Wright stutter stepped before dropping to his knees and proning out on his stomach. The sasquatch dropped a heavy Merrell hiking boot between Wright's shoulder blades, knocking the wind from him,

"Stay put," he ordered. Trisha Ray immediately wrapped a pair of zip-ties around Wright's wrists.

"Clear! Clear! Clear!" the team announced from around the house.

Wilke, on his first raid in months, was barely in the door before the all-clear was given. At least he got to hit the door with the ram, he told himself, seeking the bright side.

***

The drug house was a hole Viejo wouldn't even let his dog live in, if he had time for a dog. Crack houses all over the world are a testament to the idea that people will follow the path of least resistance. Human beings, given enough time and laziness will succumb to letting their dog shit on the same floor their kids play on, fill up a non-functioning toilet with piss and excrement, sleep on a cockroach infested sofa, eat off dishes covered in rat droppings, and forget hygiene was ever a thing. In his early years patrolling the City's human sewers, Viejo was never surprised to find a new low. Tommy Wright was no exception; the only clean items in the house were his polished pair of Nike's. Tiny, fleeing German cockroaches skittered across the warped remnants of hardwood floors, cupboards, drawers, and pillows. There was a dead rat lying in the back bedroom, apparently not worth cleaning up, only worth kicking next to the wall. There was no dog in the house but the smell of animal piss, and smears of shit ground into the carpet suggested there once was. Probably committed suicide after breathing the air in here, Viejo thought.

Tommy sat on a torn-up couch in front of him, head down, oblivious to the ecosystem of insects, bacteria, and dirt he was sitting in. The team was scattered throughout the rundown house going through years of dirty clothes, rotting furniture, and molding vents. Pulling a somewhat clear chair away from a dining room table full of digital scales, and plastic bags, he dropped it in front of the wiry drug dealer and sat down, "What's up, Tommy?" he asked. "Know why we're here?"

Tommy sucked his front teeth and crinkled up his nose. "Maan, Viejo, why you fuckin' wit me man, I ain't done nuthin'."

Viejo didn't laugh at the outright assault on his intelligence, or the masterful massacre of the English language it was wrapped in. He simply turned and looked back at the table, "The gear on the table would tend to disagree with you."

Tommy sighed, "Come on Viejo, it's just weed, that's all...fuck."

"Right," Viejo responded, then held up a heat-sealed gallon bag half full of flaky white crystals, "Come on Tommy," he said. "I actually thought you were going straight this time," he lied. "I was at your parole hearing." He continued in a cool, calm voice, "Latasha was there with the baby, your Grandma got you a job, you were gonna go to church. At least that's what you told the board. A little part of me was hoping you'd pull it off too. What was that, like a year ago?"

"Fo-teen month," was Tommy's sullen reply.

"Latasha still around, how's the baby?"

Tommy sucked his teeth again, head lolling back and forth. "Man, Viejo. Come on?"

Viejo leaned in close, "Tommy, look at me."

Wright's head rolled around one more circuit. When it came up he was able to meet Viejo in the eye for a moment, then quickly looked away. They could never hold the stare for long. "Tommy, I'm not looking to hem you up today, but I will. You know the deal. Whatta you got to trade?"

"Man shit, I ain't no rat, Viejo."

Viejo pulled the bag up to eye level again, "Yeah, but you got close to a kilo here, caught you just in time. You know how Judge Waters feels about you guys dealin' coke, and this is going to be number three since you hit the big leagues. You're nineteen now, and I've popped you twice in two years. You go in front of the judge like this now—" he paused to let it sink in. He saw the skinny little prick's shoulders slouch just a little "—you can kiss your twenties goodbye and you know it."

Wright didn't respond.

Viejo gave him a minute, leaned back in the chair, felt his jeans sticking to the seat as he shifted, ugh. "This one's an easy one Tommy. I don't care what asshole you bought this shit from. Today all I want is the asshole who shot the little girl. You know the one I'm talking about." Viejo's phone started ringing; it was Tina Winter, another of his Detective leading the raid four blocks away. "Think about it, Tommy," Viejo told him as he stood, his jeans and shirt peeling from the caked-on crud covering the dining room chair. "I'd say you got about fifteen minutes to come up with something." He nodded at Wilke, who was disassembling what was supposed to be the shitholes kitchen. Wilke dropped a molding box of Cap'n Crunch on the grungy tile floor and took over with Wright.

Viejo stepped out on the stoop and sucked in a deep breath of fresh Charleston air. Even plough mud smelled better than that dump. "Viejo," he announced as he answered the phone. "What?"

Chapter Thirty-One

One-forty-three America Street was a grey two-story wood house that listed noticeably to the right. Lead paint chipped from its once-proud wood siding which now warped and buckled at the joints. Trimmed in white, four windows covered the front— two above, two below. By looking at it, you could tell someone really took pride in the place at one time. Dried, trampled remnants of a rose garden lined the front walk, now overgrown to a bristly pant grabbing thorn bush. One-forty-three was like a lot of places on the East Side of the City. Once a proud, hardworking black neighborhood full of business owners, blue collar workers, and longshoreman, was now a dilapidated, desiccated husk of itself, infested with a malignant strain of crime and criminals.

A scared, wrinkled old face was peeking out through the blinds of the home next door as Viejo walked up to the crime scene. They looked at each other for a moment before she darted away. One of the remnants of better days. She'd probably had to watch this happen to her home town, either not fast enough to leave, or without the option as the welfare state and politics took over during the Sixties and Seventies. Now she lived as a prisoner in her own home, surrounded by a demilitarized zone full of thugs. No matter how long he'd been haunting these sad, broken down streets, Viejo couldn't help but feel a twinge for the victims interspersed with the monsters.

One-forty-three America was a panicked wreck of a crime scene. Viejo watched as two Lieutenants trampled through a blood stain while each battled to be the first to brief the Chief. Each barked into their phones, Brooks in his nasally, rat-like squeak, and Commander of the Public Housing Unit Frederick Robinson in a deep baritone, each commander just as unintelligible as the other.

Inside, the front room was a horror. He stopped at the doorway and put his hands in his pockets to fish for gloves. Looking over the scene, he didn't notice the rookie with the clipboard.

"Detective Viejo," he said.

It was the kid from the Jackson shooting. "I see you've gotten about as much time off as I have lately, how you doing?"

"Hangin on, sir," was the reply.

"Good stuff. What the hell happened here?" From where he was standing Viejo could see two bodies, black males, the uniform of the day- wife-beater and dark jeans, face down on moldy crimson-stained carpet. Each looked like he had his head caved in from behind. There were waving lines of blood crisscrossing the walls, floor and ceiling, bootprints in blood and grime leading further into the house. Viejo wondered if the bootprints belonged to one of the fearless leaders howling into the phones beside him.

"Don't know, sir," the rookie answered, pausing as if he didn't know what else to say. "Was like this when we got here."

"I bet," was Viejo's response.

Tiptoeing into the bloodbath, he carefully made his way around the corpses and the blood, camera techs and crime scene techs taking measurements, til he reached the kitchen. There he realized he hadn't seen anything yet. The dead black male in the kitchen still had half a Twinkie hanging out of his mouth. A bottle of soda had fizzed all over the floor next to him. Wide, surprised eyes stared across the floor as if he was trying to find something under the fridge. His skull was likewise caved in. Little pink specks of pulp had bubbled their way out of the bashed-in bone and stuck to the man's tight black curls like salt water taffy.

Detective Kim Winter was nosing through the cabinets in an adjoining nook as he made his way through. She stopped when she saw him.

"What the hell happened here?" he asked.

"Don't look at me, no 911 calls last night, no noise complaints, nothing."

"Rip-off?"

"Kind of." she answered. "Look at this." Winter pointed at a crust of white flakes surrounding the drain in the kitchen sink. There were also the tattered remains of a plastic Ziploc bag.

"They flushed the dope?" Viejo couldn't believe it.

Winter shrugged.

"Impossible. What about the money?"

"No money," Winter said.

"Holy shit."

Winter returned to the front room. She motioned to a scratched and faded old wooden dining room table, "Check this out."

Viejo surveyed the table; four brittle old wooden chairs were situated around it. Several empty tall boys of Bud Light were scattered around the floor, at the feet of the chairs. Around the table, a mass of dominos was arranged in a trail across the center, four piles situated around the pattern. Four half-empty beers were positioned next to the piles of dominos. Viejo's eyes lit up. "You find anybody else?" he asked.

"Nope," Winter replied. "The rest of the team is searching the upstairs right now, but we would have noticed an extra body lying around."

"Nice," Viejo confirmed, "We're missing somebody."

Chapter Thirty-Two

The other two raids that morning yielded five pounds of weed, a couple ounces of heroin, a scattering of ecstasy pills, and almost a kilo of cocaine. They didn't manage to recover any weapons, but the word got out to the street. A dead child is bad for business.

It was almost three in the afternoon by the time the street crimes unit was finished packaging evidence, booking eight subjects, and finishing the mountain of paperwork associated with an honest day's worth of cop work. By six, the team was lounging at the Manic Manatee Pub, a small, out of the way bar buried at Morgan's Marina on the other side of the harbor. The dockside bar held an astounding view of the city across the water. It was hot and humid, but the fresh air blowing in from the Atlantic Ocean cleared their sinuses of a filthy day dredging the sewer of humanity. Slouched in plastic chairs around a likewise plastic table which held an unhealthy load of empty PBR cans, the team had come to relax.

Wilke had a notable lack of empties near him when Viejo arrived. He wore cargo shorts, a set of Teva's, and a Dave Matthews Band T-shirt from the last show he had managed to catch. Wilke kicked a chair at him as he walked up and fished a can of Pabst Blue Ribbon out of a tin bucket of ice in the center of the table.

"What's up, Sarge?" Winter greeted him. She was transformed from a jeans and t-shirt wearing cop to Southern belle, dressed in a sundress, auburn hair flowing free around her shoulders. He toasted her as he popped the top off the beer. "You're just in time for the Wonder Twins' highlight reel."

Viejo took a seat and a pull from the beer. The bitter, fizzing hops and barley barely danced across his taste buds. The familiar taste signaling he was finally off duty. "Been here not even three minutes and the war stories are already flowing, huh?" he observed.

Across the table, Andy Macintyre and Dan Bolan could have passed for a Schwarzenegger/DeVito version of twins. 'Mac' was all of five-seven, maybe a hundred and fifty pounds soaking wet. 'Bo,' was a stout product of Southeastern Conference Football. A defensive end for Clemson University, a trick knee made him too much of a risk for the NFL scouts, but the perfect specimen for Southern law enforcement. Bolan stood six-three, and carried around two hundred and forty pounds of power. Each of the newest members of the unit had taken the place of officers lost the year before during the Tulley investigation. Bolan had three years on, while Mac had four. Viejo had headhunted both of them out of patrol after their respective shift supervisors—also Narcotics crime alums—had turned him on to them. They were coming along, both still looking to prove themselves, eating and breathing cop work. They still had a little too much patrol left in them, as evidenced by the crew cuts, and clean-shaven faces, but they were coming along. Viejo and Wilke had slowly been putting them into shallow undercover's, buying from bars, soliciting prostitutes. Viejo had arrived just in time to hear about their newfound glory.

"Jamal saw us coming. Don't know how a crack dealer managed to wake up at dawn, but this asshole is pissing off the front stoop of this shit hole as we roll up. His eyes bug out, does the two-step, then runs inside—still pissing on himself—and slams the door. So Knock and Announce here," Mac looked toward Bolan, "is already yelling 'police' when he jumps out of the van. So much for the stack, so much for the perimeter. I'm not even sure he bothered with the ram. He just charges through the damn door, takes the whole thing off its hinges in one piece." Mac smashes a fist into his palm. "Bam! only Terrance, Jamal's brother must've been wondering what the hell his brother was saying when he came running through the house pissing himself, because Terrance is at the peephole taking a look right as Tons of Fun hits it." Mac tries to stifle a laugh and continue, as Bolan breaks down and covers his face. Viejo, Winter, and Wilke are chuckling as the little animated Detective tries to go on. "So bam, door goes in, slams into Terrance Brantley, you know he's all of what, one-twenty? Bo gets caught up on the door, trips, and goes down on top of Terrance and the door. I get in right behind him and the first thing I see is just skinny hands and feet hanging out the sides of this door, and biggun's laying on top of it, not moving." All of them are laughing raucously at this point, tears flowing from Bolan, Mac is trying to finish, "All I could think about is that John Candy movie when the bear is bouncing on the door and Candy is trapped underneath. Brantley's squirming, crying, just his hands and feet flailing around. I thought I was going to piss myself."

The table cracked up for a minute, reveling at Bo's squirming. When the laughter subsided, Mac asked, "So what was that today, Sarge?" meaning the men beaten to death on America Street.

Viejo shrugged. "Don't know, something different, that's for sure."

Chapter Thirty-Three

The wounds on his face and inside his hairline stung like a thousand tiny fire ants taking turns biting him. He fought the urge to itch and scratch at the reminder of his humiliation at the hands of a man he had served for over fifteen years. Fifteen years, he remembered, fifteen years and now he knew where he stood with Harold Washington. Moncrief dabbed at the most painful of the numerous miniature puncture wounds dotting his body as gently as he could and grimaced.

It wasn't the first time Washington had beat him. But admittedly Moncrief had earned the previous assaults. When he had wound up under the eye of Washington in those years, he was a wild product of the street. That's how Washington had put it, a wild street dog that needed to learn control or needed to be put down. Washington had explained to him why he would beat on him at random times while he was growing up. Going to make a man out of you, he'd told him, gonna to make you right or make you nothing at all.

Part of Moncrief appreciated the early discipline Washington had harshly bestowed on him. Moncrief knew full well that without it he would have been locked up for good by now or dead in the street, and God knows the crackhead he'd called Mom would never have taught him anything.

Moncrief remembered the last time he saw his mother. It was the night she came home after being gone for four days on a bender. She had left her seven-year old son on his own for all that time. Moncrief remembered scrambling around the cockroaches and the bare cupboards to find anything he could to eat, and fighting with the door of the battered refrigerator to suck dry dregs of spoiled milk just to have something to fill his belly. Moncrief remembered the way Washington had looked at his mother. The casual, matter of fact way he'd explained that she had no rights to the child, that she didn't deserve him. Washington had put his arm around young Moncrief and led him away from the filth of his mother's home. Washington raised him, and put him in position to make money. The man had made him a king on the streets of Charleston and it was good...for a time.

Moncrief had watched slowly over time that Washington was less and less a part of the business. When he had first brought Moncrief in, Washington ruled the streets. Like a sheriff in an old Western, Washington could walk into any bar, any business, and all things stopped to wait on him. No beef in the street happened without Washington's say so. Not an ounce was able to slip from doper to fiend without Washington having an eye on the transaction.

Now Washington did nothing but tinker in that old laundromat. Taking apart this machine and that while at the same time making decrees like he was on a throne or some such. Washington still wanted to rule the streets, but he didn't want to be on them. He let Moncrief be his eyes on the street, and his muscle when Washington decided from his hideaway that something needed doing. Washington still wanted to be the man but he wanted to rule by proxy, putting Moncrief out there to roll in the gutter, while he and people like Blanding kept clean and watched from the sidelines with the same interest as they would at a USC football game. *Not any more,* Moncrief told himself.

Though Moncrief could not deny the heart-squeezing fear he still felt when Washington looked his way, he was not afraid to pull the trigger on him. Moncrief hated the effect the old man's blank, pragmatic stare held over him to the point he both feared and yearned for the day he put Washington in the dirt. There was one standout problem however that kept Moncrief from taking the throne and putting Washington down. Washington was the only guy with access to the source. Washington was not a stupid man, and he didn't rise to the top of the Lowcountry drug trade because he didn't know the value of certain things. Being the source meant you were always needed. The game did not work without you. There was no game without you. Washington kept the source his own little secret. He disappeared a couple of times a month with a pile of money and returned with a pile of dope for Moncrief to cut, package, and sell. Everyone had a role. Washington would say, "Know yours."

Moncrief could not move on Washington without knowing his source. That's why in the middle of the night he was sitting in a beat up old Honda Civic on a side street in Summerville. He'd been tailing Washington for a couple of months around the time he knew supplies were running low.

It was three months of sneaking around in the beater that he'd bought for cash in Savannah so no one would recognize the car as being his before he had any semblance of luck. He'd staked out the laundromat as he had several times over the last few months. It got to be nine thirty at night before he saw his first movement. Washington appeared out the back door, carrying a brown leather duffel that Moncrief had never seen before. The man was dressed too. Instead of the perpetual garb of blue Dickies work pants and faded flannel shirts, Washington was wearing pressed slacks and a sport coat. It was hard to tell in the darkness, but he looked as if he'd shaved and was even wearing a couple of gold rings. Moncrief never knew Washington to wear any jewelry—the man was the very definition of a minimalist. One of the richest men in Charleston dressing like a janitor and driving a rusting hulk of an eighties Ford pickup truck as if he were a living reboot of Sanford and Son. Now here he was dressed like a banker. Moncrief got excited.

Washington seemed to act natural, seemed oblivious to Moncrief's spying. The old man hopped in the old pickup and drove casually through West Ashley. Moncrief followed until he saw Washington pull up to the gate at a self-storage place off seventeen. He had wondered what Washington was up to in that the old man was way out of his normal habitat. Washington's old truck disappeared between the rows of self-storage garages and Moncrief settled in to wait. When Washington returned, it was not in the ratty old truck, but instead he piloted a gleaming black Mercedes Benz, four door sedan. Moncrief almost missed him. He was confused at first. The only reason he knew the pilot of the luxury vehicle was his mark was that Washington had to roll down the driver's side window to activate the exit gate.

Moncrief felt a dizzying mixture of excitement and dread at seeing his mentor change so drastically before him. For all his time with Washington, the one constant the man had always preached was the importance of hiding your money. He lived sparsely in an apartment over the laundromat and drove that crappy old truck. Everyone on the street knew him by the flannel and Dickies pants, and scuffed up work boots. Moncrief had even heard other boys on the block talk about Washington, that the old man looked more janitor than Scarface. They always said this behind the old man's back, of course. Regardless of Washington's outward appearance, if he showed up on the street, as seldom as that happened to be, all eyes and ears were on him, and every word was obeyed to the letter. There were numerous examples buried in the marshes surrounding the Lowcountry to remind anyone that Washington was The Man, a man never to be crossed.

A large part of Moncrief wanted to run away and hide at the sight of the changed, dapper Washington. Moncrief believed himself as close to Washington as anyone could ever be and he would have never believed the man capable of such a transformation. Moncrief's mind swam as he followed Washington's Mercedes up Hwy 61 to Dorchester County. In Summerville, Washington pulled to a stop outside a quiet, out of the way local Italian restaurant and casually strolled inside. Moncrief found a parking spot he could force the Honda into while still providing him a place to view as much of the front and side entrances that he could. As he strained to look through the windows, he noted that he could barely see where Washington was sitting, catty-corner to one of the front windows. He was able to see Washington sit down at a table but then lost sight of most of him. Only part of his jacket was visible from Moncrief's perch.

Moncrief settled in to wait, and five minutes after Washington arrived at the restaurant he watched a white male pull up to the same restaurant in a new silver Range Rover. Moncrief observed him with passing interest. Of particular note was the weird checkered pattern of the man's trim fitting blazer. It was obnoxious. It looked more like something an NBA player would wear to a press conference than something some small town tool would be roaming around in. The man with the strange jacket and close cropped blonde hair walked slowly up the steps to the restaurant and disappeared inside. Moncrief continued watching what little of Washington he could see, thoughts of the strange choice in dinnerware fading from his mind. He saw Washington rise. He could only see Washington's ring-studded hand as it reached out to grasp another. This one with a wrist cuff trimmed in a very unique checker pattern.

Moncrief smiled.

Forty-five minutes later, Moncrief watched as Washington and his dinner date exited the restaurant. They walked casually to their vehicles. The Range Rover had parked right next to the Mercedes, and Moncrief realized as he watched the two approach their cars that he hadn't even taken notice of that fact. He was across the street nestled between two raised pickup trucks. His car was hidden, and about as nondescript as could be found, yet he still found himself slouching low in the driver's seat as the two men paused between their vehicles. His heart pounded in his chest as he thought briefly about what Washington would do if he found him spying on him. He couldn't hear what was said but he watched as the two opened the adjoining doors and traded bags. Washington handed over the expensive looking leather duffel and the man in the checkered dinner jacket handed Washington a similar looking bag in black.

Moncrief could hardly believe it. Right out in the open like that? Moncrief knew an exchange when he saw one. He had thought he perfected the maneuver over the years. But this was next level. *I guess you can get away with anything as long as you got a white guy with you,* thought Moncrief. And that was it: the source for almost all of the East Side of Charleston's cocaine and crack trade was a pasty-faced white guy who drove a Range Rover and wore horribly designed clothes. He was like a hipster kingpin, or would have been if he had been sporting a pair of thick-rimmed glasses. Moncrief knew he could never tell any of his boys about this. None of them would ever believe that they all worked for some white metrosexual. It was bizarre.

After the exchange, Washington and his contact went their separate ways. Washington headed further into Summerville while the Range Rover headed north toward the interstate. For a moment Moncrief was unsure of who to follow. After so long watching his mentor, he realized he had no plan for what happened if he actually was able to see Washington re-supply. Knowing where the money was stashed would be good. But in the end, he needed the source, would need to know all there was about him if he was going to take the old man's spot. He pulled out and followed the path of the Range Rover. He had just made the corner onto the main street leading away from the small town when his phone started blaring a riff from DMX's 'X gonna give it to ya," Washington was calling.

Moncrief's breath caught in his throat and he instinctively looked in the rearview mirror expecting Washington's face to be looming over his rear window like some monster, hunting him. The ringtone repeated itself twice before he worked up the courage to answer.

"Ya," he finally said.

"How is it I hear about a rip at one of your shops from the street and not from you?" demanded Washington.

Moncrief clicked his tongue. "Man, some fiend got lucky, won't happen again. My people are trackin' it down. No way that dude gets through."

"Word is whoever it was put three of yours in the ground."

Moncrief didn't reply. He knew each one of the three men killed and he didn't feel a thing.

"Defend your streets boy," Washington ordered.

"Uh-huh," replied Moncrief. He caught sight of the Range Rover. It had shifted lanes and was angling for the ramp onto I-26.

"Also, be at the laundro tomorrow. Got a belt that needs replacing." Washington hung up.

Moncrief smiled. That was their code in the event the cops ever started listening on their phones. Washington confirmed that he had just re-upped from the white boy. He put the phone on the passenger seat and sped to catch up to the SUV.

Two blocks away from the restaurant, Washington dropped his phone into his breast pocket.

"You confirm that was him?" he asked.

A black man in a trim black suit and purple tie slouched against the front fender of a Chrysler 300 and nodded.

"Told you, you can't break a wild dog, been tellin' you that for years."

Washington didn't reply. He was quiet for a moment while he thought of Moncrief. For some reason, especially at a time like this, he couldn't help but picture that dirty little rat he had caught trying to steal change all those years ago. He remembered the spark that burned bright behind the kid's eyes. There was a gleam that Washington had seen. The kid had stood out from most of the doomed-from-birth dregs that littered the streets. He considered for a moment that that fire he had seen might be the same fire that had lead him to take aim at him. Washington wasn't sure how he felt about that. He shook his head slightly. "Well, let's not take him out yet. I wanna know who's gonna go with him when the time comes. Not even he is crazy enough to come at me alone."

"You say so," the man in the suit answered. He started for the driver's door of the Chrysler, "I be around tomorrow then."

"Hey Pell, what happened over on the East Side today?" Washington asked, referring to the rip at the stash house.

Pell looked back and shrugged. "Three of Moncrief's boys beaten to death. The dope was thrown in the sink. However much money they had in there was gone, far as I can tell. Whoever it was beat three men to death. That's what I got from my people at the PD anyway."

"They flushed the cocaine? How much? Who the hell would bust up a stash and not take the dope? Cocaine was worth more than cash on the street."

"Dunno," said Pell.

"And no guns?"

"Nope, blunt force injury, and from what I hear a lot of it."

"Something wrong there Pell," Washington sighed.

"Didn't seem like standard practice to me either," Pell responded getting in his car.

Washington sighed. "We're getting old, Pell," he said, watching his oldest associate groan and crack as he managed himself into his seat.

"Speak for yourself," Darius Pellsom hissed before he pulled off.

Washington watched for a minute as the ex-cop, his ex-cop, turned 'private detective' drove back toward Charleston. Something was wrong. Washington could feel it. Problem was, there was very little he could do about it, yet.

Chapter Thirty-Four

The halls and offices of the second floor of 180 Lockwood Boulevard were quiet. In the large open bullpen that was the Central Detectives Bureau, a single, old boxy television displayed a talking head laying out in just enough detail the latest threat to society and the reasons why everyone should hide under their covers at night. The droning went unnoticed by the four people sitting at desks in a relative semi-circle. Fenner typed fluidly on a laptop as she completed her activity reports for the day while Martin read the day's edition of the *Post and Courier*. Opposite the two homicide detectives, Viejo leaned back in one of the reclining office chairs with his boots up on Martin's desk and Wilke, arms crossed over his chest, seemed half-asleep.

"Don't offer to help the lady, fellas." Banks' voice boomed as he entered the bullpen.

"Already did, boss," Martin responded, "She declined our advances."

"I bet she did," said Banks, "Where are we?"

Viejo rolled into a forward position in the chair and dropped his boots to the floor. "We got enough crack and weed off the street to make half the fiends in this city cry, but couldn't shake anything loose. The boys know that the East Side is locked down until we get the shooter."

"Ok, what about that slaughter house on America Street?"

"That was weird," said Wilke, taking over for Viejo, "No signs that a gun was used. It looked like somebody just beat the living shit out of the three mules that were minding the store. Dope was destroyed and probably some money was taken, but no one is going to give us anything to run with."

Banks shook his head, "Destroyed the dope?"

"Looks like they flushed it in the kitchen sink then followed it with bleach. They were after the money, not the dope."

"That does not bode well, but lax security at a crack house does not trump the killing of a three-year old girl in the eyes of the mayor or the chief. Someone else can handle it. What about you two?" Banks asked, nodding to Fenner and Martin.

Before Bob could speak, Fenner looked up from her keyboard. "Deshaun Cauldwell's canteen account at the county jail was two to three times that of your local crack mule. It took a little bit but I got his records from County. He had no phone calls to speak of for the entire stretch, so I looked at the visitor log which was likewise pretty scarce. On the canteen account, he got regular deposits on the second and fourth weeks of every month, and like I said, they were fat deposits. The canteen accounts are totally wired now so there are no cash deposits at County. The deposits came in through Western Union. We had to run through some subpoena service, but we were able to track all but one of the payments to the Western Union desk at the Harris Teeter on East Bay. The deposits at the Teeter were in cash, but the surveillance system was better than most. I was able to get a snapshot of the depositor on the last two payments to Deshaun before he got out."

Fenner rose from her chair and passed a photo to each of them. "This is where I'm at. I've been working through Vice's database, and the DMV, but so far I've gotten nowhere. We're going to need to put this photo on the street and see what it shakes loose."

"Call girl," Martin said flatly.

Fenner shot him a tired look. "You're an asshole," she said flatly, rebuking the insinuation. "But that was my first thought too. That's why I went to the Vice database. Still nothing."

Wilke studied the photo as Viejo and Martin tossed around first impressions and Fenner let them know she had already considered them all. The girl was attractive, even in the low quality image. It was an overhead shot from an angle which caught her leaving the Western Union counter. A petite black woman with long hair tied up in a headscarf. She wore a white tank top which contrasted starkly with her bare skin that seemed a darker tone of a golden brown. Her tight midriff was on display between the tank top and a pair of light low-cut jeans that fit tightly to her form. The muscle definition in the woman's core was evident even in the poor photograph. Her legs and hips were shapely and firm and she wore a pair of white canvas sneakers. He didn't know why but the footwear caught Wilke's attention. He expected a drug mule's baby momma or whoever a woman wiring money to a low rent convict to be more of a stiletto pump and painted on jeans girl than a pair of simple canvas sneakers. The shoes almost didn't seem loud enough for the woman he was expecting. He committed the woman's face, wide set eyes, full lips, and just this side of plump cheeks to memory, then studied the overall of the photo a moment more. After a moment, he put the photo down.

"When you got the video, was there a dude or a chick at the counter?" he asked.

"Girl, and she didn't recognize the photo, why?"

"The person at the counter was a guy."

Fenner's face screwed into an uncomprehending and thoroughly unimpressed scowl before she took another look at the photo. Wilke watched as she recognized what he saw on the sheet. Fenner sighed.

Chapter Thirty-Five

"That's Shaunte Fields," Eric Bardom, Counter Associate at the Western Union desk located in the East Bay Street Harris Teeter confirmed. The young man had needed less than five seconds of studying the low resolution photo before recognizing the attractive black woman.

"What do you know about her?" Wilke asked.

"Not much," said Bardom. "She hasn't been in for a while."

"Good looking girl, right?" Wilke asked with a faint grin.

Bardom unconsciously flared his eyes and nodded slightly. "Not bad."

"She live around here?"

"Why?"

Wilke could see this desperate bastard looking up her details in the system and running to tell the girl the police had been looking for her. It was easy to see happening. Bardom had a shaved head, bulging, thick- rimmed glasses that gave his eyes a sort of frog-like look. And the man carried an extra thirty pounds or so. If Shaunte Fields asked him to stand in front of a bus he would do so without question. *What a doomed species*, Wilke thought. "Well, we think someone has been stealing her identity," Wilke lied to the clerk. He lowered his voice and leaned in close over the counter when he told him the secret. "Keep that quiet though, okay, privacy and stuff."

Bardom's jowls flapped when he shook his head. "No problem," he whispered. There was an awkward two seconds or so of silence while Wilke stared at the man. He started to shrivel under the unbearable quiet between the two men.

"Yeah, well anyway," Bardom said as he opened a drawer and flipped through a notebook, "here's her address and phone number. I hope it doesn't mess up Ms. Fields' credit."

Bardom froze when he looked back at Wilke.

"I thought one of the great things about money orders were that they were mostly anonymous?" asked the detective.

Bardom shook his head nervously and his jowls flapped perpendicular to his jaw. "Not so much." His voice was rising. "There was a problem with an order one time and I had to look her up, that's all."

Wilke looked at the notebook and scribbled down Fields' information. The notebook looked anything but official. He slipped the small notebook in his back pocket and turned, "I'll tell Shaunte what a big help you were Eric, thanks a lot."

"No problem," said the clerk. "Let me know if you need anything else."

Wilke waved as he left. Walking through the parking lot, heading for Viejo, he filed a mental note to check the databases for peeping tom calls in the vicinity of Shaunte's house.

Chapter Thirty-Six

Washington heard the heavy metal door at the rear of the laundromat clang shut and slid back in his chair. He sat behind a dinged and scratched metal desk and slouched in a similarly dilapidated office chair. One hand hugged a steaming cup of coffee on top of the desk and the other rested out of view on his lap. He heard the slightly off kilter slap of basketball shoes on concrete as Moncrief made his way toward him. The kid put such practice into his 'pimp walk.' He strutted just so, everywhere he went, even when there was no one around to see him try to imitate a limp. To Washington, the entire premise of a 'pimp walk' was infuriating. It was the lowest and cheapest form of show boating, something the old man had no patience for.

As Moncrief came into view, Washington's blood began to boil. Almost thirty years old, the man had a faux slouch to the right-hand side, and he walked as if he'd been hit by a car or something. The practice had started when Moncrief was fifteen. Washington, at the time, had been supporting the kid while he created his footprint on the street. He had to let it slide then so that Moncrief could properly blend with the rest of the shiftless morons involved in the drug trade. He drew the line however the day

Moncrief showed at the laundromat with a double row of gold teeth inserts. Washington had spent a lot of money on the feral child's hygiene, and healthy white teeth were not something to hide. The old man had beaten the boy until the fake teeth had flown from his mouth. The ridiculous posture and the expensive basketball shoes he would abide. Glaringly obnoxious mouth accessories he would not.

As Washington watched his protégé approach, he reluctantly took pride in the man walking toward him. Moncrief was nothing if not a predator. His strut was an act, but also a practice in energy conservation. He never saw the boy rush, or expend unnecessary energy without cause. Much like a patiently waiting hawk, or big cat, Moncrief moved fluidly and was capable of explosive acts of violence when called for. Otherwise he was calm, and moved slow while his eyes roved continuously, taking in every movement and detail around him.

Moncrief stopped before the desk.

"Hey Pop," he said.

Washington noticed the white cabbie hat covering Moncrief's head. There were still faint, rash-like outlines around the sides of his face where the wire brush had effectively relayed Washington's message earlier.

"Sorry about your head, boy," he said calmly. "One day I will explain why we need men like Blanding. Until then he cannot be touched."

"I know, he's the money guy. I'm sorry, he just disrespected me once too much. I lost it. We need him though. I won't touch him again."

Washington put on a half-smile, "He sees you again without me around and he'll probably shit himself."

Moncrief grinned uneasily.

"But you see the shit that has caused? How many times you been hit this week?"

Moncrief shifted his weight. "Couple, po-lice locking down until they get they man."

Washington reminded himself to stay calm. He felt that same fire building within him that last resulted in him beating the man before him with a wire brush. Any other moment in history and Moncrief would have been dead, sealed in a concrete filled oil drum and resting at the bottom of a swamp. Fortunately for him, the source of their product had been in flux as of late and any exigent personnel changes might have scared them into shutting down service. Nonetheless, if what Pell saw the night before was true, there would have to be a reckoning. It was just a matter of proper timing.

The two sat in silence for a moment. Finally Moncrief asked, "You get a re-supply or somethin?"

Washington leaned back in his chair. "I did," with his free hand he opened the desk drawer and withdrew two bricks of flakey white powder wrapped tight in plastic. "Before I give it to you though, I gotta know you gonna protect it."

Washington saw Moncrief sigh. He knew the boy had ego enough to fill the Galliard Auditorium. The idea that some street fiend had ripped him off and beat his men to death made him seethe. Washington wondered what Moncrief's main priority was—Washington himself, or whoever it was that ripped him off.

Moncrief shrugged, trying and failing to play off the slight, "It was no thing," he said. "Probably some crack head got a little too cooked. He'll go spend that shit on more junk and when he does we got him. I'll handle him myself."

The kid has no idea, Washington realized. Strangely, he was suddenly relieved that Moncrief would soon be out of the picture. He had known all along that the kid was a vicious street thug, he'd made him that way. That sole factor played a major role in why Washington had taken him under his wing so long ago. The wild look in the kid's eye. Even when trapped in a corner, he would still fight, no matter how doomed an endeavor. But here, in a circumstance where he should be analyzing and learning from what happened, he was simply looking for a fight.

It was Moncrief's own cook house that was hit, a place long under his control. He should know by now that the dope in that house wasn't going up the nose of some daredevil East Side drug fiend. The dope was sloshing its way through the Lowcountry sewer system, of no use to anyone. Moncrief was robbed and his men beaten to a pulp. Any leader with even a fraction of rational thought could see that this was rage, maybe vengeance for some slight the thick-headed sociopath probably committed in a random act.

Washington dropped the bricks on the metal desk, causing a dull percussion. Moncrief strutted to the desk to retrieve the supply and Washington caressed the tang of the vintage 1911 semi auto that rested on his thigh under the desk. It needed to be done, he was sure now. There was not a shred of business man in the wild street creature Washington had cultivated. Despite the shaky footing his source may be resting on at the moment, change was coming. Washington grinned at the younger man collecting the cocaine from the desk. But not yet, not yet because there was dirty business to be done on the street.

Whoever the dumb motherfucker was that ripped Moncrief also ripped him. The first rule of the dope game ever taught to Harold Washington was that you had to protect what's yours. Face had to be saved and it would be more efficient to let the wolf he'd tried to domesticate do the work he was bred for rather than Washington exposing himself. Moncrief received a pardon in that moment when he leaned over Washington's desk to collect his prize. He was granted the opportunity to continue free and vertical in the world one more day. He had a function in Washington's machine. However impermanent Moncrief's function may be, he would continue to serve his purpose, for now.

Moncrief secured the cocaine in a backpack he'd brought with him and stood in front of Washington for a moment. Washington watched him stir in the silence.

"Anything else?" the kid finally asked.

"Nah," Washington answered. "I want that trouble on the street snuffed out ASAP. We can't be having that sort of problem."

Moncrief nodded and turned to leave. As he did so, he looked toward the shadows where Pell had been waiting to flank him. The young man didn't see him, or else, Washington knew, things would have broken bad. Good instincts though, he thought, again impressed with the base survival instincts Moncrief possessed. Too bad there wasn't more to him, Washington thought, as he watched Moncrief leave. There was a lot of potential there.

Chapter Thirty-Seven

Shaunte Fields sat with her arms crossed over her ample breasts and one leg draped over the other. She wore the same simple canvas sneakers she'd worn when captured by the Harris Teeter surveillance camera. Her right foot bounced up and down as she stared at the mirrored one-way window in the interrogation room.

"She doesn't look so tough," said Bob Martin as he watched her through the window.

"Looks can be deceiving, old man," Fenner responded. She studied Shaunte's criminal history. It was only three pages, relatively short for the kind of people who normally wound up sitting inside the room with the mirrored window.

"Tell me about it. At one point, I had it in my head that you would be a kind, caring, nurturing partner. Someone who respected those senior to them and would take the opportunity to learn at the feet of a great master and make the most of it." Martin was looking at her with sadness, steaming cup of mud coffee in one hand, pad and pen in the other.

Fenner looked up from the criminal history report to see him but didn't say a word,

"Exactly," said Martin triumphantly. "Exactly." Then he turned back to the viewing window.

"If you're done," said Fenner before continuing, "Two priors for shoplifting four years ago, couple of traffic tickets, nothing big, nothing dope related." She swapped the report for her notes. "Lifelong inhabitant at the Driggers Projects. In 2013 she managed an anchor baby—she was fifteen then—and now has a taxpayer-subsidized two bedroom overlooking the marsh until the kid is eighteen. No mention of work, no mention of school in the public housing database."

"I always love seeing my hard-earned tax money going to a worthy cause," Martin said. "Who's the baby-daddy?"

"Doesn't say. That's weird, the kid's last name is hers too. Usually the future deadbeat dad wants name attribution," Fenner sighed, "You know she makes more in subsidies than a rookie patrolman's salary. How do you want to play this?"

"That's easy," said Martin. The old detective took a sip from his coffee before marching through the door. If he had a plan, he didn't bother to share it with his partner.

***

"I don't know nothin' about somebody shootin' a baby," Shaunte said.

"I know you don't, you got a baby of your own. I don't even like thinking about what that little girl went through, what her momma went through,"

Shaunte didn't respond. She fidgeted slightly as she looked to the door of the drab grey interrogation room. Martin watched her eyes float around the room, studying the plain cinderblock walls and large two way mirror that took up a good portion of the wall behind Martin.

"Shaunte, how did you know Deshaun?"

"Who?"

"Deshaun Cauldwell. He was killed the same night as little Chevante. Your little one is almost four, correct?" Martin kept his voice low and calm, trying to transmit as good a grandfatherly vibe as he knew how. It was an important trait to have in the interrogation room, where an unsuspecting subject finds themselves alone and cut off from everything known and comfortable to them. A good detective will become something familiar to their prey, something they can connect with, latch onto for safety in a cold, naturally inhospitable environment.

"I don't know any Deshaun," Shaunte told him.

"You sure?"

"Yeah," she snapped back, a little bit of heat in the word.

"You were depositing five hundred every couple of weeks into Deshaun Cauldwell's canteen account at County for an entire year. How could you not know a man you gave almost fifteen grand to?"

Shaunte froze. The woman stopped breathing, her eyes didn't blink, her muscles didn't flinch for all of about three seconds. Martin, now fairly certain that his grandfatherly approach needed some work, would have been happy to allow the silence to swell, but the girl recovered and looked to the floor. She hadn't answered the question.

"So you knew Deshaun?" Martin asked, suppressing a grin. It was always refreshing to see that the old adage that ninety percent of all communication was non-verbal play out.

"Uh-uh," Shaunte grunted, still not looking at him.

"Huh, okay, you don't want to talk about Deshaun. Let's talk about the money that went into his account."

"Don't know about no money," Shaunte responded. She was like a box turtle hiding in her shell. Martin had seen this approach thousands of times throughout his career as a cop. When confronted by a truth, hide, huddle and hope that the bad man with the badge and the evidence goes away. Martin could only figure that it was a practice everyone learned at around three years old. When confronted with a broken dish or a spilled glass of milk, a toddler will deny any wrong doing regardless of how many witnesses were standing there when the incident happened. Martin guessed that some people just didn't grow out of that kind of defense. When all else fails, deny, deny, deny.

Martin slipped the photo of her at the Western Union desk across the table, "The young man, Eric, I think it was, seemed pretty fond of you."

"S'not me," Shaunte said quietly. She leaned forward in her chair slightly to look at the photo. Her hands were still across her chest and she seemed to hold her head at an angle as if looking down at him and the photo. She was shutting down. The box turtle was going monosyllabic in her answers. Shaunte was not going to talk to him until talking to him suddenly became in her best interest.

"Shaunte, you are wearing the same pair of tennis shoes here as you were in that photo. We ran facial recognition software to match this photo to your mug shot from your last shoplifting beef." The facial recognition software was a lie, but in this day and age, and thanks to television, people believed everything. And it was a lie that she could not catch him in which made it low risk.

Shaunte stared at the floor, not moving. Her lips puckered.

"Ok," Martin sighed. He pulled out a couple of forms and laid them out in front of her. One was an application package for the Charleston City Public Housing office. The next was a registration form from Trident Technical College, the local junior college. The third was a collection of tax forms. Bob Martin watched Shaunte's eyes drift reluctantly toward the paperwork. He waited until she shot a look at him that could melt steel before speaking.

"So, Shaunte, what I have here is an enigma wrapped in a bureaucracy," He pointed to the Public Housing application. "This shows you had a baby going on four years ago. You would have been fifteen at the time the kid was born. On your eighteenth birthday, you got an apartment in the same building as your mom and grandma. That was 2014." He paused to tap a finger on the stack of tax forms. "To qualify for continued housing and welfare subsidies you must show you are working or looking for work. These tax forms correspond to a business in your name. You run a dance academy on Cosgrove," Martin flipped through some of the forms until he settled on a utility check of the location. The owner of the building was a corporation Fenner was still tracking down. "Shaunte, this is a utilities report for your dance studio. It reads that there hasn't been enough power running through your studio to keep the lights on over the past year. In contrast, you claimed a twenty thousand dollar net gain from your business, still inside the threshold to keep you in the housing system and still to fulfill your work requirement."

Shaunte was still staring at the floor. Over the table, Martin could see her twitch slightly as her knee bounced.

Martin sighed and pointed to the college application. "To solidify your status as a resident of the City's housing system you are registered at Trident Tech as a Medical Assistant student. You are registered for eighteen credit hours though the college reports you have never been to class, nor have you ever paid tuition. Seems you re-register every semester, then drop." Martin withdrew his hand from the paperwork and leaned back in the uncomfortable metal chair. He waited.

Shaunte huddled silently across the table. He stared at her with his arms crossed. He waited some more.

At first, her eyes scanned the forms before her. Then she shifted uncomfortably in her seat as if turning away from the collection of paper. She shifted a couple of more times, then looked at him. Disgust marred her normally gorgeous features. Silence for most people was unbearable. It was one of Martin's greatest weapons inside an interrogation room.

"So?" she finally spat.

Martin grinned and leaned forward. "Glad you asked. Shaunte, we don't think you had anything to do with the death of little Chevante, or Deshaun Cauldwell, for that matter. However, for us to know who killed him, we need to know about him. What was he involved in? Where had he been? Who were his friends? Who were his enemies? You are our best chance at finding out more about Deshaun right now given that you were supporting him financially while he was in jail. Now I can't make you talk to me. But what I've just laid out before you shows a high potential for housing fraud, welfare fraud, and tax fraud, for that matter. The money you sent to Deshaun alone, coupled with your fake business, will get you and your child thrown out of housing. When the investigation expands to mom and grandma, if they had anything to do with your scheme, they will get thrown out on the street too." Martin leaned in closer to her. "You have a decision to make," he said.

Without another word, he rose and left the room. The door to the interrogation room was barely closed behind him before he heard a muffled "Alright," come from inside.

Chapter Thirty-Eight

"Why do I know that name?" Banks asked no one in particular.

"He runs that church up on Huger. Remember he let us use the second floor as a perch at one point."

"Oh," said Banks. "That guy?"

"That's what I was thinking."

"It's always the quiet ones," Wilke added.

"You should talk," Fenner told him. Wilke ignored her.

Martin silenced everyone. "According to sweet Shaunte, Deshaun was in one of Blanding's reformation programs, a turn your life around sort of thing. Deshaun fell off the wagon and Blanding wanted to make sure he was comfortable while he was inside."

"To the tune of fifteen grand? Bullshit," said Viejo.

Before continuing, Martin looked at Banks. "Now I see why you hired him Captain, he's smart."

Viejo flipped off the veteran detective.

Martin chuckled, then continued when Banks gave him a rolling hand gesture. It was going on ten o'clock at night and the four detectives seated around the office had barely taken time from the job to shower and change clothes since the toddler was killed almost a week before. They needed rest—he could see it in the rings under Wilke's eyes and the way Fenner slumped just so in her chair.

"So she won't give up any more about Blanding and Deshaun other than the bullshit about the church program Deshaun was in. She did say that she had seen Deshaun around the church several times sweeping or cleaning. Doing the basic maintenance thing."

"What's her deal with the church?"

"She says she volunteers there, helps out with the Sunday school and whatnot."

"More bullshit," said Fenner. All of them agreed.

"The money?" Banks asked, but he almost feared the answer. There was only so much bullshit even he could take.

"She said it came from Blanding, part of the program's budget, taken from donations."

The four cops didn't bother responding to the line of garbage Martin was relaying.

Banks was tired, they were all tired. "Lay it out Bob, what's your take?"

Martin cleared his throat, "We're getting afield from figuring out who killed Chevante with this one but Shaunte Fields and Deshaun Cauldwell couldn't put a hundred dollars together between the two of them, on a good day. The only dude we got in her whole bullshit story with money is the church guy. Which begs the question, why do you pay to keep someone comfortable when they are in jail?"

"They're doing your stretch," said Wilke.

"Maybe."

Banks huffed, "We are nowhere on the Chevante case."

"Not yet," said Martin, "but at least we're not dead in the water. In the morning, we go and pick up Blanding. See what we can shake loose."

Chapter Thirty-Nine

Anthony Kleener woke up on his side. It was dark and humid and wherever he was smelled of mildew and plough mud. He moved to get up and a blast of panic shook him. He couldn't move! His hands were behind his back and he could feel tight bonds locking his wrists and elbows together. His legs were similarly bound above the knees and at the ankles. Looking toward his feet, he could see the shiny nylon rope digging into his jeans.

"What the..."

"Heroin?" He heard the low voice before he saw a pair of dark boots poised three feet away.

Anthony craned his neck to see nothing more than a shadow. A dark outline of a man stood before him. The only proof to Kleener that he was really there and not some ghost was the fact he could see the toes of the scuffed black boots shift ever so much with the weight of their wearer.

"Man, you are out of your mind," the seventeen- year old said, trying to look in the man's eyes.

The shadow didn't respond.

"You better let me up!" Kleener threatened. He didn't know what else to do, and it made him feel better when he was talking.

The figure moved in the dim light and Kleener cringed slightly when his body betrayed him and he involuntarily shrank away from the man. Out of the darkness came a clear plastic bag with a chunk of whitish- yellow stuff sitting inside.

"Crack," said the voice.

"No shit." Kleener hoped his teenage voice didn't sound as shrill as he thought it had.

"You cook this yourself?" asked the voice.

Kleener clicked his teeth.

A boot reached out and nudged his shoulder.

Kleener tried to squirm. "Come on, man."

"Answer me."

"No, fuck no, I just sell the shit. That all you want? Shit, all you had to do was ask and I woulda given you a discount." His comment brought the boot back. Only this time instead of a nudge, the heavy steel toe buried itself in his abdomen. Kleener coughed and squeaked a little. Whatever facade Kleener had held onto washed away as he gasped for breath, unable to move on the dingy floor. "Come on," he mumbled, "what do you want?" His voice cracked.

"When you cook cocaine into this shit, you've got to bake it in a mix so it doesn't just fry and blacken. You can do this with a bunch of stuff but usually whatever is nearby is easiest. Shit like ammonia or baking soda."

"So?"

"So you ever smell ammonia? Shit stinks. Where's your source?"

Kleener's face screwed into an incredulous grin. "You are out of your damn mind, man."

Broadstreet leaned down toward the kid, "Not going to argue with you, but ask yourself this—do you want me to let lose my crazy on you, or your boss?"

Kleener's eyes widened. "Shit, you're the guy."

Broadstreet stared at him.

"You're the one that did it. You did those dudes at that house."

"You had your chance." Broadstreet rose from his crouch and grabbed a length of rebar from the barren grimy floor.

"No, no, no, what I do to you?"

"Nothin'," Broadstreet responded. "It's not who you are, it's what you are." He hefted the metal like a baseball bat and slammed it into Kleener's ankle. There was a wet crunching snap.

Kleener howled.

Broadstreet stepped back and set the rebar to rest on the ground near Kleener's head. He tried to ignore how thrilling he found this. He knew it was wrong, but a small part of him asked, *Was it?* "Think about what comes next."

The kid was crying. "Please!" he pleaded.

"I just want your source."

Kleener snuffled.

Broadstreet smashed his knee.

"No!" Kleener sobbed, and thrashed against his restraints. "Stop!"

"That's on you." Broadstreet kept his voice calm but felt his extremities trembling with excitement.

"Brinkley."

"What?"

"Brinkley street, yellow house at the end on the right," Kleener gasped.

"This didn't have to go this way," Broadstreet told the teenager. He thought about asking for a name but he realized it didn't matter. A name didn't mean a thing.

"They're going to kill you."

"You better hope not," Broadstreet said, pulling open a dinged and dented steel door.

"Let me go," Kleener pleaded.

Broadstreet shook his head slowly, "There's no place for you here," he said. A wave of sweet ecstasy took him as the teenage drug dealer began to sniffle and plead for his life. Broadstreet hefted the rebar and adjusted his grip. Then he silenced the boy's pleas forever.

***

Broadstreet was a block away from the building when he noticed the unmistakable form of a police cruiser turn his way. The black and white rode slowly his way for about a quarter mile. He ducked his head instinctively and when he looked down, he noticed a spattering of dark droplets smearing the toe of his boot. Broadstreet's heart stopped.

Chapter Forty

Andrew Coburn watched his rookie out the corner of his eye. William Frytel was like a loaded spring in the driver's seat of the Chevy Impala. It was the kid's first night shift since graduating from the police academy in Columbia a month ago. Frytel sat straight in the seat and kept both hands on the steering wheel as if he were in driver's ed. Coburn noticed the rookies' head turn slightly back and forth like a lighthouse, scanning every crack and crevice of the street. Looking for the boogeyman around every corner no doubt.

Coburn saw someone he didn't recognize coming from the condemned Whitmarsh housing projects. The guy was dressed all in black and seemed to kind of scrunch down in his jacket as they drew closer. That in and of itself wasn't overly suspicious, in fact in this part of town pretty much everybody they drove past tried to act like either they weren't there or the police weren't there. On the other hand, they had gotten plenty of reports of copper thefts from the area since the old apartment buildings were shut down. Coburn didn't recognize the guy, and Coburn knew everybody in his beat.

"Let's talk to this fella up here, Fry," he said.

Frytel almost jumped out of the driver's seat. His neck perked up and he ripped his seat belt off like he was getting ready for a foot pursuit. He hit the accelerator just a nudge to close the gap on the pedestrian and Coburn looked at him. Frytel sensed it and slowed down, pulling to a stop almost right next to the black clad figure. Coburn grimaced. *Jesus Christ, if the guy wanted to, he could reach through the window and shake my hand, or shoot me in the face,* Coburn thought.

Not taking his eye off the black male who tried to keep walking, he exited the car. Frytel did the same.

"You forget something, kid?" Coburn asked as he stepped onto the sidewalk.

"Uhh…"

"Anybody know where we are or what we're doing?"

"Shit." Frytel fumbled for his shoulder microphone.

Coburn heard the kid give their location to Dispatch as he watched the figure slowly turn their way and stop. He scuffed his boots on the ground stirring up dust.

"How you doin' tonight, pal?" he asked.

"Ok," said the figure.

"You coming from the Whitmarsh?"

"Just passing through."

Coburn closed the gap between them casually. "Where you headed?"

Broadstreet looked at the old cop. There was something familiar in his eyes. Then it hit him. He was twelve and had just started selling crack for Zim. After acting as a runner for so long, Joe knew every aspect of Zim's business. The twelve-year old had followed the older man around, running errands, and performing odd jobs for so long that Zim had decided to give him the opportunity to earn some "real money."

Zim wasn't kidding either, thought Broadwater at the time. What was a twelve-year old kid supposed to do with two thousand dollars a month? Jordan's, clothes, sunglasses—there was only so much material property in a twelve year old's world that he could spend money on. The TV in Joe's small room dwarfed the old box set that sat glumly in his mom's living room. The speakers attached to the system were obnoxious when Joe and his friends played the newest video games on the newest game systems. But his mom didn't say anything. If Joe was taking care of himself, it was one less problem she had to deal with, so much the better. She never even asked for the money other than to put her hand out for food, booze, and cigarettes. Joe went from runt to do-boy of the most powerful drug dealer on the block to a self-styled king as soon as Zim turned on the money spigot by putting those small, off-white rocks in his hand. And he wanted more.

He drafted two of his friends, and put them to work around the small zone Zim had carved out for him. He had a system for storing and protecting his stash while the three of them sold to every passing fiend that had twenty dollars to spare. He gave his two lackey's a cut, but kept the grand share for himself, like any good business man, Zim had told him, guiding him while he built his own little empire.

By the time Joseph was fourteen, he was stashing almost four grand a month in his sock drawer and throughout the pockets and seams of his endless variety of designer clothes. His closet looked like a rainbow of colors and his shoe rack held a collection that would make a Nike executive weep. Like all things however, there were consequences.

He started to get picked up by the police. At first, he was caught past curfew and he scoffed when he was returned home and his mother stood in the doorway of their crumbling row house and laughed in the officer's face. Joe was out the back door before the cop had even pulled off from the curb.

He was usually pretty good about carrying dope when he was out on the street. Then one night he was jumped by three boys, older kids from the next block over. They knew who he was and they caught him a couple blocks too far outside his set. It was a strange mixture of circumstances that led him to fall into the trap. Zim had called him on his cell and told him that some boys selling off of Huger had run dry. Joe had just gotten a re-supply earlier that day and had a pretty stout supply of product. He didn't even think when Zim asked him to run a drop for him. It was only a couple blocks away.

It wasn't until he crossed under the fence behind his mother's house that it occurred to him he was taking quite a risk. Joe remembered how much he had sweated the walk over to the grey, condemned house on Huger Street. Each step threatened to be his last, given that he had five full cookies of crack cocaine wrapped in cellophane in an inside pocket of his jacket. The police, random fiend, or some other street creature looking to rob him could have had it all in an instant. He was out of his safety area, and on his own. He'd made it to the drop though and swapped the baked cocaine for fistfuls of cash. On the walk back, he was feeling so big with all the money in his pocket that he let his guard down and chose a side street with hardly any streetlights to use as a shortcut back to his block, his kingdom. That's when they got him.

The three boys, all a couple years older, had him surrounded before he could run and the fight was on. He dodged and kicked, and swung at any open opportunity to cause a gap in the group big enough for him to slide through and run. He knew he had broken one nose and had stunned another with a punch to the ear. He took his fair share of the beating but was just about to make his escape when the blue lights flashed. They all ran at once but there were too many units and Joe suddenly found himself tackled and in handcuffs with a swelling eye before he knew who had actually hit him.

The officer swore at him and dragged him to his feet. Broadstreet noted that his three attackers must have gotten away when he was brought around the corner to where three cop cars clogged the street. The cop cars were empty and he seemed to be the only one in handcuffs. The cop shoved him against the back quarter panel of the black and white and searched him. The guy was thorough— checked every pocket and crevice in his clothes from the soles of his shoes up. He found Broadstreet's money, and he found two chips of crack cocaine that must have come loose from the cellophane-wrapped supply he'd dropped off earlier.

The money made Broadstreet grimace. That was going to put a knock in his finances, but in the grander scheme, the fourteen-year old had the funds to cover the loss. When the officer held up the little white chunks that looked like little rolled balls of flaky dough, his head dropped to his chest.

The cop noticed his reaction. "Yup, that sucks for you," he said.

Even though Joe was a minor, they took him to police headquarters and charged him with Possession with Intent to Distribute Crack Cocaine. They couldn't house a minor at the small jail the City ran, so after charging him and taking his prints and mug shots they called his mother to come and get him. Then they waited.

Broadstreet looked at the name plate on the old cop standing before him. *Coburn*. He hadn't remembered the name but he remembered the eyes. They were the same now as they were back then, only with a flocking of crow's feet at the corners. They were alive and bright, there was a strength in them that stood notice of a steel foundation. Broadstreet remembered there had been a sadness there also. The eyes seemed like Coburn pitied the world, and everyone that lived in it.

At first, they had nothing to say to each other. Joseph sat with one hand cuffed to the chipped and faded wood desk in the lobby at the CPD Headquarters, while Coburn finished writing his report. He watched as police came and went from the building. It was after midnight and the activity in the building surprised him. Behind a glass partition, there was one police officer that didn't move all night. He stared forward into the lobby or read a paper at the desk. He did journey back once into the booking area to shout down a rowdy drunk, but for the most part he simply mumbled gravelly directions to whoever approached his window. At one point the white-haired man noticed Broadstreet watching him. He turned his head and looked at him with such grim, squinting severity that Joseph couldn't help but turn away.

When his mother finally showed up in a cab it was almost two in the morning. Coburn must have sensed the way Joe stiffened as she swung her way, unsteady on two feet, through the heavy glass doors. Her hair was all askew and her skin was ashy and pale. He heard Coburn sigh.

Then the policeman said, "Kid, you don't have much goin' for you so I get that you go after the easy money. I'm only going to say this once. You have a chance in this moment to decide the direction of your life. Your either going to keep the track you're on and end up like her" —he nodded to Broadstreet's mother whose bloodshot and glassy eyes were surveying the lobby as she swayed back and forth—"or you can look at yourself and choose a path out of this hell hole. Somewhere with a fresh start, and a new life."

Broadstreet didn't say it then, but wanted to tell the cop to go fuck himself at the time. The guy probably couldn't even pay his own rent on a cop's salary and he was going to tell the kid making twice the money a month how to live. Broadstreet stared ahead and held up his wrist. Coburn sighed again and unlocked the shackle. Joseph barely acknowledged his mother, simply waved her out the door and headed for the cab. He hadn't said anything to the cop.

Now Joe was looking him in the eye as they stood opposite each other. The younger cop was asking him something but he ignored him. Broadstreet took a step closer to Coburn, who in turn smoothly bladed his body.

"You don't remember me, but you tried to offer me some advice once and I ignored you. I shouldn't have."

Coburn squinted at him, trying to focus through old eyes, trying to remember him. Broadstreet understood. He turned to the kid who was almost yelling now, uncomfortable with the lack of attention he was getting. Without looking at him, Joe pulled out his ID and handed it to him. Then Coburn and he went back to studying each other.

They looked each other in the eye, Coburn still trying to find his face among the mire of past arrests and conflicts that fill a career patrolling a city like Charleston. At one point the young cop said that he was free of warrants and Broadstreet took his card back.

"You have a good night officer," Broadstreet said, before continuing down the street.

"You too," Coburn said, before returning to the patrol car.

Chapter Forty-One

Moncrief studied the handgun. He turned it over in his hands and dry-fired the weapon several times. This was his own weapon, a nickel plated model 1911 Colt semi-automatic. Moncrief didn't carry it much—usually the pristine gun was tucked away in a shoe box at the top of his closet. With the amount of weight he tended to have on him, it didn't pay to carry a gun on the regular. If he were caught with a couple of kilos of cocaine and a gun at the same time, given he was a convicted felon, the DA could put him away until the sun burned out. Whenever he transported any kind of weight, he had his crew trail follow him, loaded for bear. If Moncrief needed a gun at any given time, usually he would settle for some cheap piece that one of his crew could lay their hands on quick. That didn't happen as much anymore, though. In the beginning, when Washington was starting to step back there were a few gangs around the peninsula who wanted to be the new king. Moncrief outlasted all of them; anyone who took a run at him and a few he thought might challenge him, were never heard from again. Even through all those trials though, he had never fired the Colt in anger. The Colt was special, his gun was only for him.

Now he found himself sitting in a dank, musty East side row house cleaning and function checking his gun over and over as four other men scurried around the room organizing and loading magazines. Moncrief paid them no attention. They knew he had called for a hit and they were down. They didn't know who or where but that didn't matter. Every man present ran a piece of Charleston, was the authority by either block or project, and was the sole flow of heroin to his subjects. Each man in the hotel room was richer than he would ever have imagined and it was because of Moncrief. He had personally selected each one of them to be there with him because he had seen each one pull a trigger, and he had seen each one protect him when they had a chance to sell him out. These four men would be the future of the Charleston drug trade.

Moncrief cradled and felt his special gun while he considered his plan. He knew Washington had to go, and had to go quickly. Moncrief realized after his surveillance of the old man that he knew nothing of Washington's true resources. The clothes, the car, the source some preppy white guy? It was a new side of the old man that threw Moncrief for a loop. Washington had to go and Moncrief had brought out his special Colt to mark the transfer of power, but the more Moncrief thought of pulling the trigger on his mentor, he couldn't actually see it in his head. He could visualize the whole crew standing over the man, all eyes on Moncrief as he took the throne. But when he tried to squeeze the trigger, it wouldn't fire. No matter how hard he tried, the gun wouldn't fire. And even if it did fire, part of him saw Washington laughing as the round bounced off him. The old man laughed at him. Mocked him for thinking he could take his throne.

Next to him, Onre Bauer slumped into a chair and slapped his aged Mac-10 on the cheap kitchen table. The table swayed on bent and shaky legs.

"What we doin man?" he says, "We don't get to it soon this crew bout to start burnin' some weed."

Moncrief stared at the wall, noticing streaks of grime and cracks in the aged peel-offs of white paint. He saw Washington in his mind. Even in his mind's eye, Washington scared him. Then he saw Blanding there too. The fat bastard cowered in the darkness like a mouse caught in the open when the light came on.

"We take the fat fuck first," he growled.

Chapter Forty-Two

Wilke was with the shrink again and Fenner was at grand jury. Viejo in his untucked polo shirt, hiking boots, and jeans, met up with Martin dressed in a stripped button down shirt, dotted red tie, and wrinkled blue blazer. The two filled up on coffee, ridiculed each other regarding their respective wardrobes, nightlife, and general manliness, then went to Blanding's church. It was going on nine a.m. and breakfast service was just wrapping up. As part of his ministry, Blanding ran a charity breakfast in the morning during the school year. Viejo remembered from his patrol days that the place would be flocked with kids from the neighborhood every day around seven a.m. as if the man were handing out hundred dollar bills. The place would be a madhouse, though somehow everyone got fed. Viejo often wondered where all the parents were while their six and seven-year-olds were taking advantage of the charity to fill their bellies.

There were no kids picking at scraps at the moment. All of them had cleared out to filter toward the various schools within walking distance of the ministry. Now there were a handful of plump old women scraping at giant pots and pans. A couple of them had started the attempt to clean up what looked like the aftermath of the food fight scene from Animal House. Viejo took in the carnage of strewn milk

John Stamp • 230

cartons, trays, and napkins. He even noticed a gob of oatmeal slowly sliding down the wall to his right. For a moment he was mesmerized. It was like watching a giant, lumpy slug limping along on its way to the floor. It even left a slime trail on the wall.

"Can I help you boys?" The question came from one of the cleaning ladies. She leaned on a broom with a bored look on her face.

"Carter Blanding around, ma'am?" Martin asked.

"He in the back," she answered. She eyed them sideways, instinctively suspicious of the two men.

Viejo and Martin started toward the rear of the building when Carter Blanding appeared through the double doors. He strode through the doors confidently and sure of himself, a lord surveying his kingdom. Two steps past the doors that confidence melted and he came to a complete halt. He was staring at the two police officers, his jaw slack, eyes wide. Martin and Viejo continued to approach him.

"I see there's no need for introductions," Martin quipped.

"I, uh..."

"Shaunte told you we were coming," Viejo observed. "Ballsy."

Blanding blinked several times. His eyes were beady. His round face exaggerated the characteristic, given he carried an extra thirty pounds or so. He stuttered again, then said, "I'm sorry, officers. I have a very important engagement this morning. Perhaps you can reschedule with my assistant." He turned toward the double doors. "She's through the kitchen, you'll see some office space. She's right in there." He then tried to push past the two detectives who quickly closed ranks.

"We'd really like it if you could make some time for us now, Minister," said Martin. "We were hoping you could help us shed some light on a few things."

Carter Blanding squeezed past the two men. He looked at the kitchen staff sheepishly as he made for the main exit of the large room. "I'm sorry, I really must be going."

Viejo's shoulders tightened and he started toward Blanding. Martin stayed him with a hand.

"Sir, we're going to need you to come downtown with us." Martin was addressing the preacher's back.

"Am I under arrest?"

"I'd really rather not discuss that here. We're just looking for a little cooperation."

The two men were side by side as they exited the church. The swarms of school kids had dissipated and morning traffic passing by the modest neighborhood church was light. Martin caught a late model Dodge Intrepid turning their way a block up but paid it no mind.

Blanding huffed as he hustled down the steps. Martin could see he was sweating and he took that as a good sign. He also noticed that Blanding seemed a bit gray around the neck and cheeks. The minister was a light- skinned black man to begin with. The sickly pallor spreading over his features told Martin they were finally getting somewhere with this damned case.

POP! POP! POPOPOPOPOPOP!

Martin was reaching for the revolver on his hip before he knew where the shots were coming from. Blanding was just reaching a Lincoln Town car when the shooting started. The minister spun back toward him and fell. Over the din of gunfire, Martin noted a revving engine. He raised his weapon toward a black male hanging out the rear window of a blue Intrepid. The darkly clothed man, wearing a white bandana over his face, was holding a Mac-10.

Martin started squeezing off rounds. Like an automaton, the aged detective responded exactly as his thirty-plus years of training told him to. He watched in a detached, almost serene state of calm, as he saw one of his rounds ping off the frame between the driver and the shooter. Another buried itself in the door just below the shooter's elbow. He shifted the sight picture on reflex and squeezed the trigger again.

They must have fired at the same time. Before the round found its mark in the shooter's chest, a biting pain took hold in his side. The old cop stumbled around, heard the whizz pop of projectiles filling the air around him. He felt himself falling amid the din of a rapid succession of rounds and he wondered if the car had stopped. Was the shooter advancing on him? For the first time since taking up his weapon, Bob Martin felt fear and realized he'd been in his first gunfight. He tried to keep his legs under him, not wanting to be shot lying helpless on the street. Then a figure moved past him, past the Town Car and out into the street.

It was Viejo. Martin watched him empty his weapon into the fleeing vehicle. Martin smiled just a touch as he watched the younger man chase the car into the street. Then his legs gave out and he hit the ground. The pain in his side grinded and spread across his ribcage. All he could do was curl in toward the pain and groan.

***

Viejo was only a couple of steps behind Martin when the shooting started. It happened so fast that the loud pops froze him in place. It was only for a second, but it felt like a decade. He saw Martin react to the violence and saw Blanding drop to the sidewalk before he was able to bring his own weapon to the fight.

He had fired only his first shot when he saw Martin stumble. Viejo drew filled the notional frame of his sight picture on a figure in the rear of a passing car. The shooter, dressed all in black, was leaning out the rear window, firing. His face was obscured and the car was speeding away when Viejo unloaded a magazine and a half of his forty-five caliber ammunition in the vehicle's direction. He wasn't sure he had hit anything when the car rounded the next corner up the block and the engine increased power. It wasn't until the fight was over that he realized he was standing in the middle of the street.

"Son of a bitch!" Viejo cursed. He holstered his sidearm and pulled his phone from his pocket as he knelt by Martin. The old detective was folded in on himself, cradling his side. The dispatcher answered him.

"46, officer down! Shots fired at West and Drobath. I need EMS times two."

The dispatcher acknowledged him while doing her best to keep an icy, objective demeanor and began marshalling medical resources and backup to head his way. Squeezing his phone between his sweat-soaked neck and shoulder, Viejo studied Martin. He looked like he had a wound to his leg and a wound he was covering on his side.

Viejo peeled off his belt and slung it around the man's bleeding leg between a flowing wound on his thigh and his hip. Martin groaned as Viejo pushed him to lie on his back.

"Easy old-timer. I gotta do something about this leg." He pulled the belt tight around the leg and Martin let out a cry. Viejo took the man's hand and put the end of the belt in his fist. He needed something to concentrate on. Viejo didn't want Martin falling into shock.

"You get 'em?" Martin asked through clenched teeth.

Viejo got a look at Martin's side. His polyester shirt was soaked through. He pulled Martin's free hand away from the wound which elicited another cry.

"Couldn't tell," Viejo answered.

"Probably not," Martin answered, "None of you kids no how to shoot these days."

Viejo chuckled and let the old man have that one. He put a hand over Martin's wound and pushed. He felt ribs grind and give under his hand.

"Aww, fuck!" Martin yelled.

"I gotta put pressure on this," Viejo said. He noted sirens in the background, growing closer.

"Aw that fuckin' hurts!"

Within a minute, a Charleston City Fire Department ambulance pulled up on the street and Viejo was shouldered aside by a paramedic who took to assessing Bob Martin. Viejo rose slowly to his feet and stepped away so the medical personnel could do their work. Then he saw Blanding.

The man was sitting against the rear door of the Lincoln Town Car. His eyes were wide and his color pale; he sweated through the button down shirt which clung to him under his blue blazer. He held a hand to his neck as he stared straight ahead. At first Viejo thought the man was shot in the neck, but he didn't see any blood streaming from under his hand. Viejo knelt beside Blanding and grabbed for the minister's hand.

"He tried to kill me!" Blanding whispered. "He tried to kill me!"

Viejo pulled the hand away from the side of Blanding's neck and prepared himself for a gush of arterial spray, but there was nothing.

"Am I dying?" Blanding asked, wide, stricken eyes looking up at Viejo as if asking for mercy.

Viejo's brow creased as he studied the slight furrow that barely managed to ooze a weak stream of blood down to his collar.

Looking in the eyes of Carter Blanding, Viejo wondered what kind of info he'd get from the minister if he lied and told him he was dying. Finally he told his suspect, "You're gonna live. For now."

Chapter Forty-Three

Ben Wilke tried to keep his knee from bouncing but every time he took his mind off the nervous appendage, it would return to jittering up and down on his toes. It was a sign of nervousness, one that he knew Dr. Cannor would notice. He hated the chair he sat in, hated the office he found himself in, and hated the building he was trapped in. The doctor was going to be pissed now that Banks had overruled her and put him back on the street. He didn't want her to catch a nervous tick, be it his knee bouncing, chewing on the inside of his cheek, or picking at his fingernails. Wilke didn't want to give her any avenue to pry at him that he couldn't explain or run away from.

"How do you feel being back in the field?" was her question.

He searched for a hint of irritation floating on her words but found none.

"I think it was time," he responded. He felt the same in that office that he did in court, only here he felt like he was on trial for his life.

"You're still angry, still mad."

"I don't think so," he lied. He wanted to rip the drab curtains behind her desk off the wall and put his fist through every pane of glass in the room. Then he wanted to tear apart anything in the room that wasn't nailed down. Then he wanted to find him.

That was worst of all: he wanted to kick the shit out of a dead man, or dead men. Whoever was responsible for the death of Poppy Montague needed to die. It felt like a directive that Wilke could not move on from until the task was completed. But that was the damnable misery of it. There was no one left; every person they knew of that was part of the kidnapping was dead, and the Tulley's, father and son, hadn't been seen in months. He figured they fled prosecution or whoever it was they were working for. He remembered the guttural cries of the younger Tulley as Wilke tightened on the trigger, the smoldering muzzle of his gun jammed deep in the weakling's eye socket. He felt the rage building inside him, it was so hard to pull back, to tamp it down to where he could control himself. He felt like there was a bomb inside his chest and it was on such a sensitive trigger he could barely tiptoe around without setting it off. He fought to swallow the emotions; he could not afford for the psychologist to see them. Dr. Cannor was always looking for another reason to keep him off the streets. For the life of him, Wilke still couldn't understand how Banks had gotten him released for active duty. Suddenly he realized she was talking to him.

"It's okay to have anger, Ben," she said. "We need closure when tragedy strikes and when we don't get it, we have a hard time accepting. It's especially hard on law enforcement. You were trained to be the problem solver. Wherever you go, you are looked upon to straighten out the mess, fix the problem.

When we are left with a problem there's no way to fix, we find ourselves at odds with our paradigm."

Wilke nodded slightly but didn't respond.

"Are you still exercising? You said before that your runs helped."

Wilke was stuck on the last statement. His paradigm was at odds with reality. No shit. Wilke knew the woman meant well but the only product created in their meetings was the realization that he had no way to fix his world. There would be no justice for Poppy; there was no way to avenge the woman he loved. There was the heat again, building in his chest and shoulders. He wondered how long he and the doctor would sit facing each other, talking about his paradigm. She was saying something but he again had been lost in his own thoughts, something about coping skills.

Chapter Forty-Four

Wilke stomped into the Detective Bureau at 180 Lockwood drive to find Viejo and Banks staring through one-way glass into interrogation room one.

"Martin?" he asked.

"Surgery but stable," Banks said.

Wilke looked through the glass toward the object of their attention. He saw Carter Blanding sitting at the table inside the isolated room. His hands were in his lap. A square of gauze and tape covered the side of his neck. His eyes were vacant, staring into nothingness.

"Blanding was grazed, barely even bled at the scene," Viejo told Wilke.

"You recognize them?"

"Nah, they were pretty well covered. Opened up on us in front of a church of all places," said Viejo.

"He giving up anything?"

"I've been letting him cook a little bit. I wanted to make sure Martin was gonna be alright before anything."

Wilke didn't respond. All he had thought about since Viejo told him about the shooting was that he wasn't there...again. Now that he was standing there, he felt a paralyzing wave of helpless rage threaten to overtake him.

Banks, wearing a dress blue uniform, was standing between Wilke and Viejo. He leaned in toward Wilke and whispered, "You alright?"

"I'm good, Sir," he answered.

Viejo had been watching his partner with the same question on his mind when Banks beat him to it.

"So we going in there?" Wilke asked.

"Viejo and I are handling this, you watch from out here."

Viejo gauged his partner's reaction. Wilke was holding himself in check but he could see Wilke's shoulders slump just a little. He hated riding the bench and everybody knew it.

***

Five minutes later, Carter Blanding bolted upright as Viejo and Banks walked into the interrogation room.

"Did you get them?" he asked.

"Who?" Banks responded.

The question seemed to hit Blanding like a lightning bolt. He froze, standing opposite the two police across a dull, gray metal table. After a long moment he said, "If I say anything, I get immunity."

"If you don't say anything, I toss your ass back into the meat grinder. How long you think you'll last then?"

Blanding blanched. "You can't."

Banks leaned over the table. Blanding looked away as the police captain loomed over him. The minister sat down sheepishly.

Captain Peter Banks unbuttoned his jacket and took a calming breath. It had been a long time since he found himself staring down a criminal in the interrogation room. Working dope interrogations were more a business negotiation than an actual elicitation. If a dealer gets pinched, a sort of auction takes place. He considers who in his list of suppliers he is willing to give up to the police in exchange for leniency or for charges to be lessened or dropped. There isn't any real mind screwing in that world.

In the realm of personal crimes, more often than not there is no bargaining. You bring a guy or girl in that has either killed someone or raped someone and the interrogation turns into a chess game. You elicit a story and do your best to use evidence and word play to knock down whatever arguments they have installed as a defense against guilt. All the while they are listening and gathering all the information you have against them. Each party parries with alibis and half-truths until one party runs out of ammunition and is broken down. Only one story will carry the day in an interrogation room. Either the bad guy can slither out of or around evidence you think you have against him, or you pin him into a corner as you break through his lies until he has no place to turn but the truth.

Banks loved the battle, but he suddenly realized as he was about to match wits with the minister that he hadn't pinned someone in an interrogation in more than a decade.

Oh well, he thought. *Blanding doesn't know that.*

"Who wants you dead and why, Mr. Blanding?"

"I want a deal."

Banks didn't respond.

Blanding stared at him sheepishly, an unabashed attempt to elicit pity from the two police officers. The three men were silent for a long moment. Then the minister's head fell to his hands.

Twenty minutes later, Viejo, Banks, and Wilke were staring at Carter Blanding through two-way glass. Banks was dumbfounded. Banks looked at his notes for a moment. He saw the game plan scribbles left by Martin, which reminded him that because of this piece of shit, one of Charleston's longest serving officers was in the hospital battling two gunshot wounds. The story he had just heard infuriated him. He saw the notes on Deshaun Caldwell, on Shaunte Fields, the suspicion of fraud and possible statutory rape of the girl. He found himself bewildered.

Carter Blanding slumped over the table. His head hung low between his shoulders. His hands were clasped together in front of him. They trembled between muted sobs as the holy man failed to stifle a crying fit.

Banks looked at Blanding, then at Viejo. His eyes were creased and narrow. He casually sat in his chair, one leg propped against the other, a marked-up notepad resting on his lap. He was not calm, nor was he relaxed. The detective's jaw was clenched and his fist throttled the pen in his hand. He knew Viejo was struggling to keep a professional demeanor, and to anyone else he looked like a picture of professional objectivity. Banks knew him better. He looked back to Blanding,

"What you're telling me, minister, is that a toddler had to die so that you could save face." He stated it as plainly as he could, his voice the consistency of steel.

Blanding didn't reply at first, then he mumbled something.

"Sit up straight and look at me when I talk to you." Bank's voice jabbed him.

The man who had just admitted to two police officers that he used his religious organization to launder money for a heroin trafficker and was an accessory to a triple murder sniffled as he rose in his chair. His beady eyes were red, and fleshy bulbs had swollen under them. Tears streaked his face. He stared at his hands.

Wait, Banks realized. He was staring at his right hand.

Banks did not speak—he just watched. Blanding didn't look at him or Viejo; he just stared at his hand. Banks wondered where he was right then. Reliving what had happened on that night? Wondering how his life had come to this? Where he had turned left on the line when he should have turned right? Or was it darker than that?

Blanding's fixation on his right hand reminded him suddenly of a case years back. When he was still in personal crimes. He had brought in a guy he suspected in a stabbing. A random street mugging that had gone bad. It was a week after the attack that

Banks was able to track down a ring owned by the victim through a local pawn shop. Following the receipt from the transaction, he had his suspect sitting in the same interrogation room that he, Viejo, and Blanding sat in now.

He remembered thinking right from the start the guy knew he had gone too far. There are people who are comfortable with taking the life of another human being, but not many. And that guy was not one of the few. The guy mumbled answers about the ring and the stabbing, but he wouldn't come off and admit to the killing. He wouldn't meet Banks in the eyes. He just sat opposite the table from him, staring at his lap. However, every few minutes the man would wipe his left hand down his right forearm. His face would twist when he did it but only slightly, almost imperceptibly. Banks to this day didn't know how many times the guy made the gesture before he noticed it. When he finally realized the move and the accompanying expression, he asked the guy about it and the suspect didn't realize he'd been doing it. He was confused.

"Like this," Banks had said, then parroted the movement.

The suspect's eyes grew wide and his jaw went slack.

"There was a lot of blood when you stabbed him," Banks had told him, playing out his hunch. "You sliced through an artery and it gushed, covering your right arm," he'd said.

The suspect's eyes had teared up then.

"You didn't mean to kill him," Banks had said, and that was it. A sobbing confession had earned Banks a beer and the suspect thirty years upstate.

Banks thought he was seeing the same thing here. Blanding was staring at his right hand. He looked confused or disbelieving, rather than showing revulsion like the mugger. Banks wasn't quite sure. Maybe he was rusty, maybe this case was big enough that playing a hunch was too much of a gamble—he couldn't be sure. Either way, he wasn't ready yet. This interrogation was supposed to be about Deshaun Cauldwell, this was an intelligence action to get into Cauldwell's background. The plan was to get Blanding to open up so they could maybe find a direction to take this high profile case that had, til now, been foundering in a void of real leads.

Martin and Viejo were just supposed to talk to the minister until fate left one of his prized homicide investigators in an operating suite being put back together. Now this.

Banks pulled out a folder from under the pile that included the case file and Martin's disheveled mass of notes. Banks watched Blanding, who was still in a kind of trance. He wasn't looking at his hand anymore. Now he stared at the floor. He seemed to be in a cycle that took his eyes anywhere but to the pair of detectives facing him across the interrogation room. Banks thought that was a good sign; he wanted to see Blanding's reaction.

He opened the folder and slid a photo of little Chevante, lying on her back, across the table. A crimson patch covered the yellow Disney character that smiled and waved from the front of her shirt. She still had tiny berets taming her puffy pig tales that stood on the side of her head. She was so serene that Banks himself, even with all the years, all the death, and all the pain he had documented throughout this city, could hardly stomach the picture. Blanding's head was still down. Banks tapped lightly on the table. Blanding's head snapped up. His eyes bulged as if he'd been sucker punched.

"The bullet went through her mother who was running for her life. She was clutching little Chevante to her chest like this," Banks mimicked huddling the little girl to his own wide chest, "to put herself between her baby and danger."

Blanding shriveled, turning and leaning away from the photo.

"Look at the picture!" Banks bellowed.

Blanding cowed and moaned slightly. "The bullet passed through her mother's lung and ribs and muscle, punching through her chest before hitting Chevante. The bullet severed her aorta. She bled out in seconds."

"No," Blanding whispered.

Banks was silent; he let the room grow heavy.

Blanding stared at the photo.

Finally Banks almost whispered, "You didn't mean to kill her, did you, Carter?"

Blanding wouldn't look at Banks, "I didn't kill her," he moaned.

"You did, but it wasn't you, was it? Moncrief made you do it."

Silence.

"What did he do? Threaten you? Did he hurt you?" Banks asked.

Blanding was still looking in the direction of the photos, but his eyes were vacant and lost.

"Moncrief just tried to have you killed, Carter. You can't let him win. Don't let him get away with this," Banks said, just a touch more sternly. He jabbed a finger at Chevante's photo.

"He'll kill me," Blanding whispered, an eerie state of calm suddenly cooling the red and puffiness of his features, "He's gonna kill me."

"Help me to stop him. We can't let Moncrief stay out there on the streets. How many more little girls will he hurt? How many more people will he force to do terrible things like he did to you?" Banks continued the narrative that Blanding was the trigger man despite the fact Blanding had admitted to nothing, and they had no proof. In addition to all of that fiction, the idea that a prominent Charleston minister was a baby killer was on its face insane. Banks had no problem accepting that Carter Blanding was a money launderer who profited on the backs of people enslaved to a needle. Truth was that over half of the so-called ministries all over the South were nothing more than tax scams. Go online and get a certificate naming you a minister, then open a tiny store front chape,l or put a few extra folding chairs in your living room. Open the doors every Sunday, and whether people show or not, you are suddenly out of the reach of the tax collector, easy. But this was taking it to a whole new level. Part of Banks was stunned at the idea that this man killed a toddler. The very premise was an affront to what should be a solace in the world. He pictured his devout grandmother grimacing at him, hands folded over her stomach and wood spoon in hand. That's not how her world had worked and Peter Banks truly wished he knew a world like that. Yet here he was.

"Carter!" he snapped, breaking the man out of his funk. "You need to tell us how to get to Moncrief. We won't let him hurt you."

Blanding's face screwed. "Moncrief?" he jerked. "He's just as dead as I am. He's gonna kill us both." As soon as the words left his mouth, he knew he had said too much. As if the idea of being gunned down by his heroin money cow was not enough, whoever Blanding had just alluded to was the guy Banks and the rest of the CPD really had to meet.

Banks let a long pause fill the void in the interrogation room. Blanding stared at him, frozen like a jack rabbit when an eagle glided overhead. Maybe it wouldn't see him, if only he could stay still enough.

Finally, Banks leaned into him. "Moncrief, whoever else, the entire East Side of Charleston after they realize what you've done, will be after you. The list of people who want to kill you is growing faster than the national debt. Who do you think offers you your best chance of continued existence on this planet?"

Chapter Forty-Five

"Well I'll be damned," muttered Martin glumly. "Those who pray the most, sin the most, huh? True every damn time."

"How you feeling?" Viejo asked. He, Wilke, and Fenner had come to check in on the old detective one more time before calling an end to a very long day.

Breaking Blanding had only been the beginning. After the names Treat Moncrief and Harold Washington were uttered, Wilke and Fenner, freed from her grand jury duties, started sifting through files going back as far as they could find to learn everything they could about their new targets.

Blanding would not cop to pulling the trigger that killed Chevante Williams despite all indicators that even the densest, blockheaded rookie could see pointing to his guilt. Communication was ninety percent non-verbal, and throughout the day, Blanding had given a treatise on non-verbal communication. The way he sat, the way he shifted in his seat, his mannerisms, and brief, almost instantaneous micro expressions whenever Banks or Viejo would drop a trigger word about Moncrief or little Chevante. And there were many. By eight o'clock that night, the minister was sobbing under the unrelenting pressure Banks and Viejo had put on him. All three men were exhausted after almost a ten-hour siege of the mind.

Still Blanding never broke on the murder, and knowing the police were his only bet at staying alive, he never asked for a lawyer. Blanding had asked repeatedly after admitting to money laundering and a slew of other narcotics related charges if his assistance would get him out of jail time. Despite both detectives mentally lining the man up for a life sentence or two, they had nurtured his futile hope.

"That's not up to us, Carter," they would say, offering the canned answer. "It's up to the state's attorney. We'll do everything we can for you," they would say.

The glimmer of light in Carter Blanding's dark world would bring the man out of his despair for a moment. That's when Banks would again go after him on Chevante. He would put the gun in the man's hand once more.

"So, back to the little girl," Banks would interject, "We know you were the one who killed her. And we know you didn't have a choice. Doesn't she deserve peace? Tell us your side of the story." Banks would plead.

Blanding would hide again, either under his arms or he would close his eyes, or even turn completely away from the police Captain. Banks and Viejo would shift gears back to the drug investigation and start over again, reeling their quarry back in by reinforcing the threat Washington and Moncrief posed to him. How his life depended on them. The remainder of the day continued with two steps forward with new drug information, followed by two steps back when Chevante was brought up. By eight o'clock at night, Blanding was exhausted and his answers were becoming unintelligible. Banks had briefly considered going at the man again for a confession in the Chevante murder, but he knew that as enticing as the proposition was, they had been in the interrogation room for almost ten hours. They were way into the realm of a forced confession. The man had suffered a mild bullet wound. Any confession they got at this point would be shredded in court. Banks called it, then telling Blanding they would pick up in the morning. Blanding was being housed in the city jail in the rear of police headquarters for the night. Now, Banks wondered briefly how Carter Blanding was sleeping as he stifled a yawn of his own.

"So what's the prognosis, old man, besides chronic erectile dysfunction?" Banks heard Viejo ask. It was a forced joke, but not the first and not the last Bob Martin would suffer once the hospital staff allowed him visitors. As it was, Banks, Viejo, Wilke, and Fenner had barged their way in, breaking all sorts of hospital protocol so they could keep Martin informed of the investigation. Even after suffering the way he had, the detective still was in the hunt, the investigation foremost on his mind.

"You gonna let him talk to me like that, Captain?" Martin asked.

Banks shrugged. As he did, he caught a glimpse of Ben Wilke. He was there, but Banks noted the man's clenched jaw and tightened shoulders. The kid was seething. *He wants a fight.* In anyone else, he would have been happy to see that the incident hadn't suddenly made the realities of police work all too real. He'd seen it before in cops who made it years without seeing someone hurt or killed. Then when the world blew up in their face, suddenly the job of being a cop was not so exciting anymore. Danger was in their face and it scared them, as it should.

That's not what Peter Banks saw in his young detective. What he saw was a molten fury that he worried could be unleashed at the wrong time, on the wrong person. He wondered for a moment if he was helping Wilke by bringing him in on the Chevante case. A not so subtle cough alerted the four intruding police to a thoroughly unamused nurse standing in Martin's doorway. Banks watched his detective for a moment more. It wasn't vengeance for Doug Martin he was looking for.

"I think we better let this old bastard get his beauty sleep," Banks said. He looked at Martin, intravenous fluids coursing into his taped-up arm, deep bags under his eyes, his skin grey. "Get better," he said to him and offered his hand. A deep welling of guilt that one of his people was hurt while he remained unscathed threatened to overtake him. Banks knew that sensation all too well; he hated himself for something his rational mind told him was not his fault.

"Kick their ass," Martin responded, shaking his commander's hand as firmly as he could.

Chapter Forty-Six

It's way too late, Viejo told himself as he rapped quietly on the front door.

Part of him wondered if he wasn't knocking hard enough. Maybe she couldn't hear him, and he didn't want to risk waking the baby. He just wanted to see her. Another part of him also wondered if she heard him just fine, and was ignoring him. He couldn't blame her if she did.

When he heard shuffling from inside, he was at once relieved and a little apprehensive. But he wanted to look in on his little girl. Three locks clicked open in cadence and the door opened to reveal Marla. She wore an old t-shirt—Viejo noticed there was no bra underneath—a pair of pink gym shorts, her hair in a clumsy ponytail and a surly expression.

"Come on, Este," she sighed.

"I know, I'm sorry," Viejo said. "I was just hoping to look in on her. I know it's late."

"You were supposed to be here before bedtime, to spot me a little."

"I know but—"

"No buts, no more." She was irritated, disappointed, and a little bit sad. It was the sadness in her voice that bit him the most.

Viejo looked at the ground. "I tried, I swear."

She cut him off again and waved a dismissive hand in across the threshold between them, "You tried, I know. You always try, but you never come around to trying hard enough. You said you'd be home, you said you were making changes, you said this, you said that. I can't live on trying and promises." Her eyes were beginning to tear up.

"I know," he said quietly, in the knowledge that he was failing. That he had a shot at being a dad and it was slipping from his fingers hurt more than any physical pain he'd ever faced. He could barely look at her. When he finally met her reddened eyes, a switch suddenly clicked. The option he'd been toying with slipped into place like the final piece in a jigsaw puzzle. Out of the blue, Esteban Viejo's mind was made up.

"I talked to the Economic Crimes Sergeant," he said, "He said he would take me as long as the Captain signed off."

She paused and her expression flittered. Was that apprehension in her eyes? He dreaded the thought that even if he managed to swing a job that might let him be home at night, she still wouldn't want him. After changing everything he still might not be enough. Maybe it was relief, that she had just heard a glimmer of hope?

"You would do that? You could do that?" she asked.

Viejo looked over her shoulder as if trying to peer through walls to catch a glimpse of his baby girl, "Yeah, without a second thought." He knew that there would be plenty of second thoughts. He had no idea what he was going to say to Banks, much less

Wilke. He felt like he was being split in two, abandoning one family for the sake of another.

They were quiet for a long moment as they stood in the doorway to her condominium. She stared at nothing, lost in the middle distance, while Viejo shifted pensively on his heels. Finally she shook herself out of her ponder and opened the door all the way. "Come in," she said.

Viejo looked at her and though he wanted nothing more than to see his daughter, he shook his head slightly, "Nah, I'm sorry, it's too late. How about we get some sleep. Maybe dinner tomorrow?"

"I'd like that."

Viejo waited for the door to close and lock. The image of her smile and the light in her tired eyes etched themselves in his memory. The picture would be his resolve when he made the request to leave Banks and Wilke. Slowly he walked to his car, pondering the sudden strange feeling that his life had just changed forever.

John Stamp • 258

Chapter Forty-Seven

Thomas Wrightsell Aka, "Crackle" was never one to turn down a handout. Despite having a roof over his head in the spare room his mother let him stay in, decent benefits, and a disability check from the State, he often took whatever he was handed while he sat on a park bench or lounged in a doorway. Mostly white folk that either wanted him to go to church or wanted their friends to see how charitable they were would stop and ask him if he was hungry or just hand him a dollar. Crackle would take it every time. He figured he was doing right by them anyway, providing an outlet for their white guilt or whatever the jackasses on the news wanted to call it.

Tonight he was in a little bit of a bind. He'd already blown his wad for the month and he was going to have to stretch another week and a half before his next disability check came in. His benefits card was likewise short, leaving him scrounging and fighting the nod. The warm rush of sedation and flight was calling him. Morning and night he liked to have his taste, except when he was extra flush, like when he scored something good for the cops, or when he was able to "find" something to pawn. He thought about his mom's house but immediately dismissed the idea of disappearing anything from there. She'd gotten wise to him, and after the last time, she booted him for a week. No way was he going back to the shelter over some bullshit twenty-seven inch TV set in his mom's house.

He'd wandered the neighborhoods downtown earlier in the day. He was supposed to check in at Workforce this morning and he had told his mom he would, but fuck that. Day labor was for convicts and retards. He hadn't been arrested in years and he was already getting a salary from the State anyway. The neighborhoods near Spring and Congress, around the cross-town highway, had changed a lot from when he was coming up. College kids were everywhere nowdays, little restaurants, and stores. The narrow row houses were still pretty much the same, mostly sagging and not square, though most of the ones "reclaimed" by urban pioneers carried a new coat of paint in the bright, pastel style Charleston was known for.

Crackle rose to his feet and brushed off a grimy pair of black jeans. He knew those kids didn't know shit about the place they lived. They maybe lock their doors because mommy tells them to, but they don't think about the flimsy shit their doors are made of. Crackle started walking down the street, headed south on Rutledge Avenue. If the doors are too much, none of those country-fed fools were going to replace the eighty-year-old windows in the houses they bought so Sterling, Kingston, or Hayley didn't have to live in the dorms.

***

3-1 was at the wheel and One sat in the front passenger seat of a Silver Range Rover. They watched as their point of interest—Crackle—turned left on Spring Street. They sat in silence as was their custom. Even during the operation against Max DeGuello in Key West, the two had only spoken when necessary. 3-1 surveyed the mirrors surrounding the car at random intervals to see if they had aroused any interest. Thankfully, cities in the United States did not work quite the same as communities in other parts of the world. Everyone was always on the go in the States, and no one took time to get to know their neighbors anymore. Especially in a neighborhood like the one they tracked Crackle through. A mix of transients, largely oblivious college students, and the remnants of the old, failed, forgotten, and pushed aside community who watched helplessly as they were systematically removed in the name of progress. Not the greatest atmosphere for community block parties.

According to the briefing One had provided, Crackle, his street name, was a long-term heroin addict and petty criminal. Most of his charges were non-violent and the result of his habit save for one assault charge when he was a teenager. A virtual shadow, not so much going unseen as he was universally ignored as inconsequential. Just another example of a failed human in a sea of people who themselves were barely treading water. Most people simply had no time for a junkie with a couple of quirks. As such, Crackle was able to go places and see and do things the greater population could not. 3-1 could understand why the man was used by the police. The practice brought to mind a litany of faces 3-1 could remember, people just like Crackle who had very good access and information based solely on the fact the rest of the world never noticed they were there.

3-1 repositioned the car as the junkie turned off Spring Street and out of view. Carefully he rounded the corner of Coming Street and saw that Crackle slowed his pace as he passed an old but recently remodeled row house. The place was a pastel yellow; apparently the first on the street to be reclaimed in the ongoing process of urban re-engineering that was spreading across what once was ghetto. Crackle studied the front façade of the building as he passed, with an eye up the driveway. He passed the yellow pastel, then bent to one knee next to a parked Nissan Leaf in the next driveway to adjust the laces on his torn pair of basketball sneakers.

Is police work really this easy? 3-1 asked himself as he watched the heroin addict study his surroundings while appearing to tie his shoe. He finished his ploy, then without another look, skipped up the driveway abutting the yellow pastel home.

One opened the door and followed him.

***

Crackle peeked through the windows as he passed and skipped up the steps to the slanted wood porch that ran along the length of the house. He paused to look through one last window before knocking on the door. He paused for ten seconds, listening for sounds from inside. Hearing none, he knocked one more time, and after a brief pause passed the front door and headed around the back.

He was humming to himself without realizing, burning nervous energy through sound. The backyard was surrounded by an old wood fence that sagged in some places and reached almost six feet tall in others. Lawn chairs and bikes littered the backyard along with an old, party ball keg that sat dented and cracked next to a dilapidated one-car garage. He found a window sitting about shoulder height and stopped. He looked around the yard nervously, then stopped humming. He tried the window and it didn't budge. He looked around once more, then turned his back to the window. He was about to smash it with his elbow when he noticed the back door. He had walked right past it. Stepping in front of it, he surveyed the aged wood and flaking paint. He tested the knob and felt a little play. Age had loosened the door knob. He put his shoulder to the wood and it popped open with a groan and a crack.

"Hello?" he called cautiously. Crackle figured if there was anyone inside, he could run at this point without them getting too much of a look at him. There was no response.

With his hands in the front pouch of his hoodie, he wandered through a mud room, then the kitchen. Various stainless steel appliances were there for the taking. The interior of the house had been upgraded far better than the outer. He needed a decent haul to get him through til his check arrived, but given his lack of a vehicle to carry anything major he was going to be limited to what he could carry. He found a purse on the kitchen table but after he tossed it, he found there was nothing but a compact and a couple of old receipts inside.

Through the dining room and into the living room, he stopped at a sixty-inch, curved flat screen that could have brought him a mint at the pawn shop, but there was no way he could make it down the street carrying the big bastard. A Blu-ray player and Xbox sat below on an entertainment stand. Both of those were an option he kept in mind for later. The stairs to the second floor creaked, making him jump out of his skin and his heart to pound in his chest. He was out of breath by the time he reached the second floor.

Three bedrooms clearly belonging to a trio of women offered him a couple of gold chains, a set of earrings he hoped were diamond, and an iPod, all of which he shoved in his pockets. He was in the third bedroom, pulling open the drawers of a chest-high dresser. Nothing of interest greeted him until the contents of the bottom drawer made his eyes pop. Pleather and lace lingerie, a couple of thongs, and a smattering of sex toys set his mind to racing. He was holding a ball gag in his hand, curious as to the fact that he had never really believed people actually used those, when someone near him cleared their throat.

His legs trembled, and threatened to fall out from under him. A man and a woman watched him from the doorway. She was brunette, wearing a tight fitting polo shirt and khaki's, her arms crossed over her ample chest. He had blonde hair. There was a dark look in his eyes. He wore jeans and a black t-shirt.

"Shit," he breathed.

"Drop the ball gag, Mr. Wrightsell," the woman said in a tone he knew only so well. These were cops.

Crackle knew most of the cops around downtown, if not by name, then by sight, and he didn't know these two. He sat in the back seat of their Range Rover, hands cuffed in front of him, resting on his lap. He stared straight ahead. *These aren't city cops*, he told himself, a tendril of suspicion coursing down his spine.

They sat in silence while the woman piloted the vehicle out of downtown and through Mount Pleasant until she pulled to a stop at a beach access near Fort Moultrie. The guy in dark sunglasses didn't say a word either. He just stared at him through those lenses, sitting quiet like the terminator. Crackle watched them both through the rearview mirror and could not decide which of these two freaked him out more. At least the city cops would talk to him while they took him to jail. Some of them even played music for him if they knew he was going to be in for more than a few days.

"Awight, what you guys? Shit, you ain't city, so what, county? Feds?" he asked.

The woman turned in her seat to face him and held up a small gold badge. "FBI," she said with stern countenance.

"What do you want with me?" Crackle squirmed to find relief for his wrists.

"You snitch for Detectives Ben Wilke and Esteban Viejo."

"I ain't no snitch!" Crackle protested.

"You provide them information, they pay you for it, then you spend it on heroin."

Crackle shrugged, "What then."

"I need to know what Wilke and Viejo have been asking you about lately."

"Same old shit," Crackle mumbled.

"Who, what, where." She ticked off her fingers as she said the words.

"Why do you care? Why don't you go ask them? You all po-lice, ain't cha?"

The woman cocked her head sideways and stared at him through the mirror.

"No," Crackle breathed as it dawned on him. "You investigatin' them? No shit."

She looked away for a moment and removed her glasses. When she spoke to him it was in a cool, calm tone. "Here it is, Mr. Wrightsell. I can charge you with Burglary and whatever the hell else I want. I'm an FBI Agent, the charge would stick. Or you can work for me the same as you work for them. I don't give a shit about burglary," she held up two hundred-dollar bills, "and I pay better."

Crackle's eyes flared and his veins sizzled in anticipation of the magic carpet ride he was about to take.

***

Five minutes after she flashed the cash in front of the heroin junky, One and 3-1 pulled away from the beach access, leaving a thoroughly excited Crackle to catch a bus. There was a long period of silence as she piloted the Range Rover back toward the Charleston peninsula.

"Probably could have got him for fifty," 3-1 finally said.

One didn't acknowledge him.

Chapter Forty-Eight

One had 3-1 sitting on Police Headquarters, where Peter Banks was heading a task force investigating the shooting death of a toddler.

One, dressed all in black, was perched in a tree line adjacent to the modest, single-story ranch home owned by Peter Banks. It was a little past nine o'clock. She had been in position since sundown, getting a feel for the neighborhood. Banks' neighbors were quiet, save for a pair of Jack Russell terriers that had patrolled the yard next to the Banks property for about an hour before being ushered inside by a heavyset elderly man with a grumbly voice and a heavy grey beard.

Silence was creeping over the block. The random and intermittent traffic that coursed through the residential development had dwindled. The home to the south of Banks' was now dark, and only the soft blue glow of a television could be seen in a single room near the back of the home to the north. Without a sound or disruption to the undergrowth, she moved toward her target.

The sliding back door would not have challenged even a teenager who wanted to get in. She slipped in without a sound. Entering via the living room, she noticed a television affixed to the main wall, a couch, and what looked like a well-worn reclining chair. She studied the chair for a moment, pausing to look over the contours of the seat and headrest. She ran her fingers over the cushioned armrests and decided against using it.

One slowly made her way through the living area and the sparse dining room that consisted of an old dining room table that was used more as a work space. Two disassembled rifles lay neatly arranged on separate cloths with cleaning and lubricating equipment in between. At the head of the table, she noticed a binder with an unsettlingly familiar countenance on it. *Or at least the eyes, anyway,* she decided as she took up the binder with a gloved hand. The face on the cover of the binder was close but off by some detail. The eyes were unmistakable though. Biannca Dahl stared at her from the cover of that binder. One studied the police artist's rendering for a moment, but just for a moment. Memories shared between her and her former associate started to dig their way out of her subconscious and she could not have that. Not without confirmation anyway. Flipping through the binder she noted there were several attempts at an artist rendering of the assassin—however, they were all off to some degree or another. All except for the eyes. They were dead on.

Setting the binder down, she moved on to an old dusty vanity obviously ignored for some time. On it she saw pictures of Banks and others. Some in uniform, some dated where he wore a drab, green SWAT uniform. One that she spied was hidden behind the others, only a corner poking out from behind the photo of the SWAT team, of Peter Banks grinning broadly along with the rest of his special weapons and tactics teammates. She plucked the photo from behind the others. It showed Banks and a woman. He wore a black tuxedo, crisp but obviously a rental. She was radiant and seemed to be in the midst of a bright laugh with a colorful bouquet. The wedding dress was trim and exquisite. She wondered for a moment about their story. She already knew the unfortunate ending, but there was so much more to that photo than any record check could tell. She placed the photo back but left it half out of place, highlighting the glowing bride. Giving her a fighting chance against all the testosterone crowding the shelf.

Moving on, she stepped into the kitchen and looked around. Clearly the feeding place of a bachelor. Dirty dishes were stacked in the sink and a platoon of empty beer bottles were lined up against the splash guard, awaiting their transfer to the recycling bin. Before continuing, she took one of the bottles by the base and put a pen light against the glass. Holding the light at an oblique angle she could see latent fingerprints along the label and the neck of the bottle. She repeated the process, confirming the location of the prints on two more bottles.

She studied his refrigerator and found more of the same. Tupperware stacked with various leftovers fighting for space against takeout containers, and more beer. She took a beer from the fridge and placed it on the counter. She recognized the brand, Labatt Blue Light, Canadian. She thought the choice a little strange. He was basically a fan of the Budweiser of Canada. The beer seemed out of place in the Deep South.

Studying the label, she watched as condensation quickly accumulated on the brown bottle. The humidity in the Lowcountry worked fast. Almost at once there was a decent sheen and drips sliding lazily down the bottle. One retrieved a small nylon case from her back pocket. Inside was a transparent strip with one frosted backing and one clear cover. She made sure her nitrile gloves were still intact before carefully removing the frosted backing from the strip. She then placed the strip around the neck of the brown glass bottle. She held the strip firm to the glass to ensure it was affixed properly and in the general location where latent prints on other bottles showed the highest probability for contact. One gently removed the transparent film layer. Holding the bottle by the label she returned it to its place in the fridge and shut the door.

Her curiosity urged her to continue through the police captain's home, but her mission was finished. She looked around the kitchen once more to ensure nothing was out of place, then withdrew the same way she had come through the sliding back door.

Chapter Forty-Nine

Banks sighed as he entered his kitchen through the garage. The house which sat on a couple of acres off Highway 61, near the Dorchester County line, used to be on the outskirts of Charleston, SC. Now, after decades of urban sprawl, he was crunched between cookie cutter neighborhoods. The city had grown over and around what he once thought of as his getaway from the city.

He dropped his satchel that carried his department issue laptop computer and a notebook on a chair near the kitchen table. His blue and gold trimmed uniform jacket followed, being draped over the back of the same chair. Banks loosened his tie in one hand and reached inside an old, simple refrigerator for a long-necked bottle of Ying Ling. Part of him wanted to argue that he was too tired for a beer, but another part of him, the part who had seen a friend in the hospital with a gunshot wound and spent the majority of the day with a sniveling but stubborn criminal while trying to break one of the highest profile cases in recent Charleston history, told him he definitely needed a beer.

Just one, he told himself. The following morning, the team would be joined by the surveillance unit from Special Operations Command to put an eye on Treat Moncrief and Harold Washington. If they weren't spooked already that

Blanding was in police custody, they soon would be, and Banks could not afford to let them slip the noose when they were ready to strike. Banks popped the top off of the sweating glass bottle and tossed it in a large bowl that he used to collect bottle caps. He didn't bother to see if his shot found its mark.

Slowly he shuffled toward the living room where a sixty-inch flat screen mounted to the wall held court over an aged collection of furniture: leather sofa, plush recliner, and love seat. Even as he slouched down into the worn sofa he realized he would probably wake up in that same place in the morning, which was a mere four and a half hours away. He shifted his beer from left to right and before the bottle made the changeover, it crashed to the floor beneath him.

"Shit," he breathed, chasing the amber, liquid-spewing little bastard. He wheezed suddenly and shot back upright. He was hot, really hot all over, and it felt like there was a rhino sitting on his chest.

Banks tried to slide into the recliner in front of him but missed and crashed to the floor. His legs burned as if he'd run ten miles, a horrible lactic acid build-up. *Not like this*, he thought. His mind raced through all the images of the bodies he'd seen during his career, especially the natural deaths. Someone who slipped in the shower, or fell off a ladder, or just didn't wake up after curling up in bed at night; none of them had planned on dropping where they did. Banks wheezed and fought for breath, his heart pounding in his ears, arteries pounding in his neck.

I'm having a heart attack, he realized, rolling to his back. His vision was blurry. He told himself he needed his phone. *Get to your phone!* But his limbs felt like giant sacks of sand; they were sluggish and clumsy. And his head was spinning.

All Peter Banks could think about was the indignity of death. This was not how he wanted to go, not how he wanted people to remember him. He forced himself onto his side, and then his stomach. *Not like this*, he told himself. Arm over arm, he dragged himself in an excruciating effort toward the kitchen where his phone rested in the breast pocket of his dress coat. When he squinted he could see it waiting for him, as if the garment and the prize inside were observing him, seeing if he could pull off the impossible distance. Holding his head up was exhausting. He concentrated on his crawl toward salvation.

He pulled himself desperately and at a painfully slow pace. He could feel himself fading, felt the burning in his shoulders and back telling him he wasn't going to make it. He couldn't tell what kind of progress he was making, had no idea for how long or how far he crawled, he just did it. Moved one limb over the other, snaking across the living room floor to what was only vague light in his blurry eyes. It was so hard to breathe now, and his heart thundered in his chest; everything ached and he was tired, so tired. One arm over the other he moved, barely able to make even that happen. *Would they see that I fought?* he wondered. *How long will I lie here?* The vision of his bloated and blackened carcass melting in his own home spurred him on another foot or two. He was energized by sheer terror of rotting, forgotten.

Then his shoulders and back muscles just stopped. The fibrous tissue refused to go on any longer.

"No," Peter Banks moaned, almost imperceptibly, as he forced himself in one more valiant act to roll to his back. His eyes couldn't focus. It was hard to discern how far he'd made it toward his goal, how badly he had failed. His vision was a dark, hazy cloud moving in from the periphery. He just tried to breathe now. If he continued to breathe maybe he could get a second wind, maybe he could try again. *Just breathe*, he told himself when movement overhead closed in on him. He wondered, *Is this it?*

Angel-soft tendrils of hair suddenly tickled his sweat-soaked forehead, and danced around his cheeks. It was a woman, he could smell her, a lavender and fruity hint carried in the atmosphere of his home. She was leaning over him and Banks wondered if she was an angel, if angels were real, and was taking him now? Something was spilled, cool over his mouth and lips. He slurped desperately at the liquid which tasted dull and thick, but to him it was like drinking from a spring stream roiling with ice melt. He'd had no idea how thirsty he'd been.

Peter Banks felt himself begin to float. Was this it? Strangely all his fight was gone, every care, every fear, gone. He was at peace, he knew he didn't want to die, but at the same time, it was so...

"Sleep now," a voice whispered.

Peter Banks slid into oblivion.

Chapter Fifty

Pell lounged in a plush leather easy chair. He swirled two fingers of bourbon in his glass. Washington sat opposite him. He stared out a second floor window from the apartment he kept over the coin laundry. Pell was not thrilled to be there, despite the couple of ounces of eighteen-year amber fluid he sipped. He'd spent his entire life avoiding situations just like this one.

Washington was on edge and he didn't blame him. In the space of a day he'd seen everything he'd built begin to crumble, and he knew it was his own fault.

Pell looked from his glass to his longtime friend, although friend was a tough word, Pell thought. Associate, business partner, maybe; but to be a friend of Harold Washington would be a stretch for anyone to say with confidence. All that being considered, he did feel a sense of obligation to the man. He could say that he was a trusted advisor. Washington did listen to him, and even took his advice from time to time, usually when the law was involved. Pell had leveraged old contacts inside the police department time and again in an effort to deflect or get advance notice when the man was coming up on the PD's radar. Now with Blanding sitting tight in a jail cell downtown, there was no chance of deflecting an investigation, no way to keep the man sitting across from him from being a wanted man by morning. Part of him felt for Washington, hated to see anyone have to watch their kingdom burn before their very eyes. The man was a tightly coiled spring, loaded and ready to pop at any given second. A Heckler and Koch MP-5 9mm submachine gun rested next to Washington's chair. It had been in easy reach since the moment he'd heard about the attempt on Blanding's life. Washington had cleaned the weapon and loaded a number of skinny magazines and now it was permanently within arm's reach. Pell looked at the weapon. He realized that Washington had not retrieved it to protect himself. It was not a defensive measure. He was preparing for a hunt—he was going to put down the junk yard dog that had slipped the chain and turned on him. Pell was alright with that. What he wasn't comfortable with was his role.   Pell was washed out of the police department almost fifteen years ago when an internal investigation was able to catch him collecting protection money from local street level dealers. He had been in patrol, a veteran police officer, but one with no rank to speak of. He would offer a deal to the dealers on his beat, they paid and he didn't roust them, didn't go chasing them down. They continued to operate and he supplemented his meager thirty grand a year salary, a win for both interests. Then one of them got popped while he was on leave, spending some of his well-earned cash in Vegas. The little bastard talked. A kid, willing to do anything to shorten a sentence sold him out wholesale. When he returned from leave he walked in to an eerily quiet roll call room. He'd walked right into the trap, never suspecting a thing. He had avoided jail time, but his career as a cop was over.

Washington hired him shortly after he was fired. At first, Pell covered him on meetings and other dealings that Washington could not afford to have one of his underlings see. Washington had a strict rule of compartmentalization. People only need to know what they need to know, he'd say. When Pell asked him why he had chosen him, Washington had simply said, "You're an outsider. You're a cop, my boys on the street won't trust you, and you despise them. You're the perfect buffer." Eventually Pell had set himself up as a private detective, but in reality his main client had always been Harold Washington. Rather than muscle, over time Pell fell into an intelligence roll, acting as Washington's eyes and ears wherever he could find someone inside the PD that would talk to him.

Washington had made Pell a very comfortable man. He never married, owned a condo on the West Side and was never without whatever car he wanted to drive. His clothes were tailored and pressed, and he had a wad of cash in reserve in case he ever needed to disappear, a potentiality he felt was ever more likely. If he had enough money to start over, what was Washington still doing here? He knew the answer but it killed him to not at least hear the man admit it.

"How much money you got lying round?" Pell asked.

Washington sipped at his drink and continued to study the lines in the aged wallpaper that covered the apartment, "Why?" he responded.

"I just want to know how dealing with Moncrief is worth it. I want to know what you've got left to prove."

Washington put his drink down on the arm of his chair and looked at Pell. The private detective felt his guts turn. "I got nothing to prove to anybody, least of all you," he said, "This ain't about that. Bottom line is I can't go til that little motherfucker's dead. He can't have what I built. He don't deserve what I built." His voice rose. "I don't give a fuck about this business, about the dope, the cars, none of that shit. I'll leave it all behind, but not til that bitch is in the ground. After, I don't give a shit what happens to this fuckin' town." Washington turned back to the window and took a swig from his tumbler.

Pell watched the little flotilla of ice chasing itself as he swirled his own glass, "Principal of the thing, huh," said Pell. Somehow he felt better now that he'd heard the career crime lord talk about principals.

"Damn right."

Chapter Fifty-One

Viejo entered the large conference room to find Wilke leaning against a corner by himself. He was nursing a coffee in a Styrofoam cup. Viejo scanned the room for Banks as he approached,

"Where's the boss?" he asked.

"Don't know," Wilke shrugged. "Fenner just went to check his office,"

Viejo looked around the room again at the gathering group of detectives, command staff, and surveillance personnel, "Where's the Chief?"

Wilke shrugged again.

The assembled group filtered toward chairs, and pretty soon all were seated and waiting, save for Wilke and Viejo. The two stood in the back of the room for what seemed an eternity. Viejo wondered how long they could stay there without anybody saying anything.

Chapter Fifty-Two

Moncrief slouched in the car and waited. He wondered what his next move was. Did he roll in there hard and scare the white boy into telling him what was going on between him and Washington? Did he wait and break in after the dude left in the morning, figure shit out that way, or maybe, if the guy was as big a deal as Washington hinted, that the pasty fucker might have an army just waiting for someone to try him. Moncrief doubted the last idea. The guy had no one with him at the dinner with Washington, didn't have no one trailing him on the way home. The hammer on a revolver clicked in Moncrief's ear; he froze.

The man in the checkered jacket. Washington's source suddenly appeared at the passenger side window of the Honda. The door behind him opened and someone got inside. The muzzle of a weapon was returned to his skull. It now rested at his brain stem.

"Treat Moncrief," a woman said. "It's a pleasure to make your acquaintance."

Part of Treat Moncrief found it ironic that though he had a gun to his head, he was more worried about what Washington was going to do to him than what the woman in the backseat had planned. The fear that man instilled in him made him hate himself.

"I would say the same but you got a gun to my head," Moncrief tried to keep his voice steady and low.

The muzzle of the weapon receded. Moncrief did not react.

"If I wanted you dead, Mr. Moncrief, I would not have had this gentleman suffer through that dinner with your employer."

Moncrief found the statement odd, but only absorbed the fact she didn't want to kill him outright.

"I have a business proposal for you, Mr. Moncrief. Your boss, Mr. Washington, though a fine business man in his own right, does not share my vision of what needs to be done to secure our supply chain to this area. I think you might be more in line with my needs."

Moncrief cocked his head to the side. Tried to get a look at her through the rearview mirror. The woman was carefully shrouded in shadow. "Go on," he said.

"We have noticed a great interest in your organization by certain members of the police. Normally in a situation like this we would simply cut ties and move on to another distribution chain, however yours and Mr. Washington's infrastructure is sound and efficient. Rather than rebuild, I believe we should simply mitigate the intrusive force and continue on, business as usual."

"You want the cops gone?"

There was a pause, "Mr. Washington believes this would bring about unnecessary pressure and does not support that kind of action."

Moncrief felt his face flush. "That sort of thing doesn't bother me."

"I'm aware. What I propose is the elimination of a certain police unit as well as Mr. Washington. Once that is done, you and I will work directly to continue the exclusive distribution of heroin throughout the Lowcountry."

Moncrief saw himself behind Washington's old ratty desk and immediately dismissed the thought. He would never take that seat. He was going to burn that old laundromat to the ground with Washington's dead ass nailed to that fuckin' desk.

Chapter Fifty-Three

Viejo blundered his way through the operations briefing. He ummed and erred on the names of his main subjects. Stuttered when asked about target locations, and at one point looked blankly at Wilke who simply shrugged, all the while smiling at him as he floundered in front of twenty cops and command staff.

Viejo had finally been able to dole out assignments, and as the two left to gear up he'd whispered to Wilke, "You're an asshole."

"Nah, you did great," his partner had said.

With Banks nowhere to be seen and Viejo as the acting Narcotics Commander, he had been the lone figure in line to take over the operation. The hastily cobbled together operation. With Martin's injury the previous day, there was a sharpness to today's planned arrests. Viejo could feel the anger in the room as he had reminded the assembly that Martin was stable and that the crew they were after had no problem squeezing the trigger.

"We do it clean and we do it right," he had said, "But these assholes don't get the benefit of the doubt."

Viejo could feel the snap and the high-pitched whine as the bullets had zipped past him yesterday...when he was but a second too slow. He felt like a failure, and as he stood in front of the men and women at the briefing, he thought he could see it behind the ever-present façade of unimpressed grimaces cops always carry over their features. For a second he had wondered if that was how he looked during briefings. They thought he had let Martin down.

Wilke and Viejo were going to set up on the laundromat owned by Harold Washington. According to Carter Blanding, the longtime drug dealer kept an apartment over the business, and the supposed heroin kingpin of Charleston lived like a pauper. That could explain how he had ducked the radar for years. The two detectives were amazed and a little embarrassed they had never heard of him before. And how was it that one of his mules hadn't rolled on him in all the time he was supposedly running things? None of it added up, but testimony given by Blanding had provided enough probable cause for a judge to sign off on an arrest warrant, and was willing to follow up with supplemental warrant once they found Washington's stash. Blanding didn't know and the minister-turned-source who was now snugged away in a city jail cell was adamant that no one knew where the man kept his money or his dope. Washington had a strict compartmentalization policy which left the narcotics detectives with a suspect, but no place to search. On top of the fact that they were on to the scent of a supposed master criminal, Viejo and Wilke would be conducting surveillance on a man who might be either the target of an assassination attempt or in the process of arranging the assassination of his enemy, Treat Moncrief. Blanding had provided details regarding Washington and Moncrief's growing divide.

Moncrief was known to the PD. His criminal history was solid and distinguished, beginning in his early teens, though over the last few years, the career drug dealer had gone quiet. Moncrief hadn't had an arrest in seven years. Fenner and a couple of detectives from the narcotics unit were attempting to locate Moncrief, who was not only part of the growing heroin conspiracy but was also the primary suspect in the shooting of Detective Bob Martin, and of the triple murder involving Deshaun Caldwell, Heiliea Williams, and three-year old Chevante Williams. Doubts about whether Blanding was holding back about the shooting notwithstanding, the simple fact that the detectives assigned to the behemoth of a case that was the death of Chevante Williams now had a suspect was enough incentive to drive the members of the CPD to the ends of the earth in the hunt for Treat Moncrief. From the Mayor's office to the patrol units working canvas interviews in between calls all over the East Side, the entire city was involved, and they were exhausted. The rage that had consumed the city after the little girl was killed was hard to maintain. The city was tired, but would not rest until a suspect was taken down in her name. Fenner, Viejo, and Wilke wondered what they would find once Treat Moncrief was sitting in an interrogation room. Would the case of Chevante Williams go silently into the court docket? God, they hoped so. But that was for the future—today they had to find a violent career criminal first and take him in safely. Given the man's history, they figured that was a healthy enough goal. No need to start speculating before they even found the guy.

Wilke was driving with Viejo in the front passenger seat when they pulled to a stop two blocks down from the laundromat. Around them the city was waking up. A school bus lumbered from stop to stop along its winding route. Retirees and blue collar workers wandered the sidewalks, and commuters scrambled to get out before the rest of traffic. Viejo cracked the tinted windows of their department issue Toyota Camry and cut the engine. The heat and humidity of the Lowcountry morning instantly drove out the crisp air-conditioned atmosphere of the vehicle.

"Get a beer tonight?" Viejo asked as he sipped at a gas station coffee.

Wilke nodded. "You're transferring, huh?"

Viejo craned his neck at his partner, "What?"

"Heard Lieutenant Speers talking about it before the briefing," Wilke said.

Viejo sighed. This was not the time for this conversation.

"It's alright dude," Wilke said, sensing how heavy the move was weighing on his friend.

"You know..." Viejo started.

"You got a kid now." Wilke didn't so much cut him off as continue his train of thought. "This is not the life if you want things to be stable at home. I'm surprised it took you this long."

Viejo grinned. "This is kind of hard to give up," he said, taking a look at the target location. The old concrete block structure painted an aquamarine color wasn't so much run down as it was aged. He bet it was quite a sight in the Seventies or whenever the place went up. For a moment, like he always did on stakeouts, he wondered if his suspect was sitting up in one of the windows on the second floor watching him. "You know the econ guys have to wear a tie."

Wilke choked through a slug of his own coffee. "Do you own a tie?"

Viejo shrugged.

"You get anything from Banks yet?" Wilke asked, checking his phone.

"No." Viejo unlocked his own phone and studied the notifications. "That's weird."

Chapter Fifty-Four

Peter Banks floated into consciousness. From absolute nothingness, the notion that he was breathing with a slight congestion in his sinuses and pain in his chest registered. The observation of his bodily functions was distant at first, and he could not identify the significance. Then he noted that his tongue felt like sandpaper and his mouth was a desert. He needed some water.

When he opened his eyes, a shock of harsh light assaulted him. Though the only light was natural light sliding through the blinds covering his living room windows, it was still overwhelming. Wait, light, from outside...Shit! He tried to get up but his body was sluggish and sore. He groaned and paused to build his strength for another effort.

"Take it slow, old man." A soft feminine voice greeted his ears. "You've just come back from a dance with the Reaper, ease into it."

"What," he breathed, looking up through his mental fog. For the briefest of moments, he thought that the voice belonged to Karen. That changed when his eyes took in the trim young woman sitting across from him, legs crossed, wearing tights, and a simple oversized sweater, with almond-shaped blue eyes.

Almond-shaped blue eyes he would know anywhere.

They were eyes he saw at least three times a week chasing him in the middle of the night. They held a glimmer as they rained hot shrapnel and fire on him over and over again.

Peter Banks' breath caught in his chest. All pain and sluggishness was forgotten as he started in his easy chair. Instinctively he reached for his weapon, but his shoulder holster was empty.

"You!" he hissed, coming out of his chair in a charge. It was her, the girl who had almost killed him, Viejo, and Andrew Vaden just a little over a year ago. He was going to kill her. He was just gaining his feet when another figure dressed in a suit and tie flanked him, coming from his kitchen.

"Captain Banks," the man greeted him formally. "I apologize for the scare. I understand you and Biannca have previously met."

Banks paused halfway out of his chair to gauge the second intruder to his home. The fog cleared, and as he realized he was caught in a trap, the memory of the previous night's brush with death was suddenly alive in his mind now also. "What is this?" he demanded, gaining his feet. They might have taken him by surprise but he'd be damned if he was going to take whatever came sitting down.

The man crossed the room confidently with a sideways glance at the brunette and offered his hand. Banks did not take it. "Charles McKetrick, Assistant Director, Office of Logistics and Special Projects. I'm sorry we've had to meet like this."

Banks studied the man for a moment then looked to the female. "You poisoned me." The accusation was delivered solely to her.

She was smiling slightly; her toe bobbed in the air as she lounged, "I didn't know what they spiked you with." She shrugged. "I had to see what was happening before I could figure out what kind of counteragent to give you," she said plainly.

Banks was at a loss.

"Please sit down, Captain. We will explain everything."

"Start talking." Banks wondered which one of them had his gun, and if he could make it to the nightstand in a race for his back-up weapon. Another look at the girl and he doubted he could get there without a fight. And the woman was a predator; she'd already tried to kill him once.

"Please." McKetrick gestured for him to take a seat in his own living room.

"Fuck off."

"Jesus Christ, Pete, sit down." He knew that voice. Chief of Police Andrew Vaden filled the entryway to his kitchen.

Banks' eyes narrowed.

There was a long pause as the three men stared at each other while the female assassin stretched like a purely disinterested feline in her chair. After a moment, McKetrick clasped his hands in front of his waist. "Shall we get started then?" he asked.

Chapter Fifty-Five

Treat Moncrief stood in the middle of what once passed for someone's living room. Vintage, floral-patterned wallpaper peeled lazily from corners and around jagged holes where junkies and other assorted street creatures had added their own signatures of destruction over the years. There were holes in the floor around which he stood, and the carpet he stood on seemed to cling to his sneakers. There still was an owner attached to the wreck. But after being paid off in a mix of cash and heroin, the descendent of someone who once took great pride in the structure had ceded it to Washington's organization and decay as a stash house.

Stretched out on the remnants of furniture scattered around the first floor were five men that Treat Moncrief could trust. He had made these men rich in the Charleston Heroin trade. They had waited for him throughout the night—empty bottles of booze, everything from champagne to Wild Irish Rose, littered the floor. Cigarette smoke clung to the humid atmosphere of the decaying house.

Moncrief was just about to issue his marching orders when his phone chirped. A glance at the screen sent a shiver down his spine. It was accompanied by cold rage. He swiped to the right and put the phone to his ear.

"I've been waiting on you for almost twenty-four hours now, boy. You lose your nerve?" Washington asked.

"I—"

"Here's what's going to happen. I'm walking away from this business. I'm leaving it to whoever's bad enough to reclaim these streets."

Moncrief knew he had to say something but couldn't find his words.

"But I'm going to kill you first."

"Mother fu-!"

"It all could have been yours, and you know it. I wanted it to be yours. But you don't deserve it. Thought I could beat the crazy out of you boy. But you too thick, shoulda known. Now the best part of this is you still want it, and you're going to come to me. You're gonna drive yourself to your own funeral. I'm at the old place. Come here so I can put you down like the wild animal you are."

Moncrief couldn't speak. His mind spun as he tried to think through the cocaine and the fear and the anger. He finally formed a string of epithets that would make a demon blush, but before he could unleash his verbal salvo the line went dead. He stared at his phone for a long second before noticing the men standing around him. He spun and whipped the phone into the wall. He breathed in short staccato clips, and snarled, "He dies now! Get your shit!"

Knock, knock, knock.

The rapping on the door was gentle, almost quiet. The six men in the living room of the dilapidated crack house froze, all looking in the same direction. Moncrief was the first to react.

"You didn't shut this place down for the night?"

Onre Bauer shrugged. "I put the word out, ain't nobody been here all night, man."

"Get rid of it, whatever it is." Moncrief gestured toward the door. "Fuck." He looked around to see the gathering of his bleary-eyed henchmen and had the sudden urge to randomly beat people's asses.

Bauer shrugged and head low, rounded the corner to the foyer out of sight. Moncrief watched the darkened passage, his impatience building.

The door creaked open and Bauer could be heard mumbling something when a low ripping sound reached the ears of the men in the living room. Silence followed before the stumbling form of Bauer appeared around the corner. The bird on the front of his once pristine Gamecocks jersey was now a deep crimson and orange rather than red and white. Bauer held one hand to the massive gash across his throat, the other was held out flat in front of him as if trying to ask a question.

The five men stared in shock as Bauer took a couple of steps toward them.

Moncrief felt his bowels soften. Washington had found him. The old bastard had sniffed him out and now here he was to finish him off. Moncrief looked away from Onre to his empty hands as he realized his AK was leaning against a table in the next room. *Gun*, he thought, he had a forty-five in his waistband. Moncrief reached for the handgun. It felt like his arms were moving through cement. He felt Washington looming over him, felt death coming. It seemed an eternity before he felt the grip of the pistol in his palm. He looked up as he drew. Bauer was still standing, his eyes rolling in his head. Then Moncrief saw the huge shadow appear behind the dying man. It felt like the gun in his hand was catching on every fiber of his sweatpants as he drew.

***

Broadstreet gave his diversion a moment to take hold before following his victim into the room. As he rounded the corner he looked over the dying man's shoulder to see five men standing before him. Twisted faces full of disgust and horror watching their friend die before them. Broadstreet saw weapons laying everywhere, from assault rifles to handguns and loose magazines and ammunition. He suddenly realized he had entered a hornet's nest.

The one he was looking for, Treat Moncrief, stood to his left. He was in the process of drawing from his waistband. Broadstreet unleashed a vicious kick to the small of the dying man's back throwing him in a heap into the legs of Moncrief. Both men went down in a jumble of limbs.

Despite the firepower and the numbers, Broadstreet was cold, his mind quiet. He scanned the room before going in for the kill of Treat Moncrief. He saw another man reacting, bald and solidly built. He was reaching for an AK-47 that lay on the floor beneath a stained and torn easy chair. The length of cutoff rebar in Broadstreet's right hand hummed as he swung in a slash, smashing the man's face over the bridge of his nose and across his eyes. The scream that greeted him was high and shrill, not the sound a man should make. He heard the man scream, "My eyes!" before he spiked him in between the shoulder blades with his K-bar knife.

Out of the corner of his eye, he saw one man run out the back. Then he felt arms wrap themselves around his head. His assailant missed. He didn't lock in a leverage point under the chin but ended up squeezing Broadstreet's head against his body. The two spun in the middle of the floor. As the man tried to improve his hold, Broadstreet stabbed the jagged length of rebar into his opponent's inner thigh. He twisted and wrenched the metal from Moncrief's meaty leg. The pressure around his head fell away in a cry and hot fluid brushed his face. The taste of copper filled his mouth. He spun in search of another victim.

A shot rang out from behind him. Broadstreet juked to the left as a lanky man with wide eyes and gold teeth fired wildly through the room. His first salvo missed Broadstreet by a hair's width and stitched a line across his comrade's chest. The man let go of his shredded thigh and fell backwards amid a frantic wash of his own blood.

Without stopping, Broadstreet threw a table up in the path of the shooter and continued a parabolic arc that brought him to the gun hand side of the skinny black man. The rebar made a sickening crunch and the gun fell useless as Broadstreet shattered the shooter's radial and ulnar bones. Broadstreet kept his momentum, driving the rebar in a windmill swing through the base of the fallen man's head. Gold teeth clattered on the floor. The man spasmed and thrashed at his feet.

Broadstreet turned once more and, *BAM! BAM! BAM!* Three impacts ripped across his abdomen. He didn't feel the pain at first and took another step before searing fire spread across his gut and he stumbled. In front of him stood Treat Moncrief, blood dripping in dark rivulets down his nose and off his chin, his clothes covered in gore.

"Washington sends one man?" Moncrief asked, his tone a mix of fury and bewilderment. He took a step toward the darkly clothed beast of a man who swayed on one knee.

"Who's Washington?" asked Broadstreet with a groan.

Moncrief took two more steps, "Motherfucker, do you think I'm playing with you?"

Broadstreet didn't answer. He was too busy trying to decide if he could get skinny's gun in play while the drug pimp blathered.

"You hear me asshole?" The hot muzzle of Moncrief's gun pressed against the center of Broadstreet's forehead.

"Don't know any Washington. I'm here for the girl."

The gun retreated a millimeter and Broadstreet lunged, adrenalin giving him the power he needed to finish the job. One hand on Moncrief's wrist and the other plunged the hunting knife deep into Moncrief abdomen in rapid succession. He'd done it before, and knew the key would be to do as much damage as he could while he still held the initiative. Over and over again, Broadstreet jabbed with the long knife, opening up Treat Moncrief's abdomen, shredding muscle skin and organs. Stars swam across Broadstreet's vision, dancing to the tune of the drug dealer's panicked cries.

"Noooo!" Moncrief cried in rising octaves while Broadstreet stabbed again and again, twisting and wagging the knife to do as much damage as he could.

Broadstreet felt his grip on Moncrief's wrist slipping and pivoted on his foot before burying the weapon in Moncrief's armpit. Another howl and he heard the gun fall as the two of them went down in a bloody pile.

Broadstreet couldn't breathe. He could barely see and could feel his body covered in sticky fluid and gore. Beside him, Moncrief swore and moved. Broadstreet buried the knife in Moncrief's rib cage and used it to leverage himself up to kneel over his victim.

"Oh God," Moncrief whined, the fight gone from his cold, dark eyes. Now those eyes only questioned and worried about what came next. "Why?" he asked as he studied the knife handle sticking out of his chest.

"Chevante Williams," Broadstreet whispered. Blood fell from his mouth as he spoke.

Moncrief looked at him, his movements slowing, a look of curiosity on his face like the name was foreign to him.

Broadstreet freed his knife from Moncrief's ribs and wiped the blade on his sweatshirt.

"You'll find out soon enough," he said before struggling to his feet.

Broadstreet looked around the room, at the destruction he had wrought. He sighed. It was not a sigh of accomplishment, nor a sigh of satisfaction. It was a sigh signaling he was done.

Chapter Fifty-Six

Broadstreet considered staying there. Just laying down and letting things happen. He was tired, his gut was on fire, and he could taste his own blood in his mouth. He decided he couldn't. Not there, not like that, not with them. What would his daughter think? If she ever found out.

One slimy, slick boot in front of the other. He made it out of the slaughter of the living room to the kitchen. The water out of the faucet was a pale orange and the rag laying on the side of the scum-covered sink was encrusted with God knew what but the combination of the two managed to peel some of the gore from his face, hands, and neck. The field jacket was drenched in blood. It took a herculean effort to free his failing body from the garment. He was left wearing a faded black sweatshirt that itself was dark and wet. Looking around, he found a purple, red, and white nylon windbreaker hanging over the back of a scratched and chipped kitchen chair. Twisting his torso to fit into the jacket left him breathless. His pants were soaking in his own blood but there was not much he could do about it now.

He left the rebar and the knife, knowing that he couldn't defend himself with either if called upon to do so and they were just too heavy. One clomping boot in front of the other, he exited out the back of the dilapidated crack house.

It was dark but he knew the way. He only wanted to create distance now. He could feel a coldness in the back of his mind nibbling at his consciousness. Part of him was scared, part of him was relieved. There really was no place for a monster like him. Not locked up inside somewhere, and not hunting on the street. This would be best for everyone.

Broadstreet stuck to the shadows as much as he could until he was forced into the dusky pink hues of the morning at an intersection where an early morning city bus blocked his way. Broadstreet swayed on his feet as he waited for the bus to pull off. He wondered how much further he could make it. He decided he wanted to see the marsh one more time. Maybe go to the marsh and find a place to lie down? He didn't know. One boot in front of the other until a flash of bright white light shocked him out of his walking trance. He looked beyond the light to see a row of blue lights on top of the vehicle's roof. The light snapped off. Broadstreet tried not to sway. He wondered what he looked like in the morning light.

"Broadstreet," said a familiar voice.

Broadstreet offered a weak smile. "Sergeant."

"How you doin' man? You're not looking too good."

"Just tired sir, late night at work. I—"

The radio issued a piercing howl and the three men froze. Frytel's eyes were wide while Coburn looked on with a practiced, casual interest. The tone bleated three times before the dispatcher reported,

"Signal 55. Shots fired, multiple calls, in the area of Cortland and Holt Streets."

"We gotta go Joseph, be good, my man." There was a tone of concern in the cop's voice.

Broadstreet managed to smile and was amazed that he was able to move his arm upward in a weak wave. He recognized the address and part of him screamed that he had to move after the cops pulled off. His body knew otherwise. One boot in front of the other in a steady, slow procession as Broadstreet continued his walk.

"That dude seemed messed up," Frytel offered as he piloted the black and white police cruiser toward the call.

"We got other things to worry about at the moment, kid." Coburn couldn't put a finger on it, not that he ever was able to do that but spidey sense was dancing through the periphery of his senses, and the dance was a river dance. Coburn had a feeling his rookie was about to receive an education in the next couple of minutes.

Chapter Fifty-Seven

Blue lights flashed as Coburn and Frytel pulled to the curb behind the first car. Even with the heightened alert of the 'hot' call they were answering, the field training officer took note of the way his rookie responded to the situation. He parked far enough from the first responding unit with his wheels pointed out to the road that they could get out if needed. Frytel called Dispatch and announced calmly that their unit was '97', on scene. He moved smoothly as he left the car, eyes roving, scanning for threats as they approached a broken down bent crack house where a gaggle of onlookers were beginning to form.

Coburn saw that the first responding unit, Ayers and Pancek, were already trying to figure things out. Ayers was on the side of the house, still in full view of his partner while maintaining an eye on the side and rear of the location.

"Take the other side," he told Frytel, who took up a post mirroring Ayers.

Everyone, mostly old black women, and a couple of middle-aged men all in various states of dress were talking at once.

Coburn leaned in toward Pancek so he could hear. "So far I got shots fired coming from that house, not sure how many. Seems to have been quiet for the last ten minutes or so."

"You guys go in?"

"Waiting to get a couple more units, there's just too many people milling around to go in without someone watching our backs."

Coburn nodded.

The patrol Sergeant, Lou Dummo, walked up to them as another duo of uniforms moved past Frytel to set up a rear perimeter.

The Sarge looked at his two officers. "In there?" he asked.

"Yes Sir, multiple shots fired, no movement for the last few minutes."

"Jones and Kneely are around back, us three go,"

With an eye to Frytel, Coburn moved off with the other two. He could see the disappointment in the rookie's face as he realized he would not be making entry. Another chance as a gunfighter missed. Coburn hoped the kid never got his wish.

The three officers entered the front door in a tight stack and quietly spread around the foyer to cover each other. The foyer was dark and turned in an awkward L shape. To the left, a grey set of stairs led up to the second floor where only darkness could be seen. Pancek put his gun on the stairwell as the others followed. Sergeant Dummo took point followed by Coburn. Dummo rounded the corner to the right as wide as he could so as to open his field of fire as wide as possible while still maintaining some form of cover from the patchy and dented sheetrock walls.

"Holy fuck," Coburn heard the Sergeant breathe. His heart rate skyrocketed.

He rounded the corner behind Dummo and took position covering an opening at the rear of the common room. Through the doorway he could see a row of cabinets, a sink, and a few remaining areas where ancient linoleum tiles had not been ripped through by generations of drug-addled youth. Coburn felt his stomach twist as his eyes fell toward the floor. A dead man looked up at him. He could see red-stained bone through the man's neck and his eyes were glazed over. Blood covered the front of the man's shirt and pants.

"Police!" Dummo shouted, announcing their presence, "Hands up and announce yourself!"

There was no answer.

"I got rear," Pancek said calmly from behind.

Dummo looked at Coburn and motioned to a side room opposite the stairs. Coburn nodded and returned his focus to the kitchen. As his eyes swept the room before returning to his danger area, he tried to take a count of the bodies that littered the floor but lost count at four, all men, all African American, all beaten to a pulp. He returned to looking over the front sight of his Glock pistol and took a gentle side step toward the left hand side of the common room. He had to jerk his boot back as he tried to step and felt the rubbery give of a dead man's hand under his boot. The sensation, kind of like stepping on a raw chicken breast, through the hard insole of his Danner boots threatened to overcome the two-plus decades of horror that had scoured away normal human sensitivity to the horrible things people do to each other.

"Clear," Dummo announced.

They locked eyes once more and the Sergeant moved on to another small side room that was little more than a closet. He ducked inside briefly, flashlight illuminating the small space before announcing once again. "Clear."

This time, when Dummo and Coburn made eye contact, it was Coburn's turn. Dummo took up position along the opposite side of the doorway to see what Coburn could not of the kitchen.

"Back door to the left, table, window."

Coburn cut a more acute angle on the door and opened his field of view. He could see the cabinets followed the wall after the sink and turned, "Wall to the right about five feet in, button." Coburn patted his chest. Dummo nodded.

It was a maneuver they had performed countless times. Maybe it was the bodies, maybe it was the stink of the ocean of blood mixing with the years of dirt and grime ground into the floor of the dying crack house, he couldn't tell. This movement in this moment however, took an extra boost of will from the old cop to force himself forward. He took his first step and out of the periphery saw Dummo gather himself up to follow. His Sergeant looked how he felt. There was a pallor to the man, a lack of color uncommon to the regular, stoic reserve of the squad leader.

Coburn moved smoothly and efficiently passed Dummo, and cut immediately to the left to follow the wall. He charged three steps before slowing and stopping to take in the scene. He saw his own pale reflection in the window, scattered remains of empty cigarette boxes, a crack pipe, and a black field jacket gleaming with blood.

There was no immediate threat. A door to his right lead directly to the backyard and a maze of yards beyond. A bare wall was to his left, and nothing but the filthy table in front of him,

"Clear," he said, in echo of Sergeant Dummo's announcement at the other end of the kitchen. Then his eyes fell back to the field jacket. Why?

Coburn stepped back into the threshold of the doorway and looked over the bodies, giving them more than just a horrified glance. Above him the moldy timbers of the second floor thudded and creaked as officers searched the upstairs.

Six bodies strewn about the room. A single room. All black men, early twenties to thirties. He saw gold teeth and a couple of gold chains lying amongst the human rubble. Their dress was also pretty standard. Jerseys from the University of South Carolina. He saw a red-smeared, Yankees home jersey, a couple of colorful t-shirts with various loud themes printed on them. He looked back at the abandoned field jacket. It didn't fit the dress of the other victims.

Coburn leaned over the jacket. Blood permeated the coat— no clotting had occurred. He observed reddening on the inside flap as well as the outer shell. A grimy old field jacket?

"Oh, shit."

"What?" asked Dummo, instinctively reaching for his duty weapon he had holstered just moments before.

"Oh, shit. Sarge, don't let anybody touch that jacket." Coburn raced out the back of the house. "Let's go, rookie!" he yelled as he rounded the yard, charging for the black and white.

Chapter Fifty-Eight

Broadstreet watched as the spectrum of pinks and reds lightened, giving way to the orange-blue morning sun. He hadn't quite made it to the edge of the peninsula, though he could smell the sulfurous tinge of plough mud at low tide. He wasn't sure how far he had made it from the house where he had done his work but his body couldn't make it any further. Not that he didn't try.

He plodded forward until all at once it seemed his injuries had asserted themselves, and his torso had seized with such a withering pain he collapsed to the sidewalk. Maybe one of the bullets was moving inside him. Maybe something had burst. Once he hit the ground, he felt the coldness of his saturated pants against his skin. He managed to prop himself up against a telephone pole and took a moment to look himself over.

With a bloody cough and a mighty struggle, he oriented himself with a view of the east and found himself content to take in the sunrise from there. He knew he should be scared, knew with even his defective upbringing that he had sinned and his eternity was at the least a very large question. But he had long ago accepted his sins, and strangely, there was nothing bothering him at the moment.

***

"What is it?" Frytel asked, holding onto the handle above the door frame as his field training officer slung their cruiser around a corner and dug his boot into the accelerator.

Coburn didn't respond. His eyes were scanning the shadows along the street.

They reached the location where they had talked to Broadstreet and he slowed the vehicle to a crawl. "Keep your eyes out," he said.

The cruiser crept along the street, heading in the general direction they had left the limping man. Frytel put his flashlight out his window to light up their search while Coburn used the alley lights fixed to the roof.

They made it a block past where they had talked to Broadstreet when Frytel said, "There," and pointed a couple hundred feet ahead.

Coburn saw him, slumped against a light pole. It was still a dusky hue of blue as the sun climbed the morning sky. In the gloom, he couldn't see anything more than a clump of darkness at the base of the pole, a pair of legs flared out in front of the man. Coburn pulled the car over to the curb and put it in park.

"You're cover, not a word," he growled with an uncommon intensity.

Frytel nodded.

They walked up on the man who did not stir as they approached. He was slumped a little to one side, his boots extended out in front of him. Coburn turned on his flashlight and the form continued to lay still. He shined a light on the pair of black work boots and confirmed his suspicion. They were covered in dirty, crimson gore. The man coughed and Frytel almost leapt from his skin.

"Joseph?" he asked, coming up on the man's flank. He shown the light on Broadstreet, lighting him up in profile.

Broadstreet's head lolled to sort of face him. Blood and sputum dribbled freely from his mouth. His eyes stared ahead.

"I'm sorry Sir," Broadstreet said in a hoarse whisper.

"Control 225 start EMS my location, corner of Heriot and Petty." He took a step closer, "What are you sorry for, Joseph?"

"I tried to do good when I got out. Tried to be...better," he said, his voice trailing off.

"Joseph?" Coburn asked quietly.

"But I couldn't get it, couldn't even get started. Then they killed that little girl. I saw her drop, saw them drive off."

There was only one incident in recent memory that could fit that description, "You saw Chevante Williams murdered?"

Broadstreet nodded weakly.

"Who did you see do it?"

"All of 'em," he responded, choking through a gob of blood and mucus. "All of 'em, all the dealers, the pimps, the crack heads, me, all of them, all those people just like me."

"Not like you Joseph, not anymore."

Broadstreet's eyes opened a little more and he looked at Coburn clearly. His lips curled on one side in a soft grin. "You know what I did. That's why you here. I'm worse than all of 'em."

"You killed all those men?" He needed him to say it.

A weak nod. "Them an' a few more. Figured that was the only thing I had left to offer." His head rolled to the east. "Now I just want to see the sunrise, just one more time."

Coburn watched the mass murderer slowly dying in front of him. He wasn't sure what to think of the man. He remembered the night they stopped him on the street, the humble deference he had shown. The man had remembered him, and had thanked him for effectively ruining his life.

"You did what you thought was right," was all Coburn could say.

In the distance, sirens wailed and he wondered if the ambulance would arrive in time. He wondered if it should.

Broadstreet's right hand slowly started to rise from a pool of blood covering his lap.

Frytel jumped, and instinctively unsnapped his holster.

Coburn held up a steadying hand to the young patrolman, then knelt next to the stricken man. He could see in the growing light that he held a picture. Clearly him in another life, a woman and a child, a little girl.

"Yours?" Coburn asked.

A barely perceptible nod.

"Can you get that to them, to my family?" he whispered, "Tell them I'm sorry."

"I will, Joseph."

"Thank you, Officer," Broadstreet's head sagged and his body went limp.

A second later a golden sliver of morning sunlight danced between the buildings and illuminated his tattered and broken form.

The sirens grew closer.

Chapter Fifty-Nine

Viejo and Wilke sat silently in the undercover car. They studied the target building, watched the windows for movement, and tried to peer through open blinds. The building and its surroundings were quiet until an old pickup truck pulled out of an alley between the laundry and the adjoining apartment building. A middle-aged black man was at the wheel. Squinting in the morning sun, the man looked their way before pulling into the steadily increasing morning traffic.

"That's him," said Wilke, holding Harold Washington's driver's license photo in his hand. The photo was dated but the main features were plain enough. He checked his watch—it was barely after seven. He marked the time on his surveillance log.

"Hard to believe," said Viejo, firing up the Toyota.

"What?"

"This dude is supposed to be the drug kingpin of Charleston, right? According to Blanding, he's the guy. Been running the streets for years and no one has ever gotten a whiff of him, not even Banks or any of the old guys." Viejo pulled into traffic. The slow morning traffic on SC Highway Seven was tough to gauge when following someone discreetly. The instinct was to lane hop, get the hell out of the snarl as soon as possible so you could can get to where you're going. But when you're trying to follow someone without being noticed, you have to shut that instinct down. If you start to lane hop or if you get antsy thinking your target is getting away and you try to close on him, the current of motorists might put you right on top of him, or drag you right past him in the adjoining lane. On the other hand, if you try to keep it slow and maintain your distance, the rest of the herd trying to beat the congestion may start laying on their horns, bringing attention you are trying to avoid.

Viejo stayed in the same lane as Washington. They had four cars between them and their target.

"The guy's smart," Wilke said. "He doesn't flash his money or drive a lime green LTD on diamond-encrusted rims or some shit." Wilke keyed the radio he had under his shirt, "Target one is on the move heading west on Seven."

"614 copy, following from Seven and Trinity," responded the arrest team consisting of four SWAT officers piled into another unmarked. They were about a half mile behind them in the heavy traffic.

Wilke keyed the microphone again. "849 status."

Fenner and another detective from personal crimes were on the other side of the city travelling the side streets on the East Side from suspected stash house to suspected stash house trying to locate Treat Moncrief. She was approaching her third of five potential target locations.

"No joy as of yet, have not located target two," she said in an impatient huff.

Washington drove casually with the quickly thickening traffic. His old beater of a truck was relatively easy to keep track of. The rusted vehicle sat taller and wider than most of the small more efficient models that coursed through the city arteries. He made his way north, away from the Charleston Peninsula. At the intersection of Highway Seven and Highway Sixty-one he shifted to the left-hand lane and turned at the intersection. Viejo had to chop his way through traffic, cutting off a small Volkswagen Beetle piloted by a blonde female who Viejo could see swearing at him through his rearview mirror.

"She's not happy with you," Wilke observed. He clicked his microphone, "Target One turning left on Sixty-one," he said.

"Copy," was the reply.

"So fraud, huh?" Wilke asked.

"Yeah," responded Viejo.

Wilke was quiet as he watched the target.

"What?"

Wilke shook his head, "Nothin."

"You don't think I can work a fraud case," Viejo stated.

"I didn't say that."

"That's what you were thinking."

"No, it's not."

"What then?" Viejo asked as he took mental note of the intersections as they passed. Ahead, the old pick-up slid through a yellow light, "Shit," he breathed.

"I got him," said Wilke, "We're not losing this asshole because of a freaking red light," he said, "We gotta wrap this case up, we're spending way too much time at headquarters."

Viejo looked at him sideways.

It took a minute for Wilke to notice his partner. The truck was pulling away. Luckily the traffic congestion was keeping him in eyeshot. After a moment he noticed Viejo. "Wha—oh, sorry."

The department's Economic Crimes Unit was located right in between the Patrol and Administrative Bureaus.

"Not funny." The light went green and the herd of edgy commuters sped forward. "It was a little funny. Three lights up on the left."

"Ya know?"

"Come on, man. I know you can do a fraud case, and it'll be good for the kid to have you home more."

"But?"

Wilke shrugged, "I just wonder what the Econ L-T is gonna do when his use of force stats skyrocket." Wilke kept his eye on the target. "I can't remember the last time you slapped chains on somebody that wasn't bleeding."

Viejo shook his head,

"Something to think about, is all."

"You're a dick," Viejo told him.

Chapter Sixty

Eric Thompson realized he had become an early riser as he unlocked the rear door to the Charleston City Crime Laboratory. When he was on dayshift, like today, he noticed he was consistently about a half hour early for his shift, unlike the rest of the unit. He locked the mechanism in the door open so that the rest of the crime scene staff could get in, and wandered to his office where he dropped his backpack on an extra chair he'd snagged from one of the storerooms, then made an about face. Coffee was the priority. He made his way to a break room where he loaded and started coffee percolating. He wondered why he had drifted into the lane of being first into the office. It wasn't like he had given up being a night owl in order to make it into work early. Despite himself, he could not make it to bed before midnight on any given day. His sleep was short before he was back at it again. Yet over and over, here he was.

The building was silent, which at the same time was both peaceful and a little unsettling. The metal building was not much more than a warehouse carved into a cluster of small offices, a conference room, a cavernous garage bay, and a pair of laboratories. The aluminum shell of the place had a tendency to pop and groan when the wind blew or the sun beat down on it. He had been at Crime Scene for a little less than eight months now and he still wasn't used to the strange sounds the building made when it was quiet and no one else was around. He piled coffee grounds into the basket and wandered out of the break room to let the machine do its work.

Leisurely, he wandered out of the break room and headed further into the building. In the main entryway, he turned on the lights and continued passed the conference room to the first lab. Without heading in, he reached inside and flipped the light switch, inducing a low thrumming as the overhead halogen lights began to warm up. At the next lab, he wandered inside flicking on the lights as he passed the threshold. The bulbs likewise had to heat up. Under the dim lighting he went to a large drying cabinet and checked to see if the ventilation had stayed on overnight, keeping a steady current of air flowing over a pair of muddy jeans and a grimy t-shirt that had been collected the day before on a missing person's case.

The clothes supposedly belonged to an eighteen- year old tweaker who was reported missing three days ago by a forlorn and exhausted family. Thompson had accompanied the detectives to the family home in one of the more upscale developments on John's Island. The kid's mother had given them the report and a statement along with a description of her son who had run out on a last-ditch intervention. Sitting at their spotless and smooth oak dining room table, surrounded by ornate décor, he had noticed the woman's defeat. How strange it had been to see that side of the societal gutter that was the drug world. A mother with no hope, someone who was sliding away from the boy she'd given birth to. Tired of the endless fall of an addict, a woman with no more energy to fight the monster that her son had become. In his old life, Thompson would have been wondering if the kid would have any information he could use, if there was enough left in his fried brain to keep him on point long enough for a debrief and a couple of buys. Now he was almost sad; he wondered if he felt for the tweaker or the family left in its wake. The despairing woman had given them a description of what he was last wearing and an idea of where he was known to hide out when he went on a bender.

The area detectives searched based on the mother's description was well known. A series of dirt roads wound through a copse of trees and swamp on the land of a John's Island development that was never built. The corporation that owned the land had gone belly up during the real estate collapse of 2008, leaving behind an area just enough out of the way to provide an excellent infrastructure for all manner of low life. Piles of garbage could be found in random places along the rough dirt cut-outs, soiled and decaying mattresses here and there, a homeless camp in one spot. The place was also a good bet for finding stolen cars every now and then. Drug paraphernalia littered the ground. There was blackened aluminum foil, broken car antennas, shreds of plastic baggies. This was a place people came to disappear, whether from the rest of society or from themselves. He could imagine the kid laying on one of the stinking, rotting mattresses while chasing the dragon with whatever mind-altering substance he were able to steal enough to afford.

Detectives searched the area with a K-9, using a sample of the tweaker's clothes they were provided by his mother. The search lasted hours until the dog alerted to a tattered t-shirt and a shoe that vaguely resembled the clothing description offered by the family. The items were caked in thick black mud and sand, almost undistinguishable from any other trash scattered around the area. Thompson had collected the soaked and stained articles and left them in the drying hood overnight.

He looked at the items now, trying to see if he could make out any stains or damage that would tell him anything. A rip, or a hole left over from a gunshot, maybe some blood. Despite the horrible story the clothing might tell about their missing drug addict, Thompson couldn't help but be a little excited at the same time. He was going to add to his arsenal of forensic weapons today when his supervisor got in. The unit had just received an infrared- enabled camera which could image everything from gunshot residue to blood, even under the layers of stains and permeating junk distorting the clothing.

A ring sounded over the intercom, interrupting Thompson's examination of the clothing. Someone was at the front door. Hustling back to the front of the building, Thompson noticed a uniformed FedEx courier holding a box. It seemed a little early for a drop off but Thompson didn't give it a second thought. A lot of the evidence they shipped back and forth between the State lab in Columbia was sent priority. If it was something sensitive, FedEx might want to get it off their hands sooner than later.

Thompson swiped his card against the reader and opened the door. The courier was average build; strong muscles snaked around his arms. White, with stark blue eyes under close cropped blonde hair. The man handed him the package, a cardboard box wrapped almost entirely in clear packing tape. The label read State Law Enforcement Division Crime Laboratory and was addressed to him. Without a word, the man pulled out a scanner. He deftly scanned the bar code on the package, then held the scanner for him to sign. Thompson took the small stylus and scribbled "ET" on the pad.

"There you go," Thompson said.

The courier nodded and turned, then he halted in place for the slightest of a second. Coming from the parking lot, wearing jeans and a polo shirt on a weekday morning, came Captain Peter Banks. The courier waited for him to pass before continuing toward his truck. Banks nodded to the man as he came past.

"What's up, Cap?" Thompson asked, "What is it? Casual Friday and no one told me?"

"Not quite," Banks said. "Let's get inside." He looked at the package. "What's this?"

Thompson shrugged. "Just showed, from the crime lab."

"It's not even eight o'clock yet."

"I know, must be priority."

Banks turned from him and reached for the buttons on his polo shirt. "You clock the FedEx guy that just left here?"

"No FedEx guy here." Biannca's voice still made his skin crawl. An unbelievable reminder that his world had been flipped upside down.

"Not even a truck?"

"Nope."

"What's goin' on, Captain?" Thompson asked.

Banks turned back to him and looked at the box in his officer's hands. "Get inside."

They retreated into the building and slipped past the desk, heading for the lab. Thompson led his commander down the still quiet and dimly lit hallway. He was now tiptoeing with the unnerving package in his hand, "I feel like I should be let in on something," he commented.

"You got an isolation chamber?"

"Yea..." Thompson paused when he noticed a stunning brunette wearing tight-fitting jeans and a halter top walking casually toward him, "What the—"

"She's with me," Banks answered.

"What's that?" she asked.

"I was hoping you could tell us."

Banks pressed Thompson to move and they made their way to a chamber near the rear of one of the labs. "It's a vacuum deposition chamber, used to bring out fingerprints using a mix of zinc and gold particles. Best I can do. Is this thing about to blow up or something?"

No one answered him.

"Can he put this down?" Banks asked the brunette.

She shrugged. "Dunno, depends on what it is."

"Not helpful," stated Thompson flatly. "Boss, what the fuck?"

"Shit," said Banks. "Hell with it. Put that thing inside."

As gently and as quickly as he could, Thompson deposited the suddenly, very intimidating cardboard box into the twenty-five thousand dollar chamber. When the box was inside and the chamber sealed, Thompson realized he'd been holding his breath. "Now what?" he asked.

Banks looked to Biannca.

"It's not a bomb," she stated, cocking her hip to the side as she studied the package. "They can't go around blowing cops up. There's too many of you in a confined area. If they are going to take you out, they have to be subtle about it. You feeling anything at the moment?" she asked Thompson clinically.

"Not sure where to start," he responded, "How did you get in here anyway?"

Biannca ignored him.

"Eric, the guys we took down last year?" Banks asked.

"Yeah?"

"They put a contract out on us."

"Us?"

"All of us."

Thompson felt his blood boil and his stomach churn at the same time. He didn't like being threatened, but those people came within a hair's breadth of killing his whole team. An image of Poppy Montague flashed in his mind and the fear was suddenly quelled by a roiling flood of hatred.

"So who's she?"

"One of them?"

"I'm not one of them," Biannca blurted without taking her eyes off the package. "You got a biohazard suit? Full containment suit?" she asked.

Ten minutes later, Biannca stood covered head to toe in white Tyvek. She wore a re-breather mask and her hands were double gloved. Banks and Thompson stood just outside the lab, watching through the glass door.

"What the hell is going on, Captain?" Thompson asked, a real chill to his voice.

Banks leaned against the door jamb with one hand resting on the butt of his gun, "She's the subject who escaped the snipers' nest during the take down last year." he said matter-of-factly.

Thompson took a second look at the woman who was swabbing the outside of the box. She went about her business clinically, as if she were putting together a less than exciting jigsaw puzzle. Though he had been fighting for his life in a hospital bed during the episode where Banks and Viejo had almost died, he knew what happened. They had all dissected and rebuilt that case over and over again trying to figure out what went wrong, how not only she but another subject had escaped. "No way," was all he could say.

"She saved my life last night." Banks nodded to the package. "I grabbed a beer out of the fridge and woke up on the floor this morning. She had the antidote and a suit with her. We're in trouble here, Eric. These people have already taken out Burgess and Max."

"DeGuello's dead?" The words were vile. With everything else, he was trying to process the new information. It made his knees weak, and his guts twist. He suddenly heard Max DeGuello's wiseass laugh in his head, and could see his dead friend swilling a beer while lounging in a deck chair behind Sammy's bar. Thompson was enraged. "How do we get 'em?" he asked.

"Working on it."

Biannca studied a glass specimen tube, one she had taken from a small kit she had brought with her. Banks guessed it was the same one she used when she brought him back from the dead. She waved them inside.

"This isn't the same thing they got you with, big guy," she said to Banks matter-of-factly. "The tape was laced with polonium. You were wearing gloves when he dropped it off?"

"Still wearing them," Thompson said.

"Get rid of them, now," she ordered.

Thompson stripped the gloves off his skin carefully and dropped them in a biohazard can. "What would that have done to me?" he asked.

"Polonium-210 is a radioactive isotope. Basically the radiation would have destroyed you at the cellular level. Eating you from the inside out. Your last month would have been excruciating. That would have started today."

Thompson was silent.

Banks suddenly had the stray thought that he was lucky all they tried to do was give him a heart attack. Things had definitely become surreal over the last twenty- four hours. "Alexander Litvenenko," he said.

"Exactly," she answered.

"Wasn't that the Russian's who killed him?"

Biannca shrugged. "When something works..."

"So the CIA is killing people using Russian methods now. Makes me proud to be an American."

"Oh, it's not CIA actual that is hunting us. Maybe someone on the inside is coordinating. But these are contractors. McKetrick will figure it out eventually, but the South Africans and the Eastern Europeans have been getting the majority of the work lately."

Thompson, listening to the exchange, slouched against the wall. His voice was suddenly quiet. "Is this what they did to Poppy?" he asked.

Biannca cinched her kit closed, "I wasn't in on that. Whatever Davidson used on her was quicker than that."

"Davidson?" asked Banks

Biannca looked him in the eye, "Don't worry about him, he didn't make it."

Down the hall, a door latch clicked and whined as the door from the offices was pulled open. Banks and Thompson jumped and reached instinctively for their firearms. Sergeant Bill Thomas, a fifty-seven year old overweight man with wispy grey hair and a bushy mustache, dropped his Styrofoam coffee cup and froze when he saw the alarmed looks on Banks' and Thompson's faces.

"Bad time?" he asked.

"Gonna need Detective Thompson today, Sarge," Banks said as the three filed past him.

"You're the Captain, Captain," Thomas said, stepping out of their way. As the trio filed past, he noticed the hot brunette ripping off a Tyvek suit as she went. He wondered if they had gotten a new intern he hadn't heard about. She smiled at him as she walked by.

Chapter Sixty-One

Washington wound through the busy streets of West Ashley for another fifteen minutes before bringing the old pickup truck to a halt outside an abandoned mill. The plant was an old textile company that went out of business long ago. The old brick and wrought iron fire escapes that poked from the four sides of the square structure were slowly decaying from neglect. He parked the old pickup around the side in the loading dock. A lock twenty-five years younger than the door it was affixed to stood out in stark contrast to the rust and grime. Washington bought the building years ago through a dummy corporation he had created, as he rose through the ranks of the local illicit drug community. He had realized early on that the men and women around him, his peers in the Charleston underworld, got caught because they flaunted what they had.

High rolling Cadillacs, tailored suits in the ghetto, and flash rolls of ten thousand or more attracted the attention of the police. They stood out from the surrounding ecosystem they preyed upon and as such ended up in prison or worse. Washington would never be a man to deny he was tempted and even had slipped from time to time. Luck was a part of his rise to the apex of that world, as was timing. Though once he found ways of hiding his cash and removing himself from the supply chain, he had thrived while others fell.

No one could distance themselves fully though. He still had to keep his hands in the pot. This building had served as the hub of his enterprise for almost two decades. He was going to be sad to see it go, but then again, he was himself on his way out. All good things…

Washington looked around casually as he exited the truck and walked up the cracked concrete ramp to a rusted steel door. The building was surrounded on two sides by marshland that stretched as far as the intercoastal. John's Island and the bridge leading to the west side of the island stood against a green backdrop of marshland. A little haze of a Lowcountry morning hung near the wetlands. To the west of the building was a neighborhood of old, concrete block ranch houses that bordered a stand of trees and an old industrial park.

Washington noticed the lock on the door was still engaged. If it had not been, he would have immediately fled the scene as was his standing rule since the day he started using the place. He disengaged the lock, pulled open the door, and went inside.

The old brick building looked like a multi-story factory from the outside with its rows of windows and fire escapes attached to the façade, though in actuality the building was little more than a shell of what it once was. On the ground floor, a couple of sheetrock walls that were once administrative offices were still intact, and an assortment of heavy equipment forgotten by time and left behind by technology sat collecting dust and rusting into oblivion. The remainders of what once were five floors of production were now barely more than scaffolding supporting the frame of the building. Metal walkways stood for no other reason than to offer the ability to inspect the outer walls for structural integrity that had not been done since he surreptitiously bought the property years ago.

The building was silent. Washington stood in the shadows for a long moment to allow his eyes to adjust from the morning sun of the outside world to the gloom of the dead building.

Once he could see clearly, he called out, "Pell, where you at, man?"

Washington started moving toward his powerful collection of weapons that were stashed in a subfloor hovel he'd dug out in one of the offices toward the rear of the building. Part of him wondered if Moncrief would actually show and meet him head on. The boy was vicious, but Washington knew the kid feared him. There was no answer from Pell.

"Pell!" he called out again, looking toward the scaffolding above.

No answer.

He stopped in the middle of the floor and searched the walkways above. That primal alarm that had served him so well over the years was starting to warm up at the base of his skull. Washington took a couple more steps toward the office. His steps grew faster, in a staccato tempo. He took his eyes off the metal walkways above and turned toward the office. He was reaching for the nine millimeter Beretta in his waistband when he froze in his tracks.

Standing in front of him was a dark-haired female. Her high cheek bones, pearl-hued skin, and piercing blue eyes stood in stark contrast to the gloomy atmosphere of the building. She held an SKS assault rifle and was watching him without a word. He had the Beretta in his, but did not raise his weapon toward her.

"You're in the wrong place, miss," he said. Hearing a movement behind him, he spun to see a man with close cropped blonde hair. He was clothed in khaki cargo pants and a black polo shirt. He also held an AK style rifle. He didn't say a word either.

"What is this? Where's Pell?" Washington demanded, instinctively rubbing the hammer of his pistol with his thumb. The man's eyes drifted up to the walkway above. Washington could see two more men with rifles. At their feet was a body, head hanging from the side of the metal walkway. Washington's breath caught in his throat when he recognized his man.

The man flanking Washington mumbled something, then looked to the woman.

"They're here," he stated. "Targets plus four."

She nodded absently, as if doing calculations in her head. She looked back at Washington. The connection between them was so clinical. He could feel that she was going to kill him. However, he also got the feeling he was a minor part of whatever was about to happen. For the briefest of moments, Washington could see the gleaming crystal waters of Fiji lapping at warm white sand, his little bungalow just off the beach. He sighed, and raised his weapon to the bitch's head.

Chapter Sixty-Two

Viejo circled the building and pulled into the lot between the old textile mill and the highway. Washington's beat up old truck was just visible on the side, parked in the loading dock. The arrest team took up position on the opposite corner of the lot.

"You know, I'm actually really looking forward to talking to this guy," Viejo said, studying the building. He fidgeted, trying to get comfortable in his bulky tactical vest.

Wilke was watching the truck and didn't seem to suffer from the stiff ballistic material digging into his sides and scratching at his neck. "A guy that careful isn't going to say shit to us." He picked up the radio to give Fenner their location but was greeted with only static. They looked at each other.

Viejo looked up at the sky. Barely a cloud cluttered the bright blue above them; the sun was gleaming in the east. "It's a really high ceiling, maybe we're too far from a repeater," he said.

"We even still in the city?" Wilke asked, looking around for landmarks.

"I think so?" said Viejo, "West Side is not my thing."

"Mine either." Wilke motioned to the arrest team and put his finger to his ear and tapped it.

The driver, a corporal from the SWAT unit, stuck a black gloved hand from his window with a thumbs down.

"Shit," said Wilke. It was one thing to lack equipment in the field. Most police departments made do with old or out of date cars, computers, etc. But when your communications went out, that gave any cop chills.

"Think this is his stash house?" Viejo wondered.

Wilke was about to respond when several shots rang out. They all seemed to be coming from the building. The SWAT officers were out of their car and on the charge.

"Damnit!"

"At least we don't need a warrant anymore," Wilke observed as he charged his M-4 carbine. Viejo did the same.

***

One was standing over the body of Harold Washington when 3-1, manning one of two identical Range Rovers secluded across the highway from the textile mill, advised that the targets were incoming.

She looked to the lead mercenary.

"Start the clock." As part of her research for the operation, One had studied the response times of both Charleston City and County law enforcement agencies. Given their relatively remote location within the city, she had determined the operation had four minutes before the police would be on their way. She did not like the tight time frame, however if they were going to create the image that the ambush was an effect of local radicals, no one in her element could be caught. She took up a position behind one of the large abandoned machines scattered about the production floor, and watched the rear door as the perimeter team advised her of the targets.

***

Viejo and Wilke met Corporal Andrew Jane, a hulking, bald-headed black male as they lined up on opposite sides of the loading dock door.

"You got any comms?" he asked the two detectives.

Viejo shook his head.

"We're pretty far out here," whispered the man behind Jane. Billy Conway, a blonde haired boyish detective from the upstate. The two final members of the arrest team, a black male named Gregory and a white female named Kim, kept their eyes on the windows and surrounding area. All four of the SWAT team members carried their duty pistols and M-4's.

Viejo was on point in front of Wilke. He nodded to Jane. "Cross, on me."

Jane simply held four fingers up along the stock of his M-4.

Viejo ducked under the muzzle of Jane's weapon and slid inside the door. As he moved past, Jane seamlessly crossed the threshold covering the opposite side of the wide and open floor. Conway and Wilke likewise zippered their way through the door and the others followed.

Viejo and Jane covered their respective walls and corners around the perimeter of the dusty industrial floor while the rest of the arrest team covered complimenting areas of fire. The last officer through the door, Kim, covered their rear with her M-4.

Wilke's eyes danced from potential danger zone to potential danger zone so fast that he soon realized the scattered remains of commerce that used to go on at the location created a buffet of potential ambush points.

"City Police!" Viejo shouted. "Come out with your hands up!"

Wilke turned to cover the interior of the building as Viejo ducked his head inside an abandoned administrative office. After a moment he heard, "Clear!"

As Wilke's eyes swept the area, he saw Jane and his four officers on the opposite side of the expanse doing the same, hopping from one open door to the next. He also couldn't help but notice the graffiti smearing the bare concrete and brick walls of the old building. He saw various anti-police quotes: "Wings on Pigs," "Fry like bacon," and the like. *Enemy territory*, he told himself.

He was returning his scan to Viejo when he noticed the limp form of a man adjacent to a blocky, rusted stack of forgotten mill equipment.

"Body," he said in a low voice. "Your three o'clock."

Viejo looked over the rest of the unexplored perimeter and did not see any further offices. There was cover toward the interior of the building in the form of several workbenches and abandoned machinery. "Go," he said.

Wilke cut from a shadow and skittered to a large work bench adjacent to the body. He took a knee and looked for targets. He noticed Conway who nodded in his direction. Out of the corner of his eye, he saw Viejo move past and kneel over the quiet form lying on its face.

***

Viejo slipped his rifle around his back as he knelt next to the fallen black man. It was Harold Washington— he could tell by the man's dress. The jeans and plain shirt that had so impressed them in their normalcy when they first observed the trafficker. Blood pooled under the man's shoulder.

"Police," he whispered. "Sir, you okay?" Viejo rolled him over and almost cried out when the man gasped. His lips were blue and his eyes bulged as he fought to breathe through a frothy mixture of blood and spittle that burbled out of his mouth.

The two locked eyes for a brief moment. Viejo could barely hear the words as Washington coughed, "Ambush."

The officer's breath caught in his throat. Then he noticed the two sets of dusty footprints flanking the fallen man. He was about to call out when all hell broke loose.

***

The concussion of automatic weapons fire battered his ears. He felt it in his teeth. Rounds seemed to come from everywhere at once. Over Viejo's shoulder, Wilke saw muzzle flashes. Viejo fell backwards, away from Washington, and scrambled for cover. Wilke turned his weapon on the flashes from a darkened corner. Six rounds in quick succession were fired at the amorphous figure behind the opposing muzzle flash. He was greeted by returning fire not only from his intended target but he found himself suddenly engulfed in a swarm of snapping, banging hornets as someone opened up on his position from behind him.

He moved. Firing on the known position, he charged for where he last saw Viejo. He halved the remainder of his thirty-round magazine at the shooter directly in front of him. He thought he saw his opponent stumble before the enemy weapon went silent. Finding Viejo crouched beneath a massive tool box and firing to his rear, he banged into the tool box and dropped to a knee.

"What the fuck!" he yelled.

Viejo kept firing while Wilke did a tactical reload, removing the magazine that still held a number of rounds for a full thirty round magazine. When he didn't respond and Wilke no longer had a target forward, he looked at his friend. Viejo's jeans were coated in a growing blood stain spreading from about a hand's width above the knee.

"No, shit!" He slid toward the wound when Viejo yelled, "Get down!" Wilke dove to his right as

Viejo's muzzle swung just over his head. The shattering sound of 5.56 rounds blazing right over his skull was paralyzing. Before Wilke could move, a massive form bounced off his back. Instinctively he rolled and battered the body with elbows until he could get away. Getting his weapon back up, he found himself looking into the remaining good eye of a stranger with a shaved head, covered in body armor. The image did not compute in his overloaded nervous system so he put it away and moved to Viejo. Rounds still crackled around them and he heard yelling from his one o'clock position. *Jane and the others?* Blood was now spreading to cover the majority of Viejo's thigh. That was something he had to deal with.

"This is gonna suck, pal," he said and Viejo cringed as he continued to pop off rounds as bullets pinged and whacked above their heads. Wilke ripped a tourniquet from a Velcro release on the shoulder of his vest and shook it out. Viejo ground his teeth and quieted a scream as Wilke moved the nylon band over his boot and up his leg. When he passed over the wound, Viejo grimaced and hissed in pain, but gritted his teeth and kept firing. Wilke almost had it when out of the corner of his eye he saw movement. His hand moved like lightning, freeing his Glock from its thigh holster. As he raised the weapon, he saw his target collapse to a knee. He was white, with short cropped black hair, and had a goatee. His eyes were wide as he presented himself. Wilke shot him twice in the chest and once in the throat before the man fell.

Moving back to the tourniquet, he cranked on a plastic dowel to cinch down on a nylon band. He unceremoniously increased pressure on Viejo's thigh until blood no longer flowed freely from the wound. His partner gasped for air as Wilke secured the pressure rod in a Velcro strap and gathered his rifle.

"You ok?"

Viejo just shook his head in the affirmative though he was unable to speak through the pain.

Wilke thought he should say something but there were too many people trying to get at them. Bullets sang overhead beating on their meager barricade, shards of metal and wood flying.

***

One stood just inside one of the administrative offices watching the mercenaries flank her targets. There were three gunmen; she forgot their call signs and for the most part, identifiers did not matter. She knew at least one had fallen as a result of the four other officers that had entered the kill zone. The four were disciplined and worked as a unit; however, her mercenaries held them at a disadvantage. Two of her men had the officers pinned down in a room on the far side of the engagement. One checked the lighted dial of her watch: fifty-two seconds since the ambush was initiated.

"Three minutes," she advised 2-2. Despite the distaste men like the mercenaries caused her, she did know this one's name. They had been assigned operations together in the past which was one of the reasons he was standing next to her now. They understood each other. The man cared only for money, and had a taste for blood. He could be truly cruel given the proper contract stipulations. That was why she both despised him and respected his results.

2-2 was watching three of his men move in on the two targets through a scope affixed to his mission-specified AK-47. He responded by giving her a thumbs up.

"The casualties need to be cleared when we exfil," she reminded him.

Another thumbs up.

"One minute thirty seconds," she said as she fought the nerves rattling her insides. This mission could not fail.

***

Banks, Biannca, and Thompson, who was trailing the other two and still trying to wrap his head around what was happening, were in the parking lot of the forensics lab. Banks had his phone to his ear, trying to get ahold of Wilke or Viejo when an alert tone sounded from the radio on Thompson's hip. Three stark beeps that made every cop's heart race. It meant there was a hot call coming, or someone, one of their own, was in trouble. Thompson pulled the radio from the holster on his belt and turned up the volume.

The tones stopped after the third shrill beep and veteran dispatcher Margaret Kennedy's voice came over the air, "All units, signal 55, shots fired in the vicinity of 17 and Dorridge. Multiple calls and report from shot spotter. All available units Westside respond."

Banks and Thompson were moving for their cars.

"Don't fuck around Eric, these guys are bad," Banks said, dropping into the driver's seat of his city issue Impala.

Thompson only nodded his head as he heaved himself into his black and white Chevy Tahoe. He looked around for a moment as the engine came to life. Part of him couldn't believe he was in it again, that some faceless group of assholes wanted to kill him and his, for what? Thompson had no idea, and he couldn't wait to ask them. In a cloud of dust and smoke, he tore out of the parking lot on the heels of Bank's unmarked Impala. Both had their lights and sirens flashing.

***

Wilke had two shooters flanking him. He raged as every second it seemed they closed on him, their fire growing more and more accurate and there was nothing he could do. Every time he tried to fire back, a flurry of popping and cracking rounds impacted all around him. The heavy bench they used for cover was crumbling under the unceasing attack. In the back of Wilke's mind, the detective was still at work despite the chaos and fear engulfing the world around him. There was no way these guys were just some rival gang. These guys were crisp and methodical in a way that made Wilke want to run away screaming. They were closing on them and they were helpless to do anything about it.

Wilke poked his head up and loosed a burst of rapid fire with his rifle. Aiming wildly, he hoped if nothing else his rounds would at least slow them down. He could see the two men slipping and sliding from position to position while one covered the other. He jumped and rolled against the bench as a round furrowed his shoulder, missing his face by an inch. He pressed himself against the barrier, trying to flatten himself. Another round creased his forearm as he reached to staunch the blood flowing from his shoulder.

"Fuck!" he yelled. The realization that neither he nor Viejo were going to make it out of this was fighting to overwhelm him. He fired blindly at the men coming for him, and looked to Viejo.

His partner sat in the position Wilke had left him in. He seemed to have a good nook in between the bench and a large textile machine where the rounds were unable to get him. His skin was pale and graying, but he continued to fight.

Wilke could hear their boots tramping the concrete now. They were getting close. The sound all the more enraged him. He switched out for his last magazine and leapt to his feet. If he was going out, he was taking both these fuckers with him.

The sudden move must have surprised the two men. Wilke locked eyes with one no more than seven or ten feet away. The man was looking at the ground when suddenly the guy looked up at him. Wilke fired as rounds from the second man blistered the air around him. The shooter in his sight picture caught two rounds in the abdomen and Wilke saw a chunk of flesh fly from the side of the man's head.

Then Wilke went down.

Whether fire from the man he'd just stopped or from the shooter on his flank, a massive impact caught Wilke in the chest, dropping him to the floor. He couldn't breathe, he tasted copper and dust. Panic ate at the fringes of his rational mind. He freed his hand gun from his thigh rig. Eyes blurry with tears from dust and smoke, he wasn't sure where he had fallen and scrambled for cover until he banged up against an I-beam. He held the weapon up, trying to focus on the front sight through a wash of dull color and streaks of white. Then he realized he was breathing, though it hurt like shit. He was able to hold the gun steady with one hand while he slipped a gloved hand under his vest. There was no blood when he removed his hand. The data should have brought him joy or at the least a relief but Wilke felt nothing. He understood nothing except there was another target. Weapons fire sounded from what seemed to be everywhere but there was no target for him to shoot at. He prepared to move when he caught movement over his front sight. His right index finger started to squeeze. When he focused on his target, he noted CPD issue body armor and a gloved hand pushing air toward the floor. It was Kim peeking out from behind a workbench. What was she trying to tell him?

Chapter Sixty-Three

When the shooting started, Jane and his team engaged just like they had trained for. It was a bit shocking to the police corporal how quickly he had taken to trying to kill another human being. He had never been in a firefight in his decade-plus career, but he squeezed the trigger and moved forward toward the muzzle flashes. Behind him he could hear Conway and Kim doing the same—he even felt the concussion from his rifle as Conway fired behind him. Three, four, five shots and three steps forward before a string of rounds pinged off the concrete wall beside him and he had to take cover. He ducked behind a support strut from a textile machine and snapped off another two rounds as Conway bounded past him to the doorway of what used to be an office. Jane stole a second to check on him and looked up just in time to see him flailing, falling backward into the office.

"Shit."

He and Kim fired. Jane bounded to the office where Conway disappeared, while Kim took up his prior position to give the two men cover. He entered the room and dropped to his knees as rounds sizzled the air over his head. Conway lay coughing on the floor. His hand dug under his vest in a panic while he rolled over a shattered pile of wood planks. Jane was over top of him searching for wounds when he saw something under Conway's left shoulder. Jane shoved his man aside to see that Conway had fallen on top of a hideaway in the floor. He tossed some of the old mildewed and rotten wood aside and smiled, momentarily oblivious to the chaos around him. He broke from his fog when he heard Conway over his shoulder.

"Is that thing real?"

Jane grabbed the heavy gun and the box sitting next to it and retreated to a corner of the office while Conway and Kim covered him.

"I see four, and I think another may be hiding across behind some of the equipment on the other side of the floor. They've got Wilke and Viejo pinned down. You know how to use that thing?" he yelled.

Jane broke open the box of linked ammunition and tried to remember how to load the weapon. "I shot one at FLETC once during the SWAT Operators course," he responded.

"Great," said Conway. A void of confidence was apparent in his response.

***

Wilke's eardrums split and his teeth rattled as the pervasive pops of semi-automatic rifle fire was suddenly drowned out by a massive, uncompromising roar of automatic weapons fire. A shower of splintering metal and wood covered him as Jane fired across the production floor in an unceasing rage of bullets from an M-249 Squad Automatic Weapon. Wilke tried to cover himself as the world around him ripped and came apart under the concussion and violence spreading from Jane's hand.

***

From her place of command inside the doorway of one abandoned office suite, One was watching time click down on an operation that had taken far longer to accomplish than she liked. A back channel in her mind went through a list of variables she had failed to anticipate, namely that her primary targets had put up more of a fight than she had expected. The mercenaries were moving on them and she gauged that they would finish the kill soon. However, things were messier than she had planned for. It was the location, she thought. Too many heavy pieces of equipment for the targets to hide behind.

"Twenty seconds." No sooner had she made the announcement into the microphone on her lapel then the entire production floor lit up in a madness of automatic weapons fire. She looked toward the familiar, yet grossly out of place sound of the weapons platform to see tracer rounds and heavy, full metal jacketed bullets tear through one of the mercenaries. With a microsecond to spare, she dove from the door frame to cower on the dusty floor as a wash of destruction tore apart her office. Immediately she knew the mission was a failure.

"Withdraw!" she yelled into the microphone, barely able to hear herself over the hellish bark of the automatic weapon.

Chapter Sixty-Four

Banks dove between vehicles on the crowded artery that fed the Charleston metro area. All around him, commuters sat, pissed off, sipping coffee, ignoring their carpool-mates, or doing their make-up at thirty miles an hour, all oblivious to the fleet of police cars converging on an area right on the limits of the city's jurisdiction. Biannca braced herself with one hand on the door frame and one on the dashboard. Tires squealed as the police vehicle fishtailed around a grey minivan that seemed paralyzed by the police cars zooming around it. The radio blared updates as units from downtown and the West Ashley area called that they were in route. From the forensics lab the location where the call had gone out was almost five miles. Time seemed like an anchor slowing him down, as Banks willed the car to go faster through crowded traffic that seemed to clog the pavement at every turn. Dispatcher Kennedy reported more calls coming in from around the area. Some of the updated locations she put out included a boat storage company, the marsh, and a small trailer park as citizens called in with various guesses as to where the sounds they heard originated.

"This is kinda fun," Biannca said from the passenger seat as Banks dodged a tangle of sedans. They were a little less than a mile out from the scene.

Banks didn't acknowledge her. He thought about the fact that she was accompanying him to a possible gunfight and she, to his knowledge, was unarmed. He thought about telling her about the backup gun he kept in the glove compartment, but couldn't bring himself to offer it up. The woman sitting next to him was a psychopath, regardless of what some suit said, or the fact that she had saved his life. That girl was bent, and the sooner she was behind bars the better. Giving her a gun would do nothing to help that eventuality.

Banks tried his phone one more time as they closed on the location. He thumbed Viejo's number and swore. To his amazement and relief, there was an answer.

Chapter Sixty-Five

Wilke poked his head up through the dust and detritus that covered his head and shoulders. He immediately saw Jane and Conway with the monster assault rifle, moving toward the exit from the production floor. Wilke scrambled to his feet to give chase but fell back to his knees when he noticed Viejo lying on his side next to him. His breath caught in his throat as he rolled his still friend over.

Viejo was gripping the tourniquet dowel in his left hand and gritting his teeth. "Don't let those fuckers get away."

Wilke nodded and Viejo managed to grin through his pain. Then Viejo's phone vibrated in its pouch on his vest. Before his friend could, Wilke grabbed it. He saw Banks' name on the screen, and took off running.

"Hey!" called Viejo.

"17 and Bee's Ferry. We were ambushed. Viejo's down, GSW to the leg. Whoever they were. They killed Washington and they were good."

***

Banks shook his head under the sudden flood of information as Wilke filled his ear, details rolling like a thunderstorm through the speaker.

"Ben, Ben! I copy!" Banks yelled, trying to calm him down.

"In pursuit!" was Wilke's response.

"Negative!" Banks boomed. "Negative, detective," Banks tried to fill his officer in on the details.

***

Wilke had bolted from a side door, phone to his ear, rifle in his right hand, closing on Jane and Conway as they pursued three men and a woman as they fled toward two silver Range Rovers. This was his first good look at them since all hell had broken loose inside. Banks was still talking in his ear. Wilke's senses struggled to parse all the data he was taking in.

Then Banks' voice broke through the stupor. "...them, the same assholes that were with the Tulley's...killed DeGuello...Burgess..."

Wilke stopped dead in his tracks. He didn't even notice a couple of errant rounds zipping past him as one of the men snapped off a couple of shots to cover the rest of the assault team's escape.

Them. The term froze Ben Wilke. *It's them.* He felt like a man stumbling through pitch black darkness only to suddenly feel his way around a corner and discover a sliver of light. *THEM.*

More bullets dug chunks out of the pavement at his feet. Conway and Jane engaged from behind a dumpster. Wilke found himself running for the Range Rovers without a conscious thought. One pulled off in a cloud of smoke while the other, disabled by a torrent of fire from Conway and Jane, stuttered and died before making it to the highway. Wilke gave chase to the fleeing vehicle. Ditching the phone for his rifle, he fired as he ran only to see the SUV escaping him.

Sirens sounded from everywhere. Out of the corner of his eye he saw a marked SUV burst around the corner and come right at him. He had to stop as the Chevy cut off his pursuit. Thompson dashed around the hood. He was saying something but Wilke ignored him. He passed his friend without so much as a word and leaped into the driver's seat.

"Wilke!" Thompson yelled as he jumped into the passenger seat. Wilke slammed on the gas.

He tore out of the parking lot and jumped a curb onto Highway 17. The Range Rover was ahead by almost a quarter mile.

"Wilke, be cool," Thompson pleaded.

At seventy miles an hour, Wilke dive-bombed his way through traffic, "It's them," he said.

"I know," was the response. "Goddamnit, we don't have the gear they do."

"They shot Este."

Thompson grabbed Wilke's remaining magazine from his vest and switched it out with the one in Wilke's rifle. Then Thompson retrieved his own forty-five from his hip, "We need to think this through, Ben," he said.

"They are not getting away," Wilke responded, voice cold. Eyes focused on the road ahead.

Part of Eric Thompson felt like he was on a runaway train. Like everything was out of control, moving too fast. Then he pictured Esteban Viejo laying on the ground bleeding to death. He saw Max

DeGuello's flirting with his nurse. Poppy Montague smiled at him. "Fuck," he breathed. He grabbed the radio microphone from the dash mount and called in the pursuit.

***

Banks and Biannca slid into the parking lot adjoining the dilapidated textile mill on Thompson's heels. Banks saw Wilke going for Thompson's vehicle. He saw the look on his face. *No,* he thought. Then his windshield was stitched by a line of fire from the disabled Range Rover. He and Biannca dove beneath the dash, and the sedan slid to a halt. Banks peeked through the spider web of cracked laminated glass to see Thompson's Chevy Tahoe squealing onto Highway 17, heading south.

"Right there," Biannca said. "Her, we get her."

"Wait, what?" Banks could just see a trio of bodies disappearing through a thicket of trees between the textile property and a rundown collection of mobile homes. Biannca was already gone.

Banks sprang from the car, ignoring the bullets zipping around him. More units were arriving. It sounded like every set of blue lights and sirens for fifty miles were singing at the same time. Jane and Conway were immediately at his side, watching Biannca flee. They were about to follow when Banks called them off.

"No, see to the wounded, secure the scene." He took off after her. "She's with me." He heard the words but couldn't even to believe he said them.

***

"Wilke, I know what you're doin' man, but we need to be smart."

Wilke didn't respond.

"They didn't just kill your girl, they shot me up too, and I'm telling you to lay back!"

He was closing in when the Range Rover came upon heavier traffic. They were outside the crunch of Charleston's urban sprawl, outside their jurisdiction by a couple of miles. The crowd of commuters was thinning, the landscape becoming more rural.

It wasn't that Wilke was ignoring his friend, or that he didn't care what he said. He heard everything Thompson said, and he was right. It was just that the silver Range Rover and her occupants resembled a relief valve of sorts. The moment Banks said the words. The moment he heard of DeGuello and Burgess's deaths. That whoever had laid the trap for them were connected to the conspiracy almost a year ago with Congressman Tulley, it was all over. Those men killed Poppy Montague, the woman he loved, and she died because he was late.

The pathologist had noted an unexplained, massive cerebral disruption had occurred in Poppy's brain before her death. But what actually killed her was asphyxiation. Wilke's rational mind told him over and over, just as the department shrink, and even Viejo at one point told him her death wasn't his fault. Rationally Ben Wilke knew that there was nothing he could do to save her. But a deep, dark voice his soul wondered about those few minutes. He was less than a mile away from where Poppy was held prisoner waiting for the order to execute when she died.

Wilke saw Poppy's vacant stare, the last image he had of her. She was wrapped in plastic and locked in a trunk. He gripped the steering wheel tighter. Thompson was trying to talk to him but it didn't matter.

How long had it taken from the moment the last shooter in that mass of twisted metal and screaming civilians on John's Island was down before he got to the trunk? How many of those precious moments could have been saved if he had just been faster? Faster in the car, faster on the draw, more aggressive in engaging the men who had put her in the trunk in the first place.

Wilke realized the roads were clearing. They crossed a low bridge that passed over a marshland. In his rearview mirror, he could see blue lights sparkle in the distance.

Chapter Sixty-Six

Biannca flashed through the woods in pursuit of a woman she had never in a million years thought she would see again. The hair was different now, but then again so was her own. She was still trying to sell those fake librarian glasses, Biannca thought, even on a tactical Tuesday or whatever day it was. Biannca wasn't even paying attention anymore. The day didn't matter; who she was chasing didn't matter. The fact that they carried smoking AK-47 assault rifles and she was carrying a Walther sub compact did not even register as a problem with the woman known as Biannca. Ahead was the problem. Biannca could not get away from the asshole suits or the asshole cops until the problem was solved.

One of the men that fled with Andrea Van Reimer pivoted and fired. Biannca ducked the move and using a wide, pine needle laden scrub bush for concealment, dropped the guy with a round to the neck without breaking stride. She considered slowing briefly to take the dying man's weapon, but didn't want to lose time on her target.

She wondered briefly what the fallout would be if she just put her former roommate and friend down. The woman had more dirt on Biannca than anybody on the planet, and it went without saying that she deserved to die painfully. Andrea was tough, and she was dangerous, but she wasn't in Biannca's class, never could be. McKetrick might screw her over though if she didn't bring her back still breathing. Bottom line was she had to take care of this lingering problem, and as much as she hated it, she had to bring McKetrick someone to work on.

Biannca stayed off the path Andrea and her cover, who seemed to shuffle more than run, were on. She could see them dodging and turning around trees as they moved behind a set of trailers she thought only a crowd of hillbillies from *Deliverance* could love. Ahead the trees, and her cover, gave way to an open gravel lot and stacks of motor boats and trailers. She was too far from them to stop them before they reached the clearing. Things were suddenly getting a lot harder.

***

Banks was huffing and puffing by the time he reached the body of the dead mercenary. Close cropped hair, well-muscled, wearing a polo shirt and a pair of jeans, a pool of dark blood was settling into the sandy soil. Banks could see the wound to his neck. He paused for a moment over the body, conflicted, as his police instincts told him to preserve evidence while another side of him warned him not to let Biannca slip away. He grabbed the rifle lying next to the dead man and stripped out the magazine. Then he retracted the bolt and launched one unspent casing into the air. Dropping the rifle, he moved on.

***

One, also known to a very select few as Andrea Van Reimer, scanned the area as she dashed through an open chain-link gate into the boat storage facility. She was looking for a vehicle, and ironically, she was surrounded by them. Unfortunately none of them could help her on land. Stacks of speed boats were kept on scaffolding that rose four levels, around fifty feet in the air. A metal building rose over the scaffolding to her right. She made a turn in the maze of racks toward the building.

Behind her she could hear the stomping of boots on gravel as the leader of the team—she didn't know his name, also didn't care—followed her. Andrea could not believe the magnitude of how utterly and completely the operation had failed. There were only two targets of consequence for the failed operation and they had both walked directly and willingly into the ambush. The trigger pullers she had been saddled with had only one job. They had the surprise, every advantage, and still they failed. The mouth breather behind her was getting winded; she could hear him wheezing behind her. A professional solider, a private contractor whose job it was to be ready for any operation at any time was tiring after less than a mile over level ground.

She turned a corner and saw a truck sitting alone near the large bay opening of the metal building. The truck was old, dented, and rusting around the frame, a well-used piece of equipment, but if it would turn over, it would do the job. She had her exit strategy. The man following her stayed on her heels, no doubt seeing his paycheck in their escape, rather than covering her as was his job description.

Andrea decided she no longer needed a shadow. She stopped and ducked behind a rack of boats only fifteen feet from the truck. The mercenary joined her, rifle trained on the rows of boats and the direction they had fled from.

"We get that truck, we get outta here," he wheezed. His back was to her.

She put the muzzle of her pistol to his brain stem and fired. She then casually peeled off the dark wig she had been wearing since the beginning of the operation, and her shirt. She was now a blonde female wearing a tank top and jeans as opposed to a dark-haired operative fleeing a crime scene. She left the accessories soaking in the blood that flowed from the dying mercenary and ran for the truck.

Andrea had only made it around the corner of the rack before she slid to a stop on the loose gravel.

"I was hoping that was a wig," said Biannca, perched on the hood of the truck, legs crossed. "Otherwise you were like a more awkward Zooey Deschanel." Biannca twisted her face in scorn as she hopped from the hood.

Andrea said nothing but smiled.

"I can't believe you took a job on me," Biannca said.

"Like you would have done any different," Andrea responded and charged.

***

Biannca felt the wound in her side protest as she pivoted away from a low kick to the knee. She answered the strike with a downward elbow that was blocked; she then caught a combination jab and upper cut and stumbled away, banging into the hood of the truck. Her vision was blurry but she could see Andrea closing. She twisted off the vehicle in time to evade a front kick that added a new dent to the worn quarter panel.

"How did they get you?" Biannca asked.

"Met my asking price," responded Andrea.

"What are you going to do when they find out you failed them?"

"I haven't failed at anything. In fact, you showing up shaved a great deal off my timeline. I thought I was going to have to find a new set of mouth breathers to sic on you. But here you are."

"Here I am," breathed Biannca with a grin as she attacked. She feigned a haymaker and spun when Andrea took the bait. Going low, she swept the woman's legs and dove her into the ground.

Biannca straddled her old friend. Andrea bucked from side to side trying to dislodge her opponent. However, since they both had received their training at the same place and from the same instructors, Biannca was ready for the move and countered it. She dug her heels up under Andrea's thighs and delivered a straight punch to her diaphragm. Andrea coughed with a whoosh and wheezed before covering her face in her forearms. Biannca giggled as she batted the arms away and showered the assassin with blows to the face and head. Andrea grabbed and pulled at Biannca's hair. She got a handful and wrenched her head back.

Biannca jabbed a thumb—armed with a flawless, sharp, enameled nail—into her eye socket. Andrea barked in terror at the assault, her free hand clawing at Biannca's face and neck. Biannca felt the deep furrows being dug down her neck and arms, and felt the warm juices of her opponent's eye socket begging her to drive deeper. She sighed as she released tension only enough to allow Andrea to raise her head a little. Biannca unleashed a thunderous forearm strike to the bridge of her nose. Andrea's head bounced off the gravel with a sickening knock, like two baseball bats being struck together.

Just as she landed the blow, however, something registered with her senses. Something distant but alarming to the extent the sensation could break through the euphoria of victory in mortal combat. It seared her back and shoulder. Biannca disentangled herself from the recovering Andrea and felt around at the point of the wound. Reaching around her left shoulder with her right hand, she felt the wetness, cringed at the ragged gash and free flowing blood she felt under her shirt. She tried to stand but couldn't get her legs under her. Tried to brace herself on the ground but the world spun around her. She just couldn't get any traction.

She looked at Andrea: the woman's eye was black and swollen, blood trickled from both sides in a steady stream. She smiled a bloody smile, and a six-inch dagger danced in between two fingers.

"What was it?" Biannca asked, fumbling until she could brace herself against the front wheel of the truck.

"You're going to love it, I promise," Andrea responded, trying to rise herself on wobbly limbs.

Biannca coughed up a mouthful of blood and ooze from her damaged insides, and felt like she could sense where the poison was as it raced through her system, "Yeah, well I know something you're gonna love too," she said, grinning through bloody teeth at her one-time friend.

Andrea's head tilted just so, like a fox hearing a mole under a layer of snow.

Biannca tried to think of something funny to say, tried to think of anything, but it was all so hazy. Her world was spinning down into a blurry smog, "Ah, fuck it," was all she managed. She could barely keep her head up, much less look into her killer's eyes.

Andrea's face contorted in a twisted grin and her eyes bloomed as she watched the stricken woman fade away. Biannca was just able to see her dimming features, but could make no sense of it.

Banks belted the woman on the back of the head with the slide of his pistol, and she went limp. He gave Andrea a cursory look before hitting his knees at Biannca's side. The assault made Biannca smile in a sleepy way. She was surprised to see genuine concern on his face. Maybe he couldn't help it, she thought. Cops, the sirens, and driving fast is fun and all, but the unequivocal empathy was a deal breaker for her.

"Back pocket," she whispered.

Banks rolled her over slowly and retrieved a small nylon pouch. It was the one he had seen her using at the crime lab. She sat straight and he put the pouch in her lap.

He applied pressure to Biannca's shoulder, freeing her trembling hands to work the small thin zippered pouch. Her fingers didn't want to respond. It seemed like hours before she was able to get the bag open. Once open, she scanned the half-dozen ampules of varying color liquids. She could barely see at this point, her vision closing in from the periphery. *Won't be long now*, she thought.

"What's the problem?" Banks' harsh question broke through the growing fog.

"I don't know what was on that dagger," she answered calmly.

Banks was silent for a moment. Then he blurted, "Pick one."

"I choose wrong, I might kill myself," she protested.

"You don't choose one, you're dead anyway,"

"Yeah," Biannca felt herself drifting, her vision dark now. The world nothing more than fluid shadows.

"Ah, fuck it," she heard, and winced when something punched her in the neck. Then everything stopped.

＊＊

365 • Where Angels Sing

Banks checked the girl's pulse and found it was slow but steady. Her chest rose slowly. He found himself conflicted over the relief he felt that the mercenary who once threw a pair of live grenades at him was alive.

He left her there and moved with caution to the bleeding woman who moaned unintelligibly. He retrieved his handcuffs from the small of his back and dropped a knee in between the woman's shoulder blades, pinning her to the ground. The harsh move elicited a gasp, but if the woman was anything like Biannca, he would take no chances, no matter how injured she appeared to be. He ratcheted the metal restraints tight on her wrists, binding them behind her back. He was about to roll her over and search when he felt a sting in his calf.

At first, he thought it was an insect bite and he batted at the offending sensation. When his hand knocked a small object from his leg, he spun and rose to his feet.

Biannca was circling him.

"Wha..?" Banks' vision grew bleary.

"Don't worry, it's just a sedative," Biannca said with a wry grin. "You thought I was going to kill you, didn't you?"

His legs went numb and he dropped to a knee. "You bitch." He tried to reach for his gun but he couldn't coordinate his hands.

Biannca unceremoniously yanked her dazed adversary to her feet by the elbow and grabbed a handful of hair. Andrea Van Reimer shifted unsteadily under her control. Banks watched her, swaying himself as Biannca escorted Van Reimer to the passenger side of the pickup. She bounced Van Reimer's head off the door frame before throwing her across the bench seat.

Pinpricks danced across his vision as Banks floundered again for his gun. Biannca seemed to ignore his attempt to arm himself as she rounded the front of the truck and knelt next to him.

"You know what, Pete, I bet me and you could have really had something if things had been different...and you weren't like a hundred years old."

"You wish," Banks whispered as he fell to his side.

"See you next time, sweetie," was the last Peter Banks heard before falling away into a spinning darkness.

Chapter Sixty-Seven

With the highway opening up before them, the chase came down to a matter of horsepower. Wilke didn't know what the Range Rover had under the hood but he could feel the response of the Tahoe's engine as he mashed the gas pedal to the floor, and didn't fill him with confidence. The sides of the road were a mix of marsh, cypress swamps, or farmer's fields which stretched for miles before the highway neared Walterboro.

He was closing, but not by much. The Range Rover came upon a small cluster of cars. The SUV had to take to the median when the oblivious or annoyed drivers did not respond to the flashing lights and horns.

Wilke was within a couple of hundred yards and gaining when Thompson yelled, "Shit!" and lowered his window.

Wilke took his eyes off the road in front of him for a split second, and saw the head and shoulders of a man out the passenger window of the Range Rover. He raised one of the assault rifles and opened fire on a Volkswagen Jetta that failed to yield to the Range Rover. The driver's side window of the Jetta was obliterated. The small car juked to the right, fleeing the assault and sideswiped an old Mercury next to it. The move cost the SUV momentum but left a tangle of smoking cars clogging the road.

Thompson popped off a string of rounds from Wilke's rifle at the Range Rover. The rear window splintered and the left brake light fell from the SUV in red shards. Thompson fired several more times until a puff of white smoke blew from the right rear tire. The rear of the Range Rover wagged like a dog's tail as it lost speed. Thompson returned to his seat.

The Jetta, Mercury, and another sedan sat crumpled together in the right lane of the highway as they flashed past them.

"Motherfuckers," Thompson breathed.

Wilke could see one of the victims pleading for them to stop, then throwing their hands in the air as they passed by. They were within four car lengths now as the driver of the Range Rover tried to keep the vehicle going at speed on only three tires. Wilke appreciated that the driver was still holding it together at over forty miles an hour, but it wasn't going to last long.

The Range Rover was flagging. The men inside had no place to go, no means of escape except for miles of marsh and swamp that would do nothing but make them fair game for the army of bloodhounds that the locals would unleash on them. Wilke knew that sooner or later one side or the other would have to take the initiative.

"I'm taking them out," he said coldly. Thompson braced against the frame of the door and the dashboard.

Wilke tried to mash the accelerator through the floorboard. Though the department did not like pursuits, and almost never let a pursuit even happen, Wilke had been trained in the pit maneuver at the academy. The idea behind it was to nudge the other vehicle just enough to break the target's traction, causing a spin-out. He was taught to match speed and take action slowly, applying force with his vehicle on the quarter panel of the target. Slow and easy, he could hear his instructor say. *Sure,* thought Wilke.

He gave the Tahoe a slight juke to the left as he pulled up alongside the Range Rover. He saw bodies inside leveling weapons, but they were too late. With around three feet of space between the right front of his Tahoe and the left rear of the wiggling Range Rover, he slammed the steering wheel to the right, driving the corner of the Tahoe through the left wheel well of the Range Rover. With no support on the flat right side tire, there was no chance of a counter move. The right rear rim of the Range Rover sparked as it dug through the hot asphalt. Almost immediately, the SUV began to tumble.

Wilke fought the police vehicle for control, feeling it fighting to slide out of control and join the crash. Letting off the gas and easing the shake the impact had caused, he watched as the Range Rover rolled once, twice, three times before catching a utility pole broadside. To Wilke's surprise the pole held, the destroyed SUV almost folding around it. Wilke stopped the Tahoe twenty yards from the crash and the two exited the car.

Wilke stepped from the cover offered by his open door and heard a crack. The passenger behind the driver managed to get a round off before Thompson silenced him with three rounds of the rifle. With a nod, Wilke took the left while Thompson flanked the right. Smoke rose from the engine compartment; fluid and shards of plastic, glass, and metal strewn across the road crunched under their boots. He saw the driver twitch. The man was covered in blood, his right arm and head hanging from the open passenger window. The driver watched him as he approached.

When Wilke got to within a couple of feet of the driver, he lowered his weapon. The man was conscious as he convulsed, blood trickling from his mouth and nose as he tried to breathe. Wilke stepped back, cringing, as fire whooshed and rose from under the hood, and smoke drifted from the dashboard. He looked the man over, the man who had tried to kill him only minutes before, the man who might have been the one to kill Burgess. He may have put a bullet in Max DeGuello, Wilke couldn't be sure, but it didn't matter. The man had blonde close cropped hair, his face was swelling and bloody, one eye sealed shut. Ignoring the flames flashing and snaking around the engine compartment, Wilke approached him. Within a foot, he could see the flayed remains of the man's legs. He had a full sleeve of tattoos covering his horribly twisted arm. Wilke noticed a splinter of bloody white bone protruding from the center of his bicep. The man's body quivered and spasmed.

"Holy shit," Wilke heard Thompson breathe.

He looked toward his former partner.

"That's him, dude tried to poison me."

"Do it," the man choked, his eyes flickering from Wilke to Thompson, to the growing fire that crawled from the dash like the glowing tentacles of an octopus searching for prey.

Wilke studied the man, then the fire and smoke reaching for him. "You killed my friends," he said, his voice and gaze ice cold as he stared down his enemy. The stricken man was watching the flames. Sirens were growing louder in the distance. Wilke leaned inside the compartment, his mouth inches from the bleeding mass that was the man's ear. "You hear that?" he asked. The man gurgled a clipped squeal as the fire took his boots and started climbing his shattered legs. "I think I hear angels singing," Wilke whispered.

The man's eyes were wild with a helpless terror. He looked at him before he screamed. Wilke watched the blonde man's agonized throes until the heat forced him away. He turned his back on the man and found Thompson watching him from a safe distance. His friend had a look on his face Wilke did not remember seeing before. The two didn't say a word to each other as they waited for the fleet of racing police cars narrowing the distance between them.

Chapter Sixty-Eight

Two Months Later

Viejo was still walking with a limp, but the damage to his leg was nothing that would take him out of service. Banks watched him like a hawk as he, Wilke, Thompson, Fenner, Martin, and Chief Vaden walked down the steps from the South Carolina State Courthouse. They cleared the throng of observers and reporters waiting for the District Attorney to comment on the plea entered by Carter Blanding on what was supposed to be the first day of a trial by his peers. Blanding had been charged with Accessory to Commit Murder in the death of Chevante Williams, her mother Heiliea, and Deshaun Cauldwell. Accompanying those charges were a host of fraud and narcotics trafficking charges, and a statutory rape charge once it was proven Shaunte Fields' child was also Carter Blanding's. The minister's involvement in the death of a three-year old girl was all the news had been focused on since his arrest, shortly after the death of Harold Washington and Treat Moncrief, the co-subjects of the investigation. The District Attorney was more than happy when they received the call from Blanding's defense attorney querying him to the possibility of a plea. Carter Blanding agreed to twenty-five years incarceration with a possibility of parole in twelve. In open court, he plead guilty to all counts. This elicited shock from some, disgust and hatred in others who amassed in the humid and hot courtroom.

Banks had watched the proceedings from the rear of the room, Viejo, Wilke, Fuller, and Martin flanking him. As the gavel struck, he looked to his left where his two detectives watched dispassionately. Banks had another reaction. *This is how it ends*, he had told himself. The group watched as the DA addressed the crowd on the steps of the courthouse. Martin was the first to break the silence.

"Fraud. Really, Esteban?"

Viejo shrugged. "Gotta grow up some time, old man."

Banks knew it was only in his own mind. But to see his people, what remained of his people, splitting up to different units felt like a family was breaking up. Though Wilke and Viejo were the only two remaining officers from what was once his narcotics unit, Viejo's move to fraud was the final nail in the coffin of his old unit.

"What about you, kid?" Martin asked Wilke.

Wilke looked at Banks with that wry smile and sneaky way that he had somehow recovered as of late. Wilke's demeanor had lifted after the Washington case wrapped up and Banks knew why. The kid had gotten a chance at payback against the people who, however disconnected, were aligned with the group that had killed Poppy Montague. Revenge had soothed the kid's soul. That fact terrified Peter Banks.

Wilke nodded across Broad Street toward a gleaming black Mercedes Benz S Class. The front door opened, and out of the driver's seat popped a stunning blonde. She wore tight fitting jeans, black stiletto heels, and a gleaming black leather jacket as she cocked a hip onto the hood. She smiled and offered a casual wave that seemed to be directed at Banks in particular. In the frame of the passenger side door stood Charles McKetrick.

"That woman's got balls," Thompson said, recognizing Biannca.

Banks took a deep breath as she smiled at him. The sight of the beautiful woman made his blood pressure skyrocket. He couldn't help but grin, at the same time fighting the urge to laugh out loud and open fire.

Wilke told him what he was going to do over a beer the night before. When he showed Banks what he'd been doing since the Tulley investigation, Banks told him he was out of his mind. That the two very people he was now staring at would not have his back. They would get a man he thought of as a little brother killed. Banks' plea fell on deaf ears. Benjamin Wilke was looking for something he would never find if he stayed in Charleston. Unfortunately, what the kid wanted was revenge—it was eating him up inside. Banks knew he could do nothing but hope the kid found his way home someday. The predatory grin turning up Biannca's lip made the police captain believe that it was a long shot he would ever see Ben Wilke again. He felt like a failure.

"I'm going with them," Wilke said.

Without giving anyone in the group a chance to object, Wilke smiled and crossed the street against traffic. He opened the door and got in behind Biannca. The blonde assassin winked in Banks' direction. The Mercedes sped off.

END

About John Stamp

John Stamp was born and raised in the Fingerlakes region of upstate New York. He is a graduate of Charleston Southern University with a Bachelor's degree in Criminal Justice and he holds a Master's degree in Forensic Science from the University of Florida.

John began his law enforcement career as a Police Officer serving the City of Charleston Police Department, Charleston, South Carolina. While in Charleston he served as a Patrolman, Narcotics Investigator, a member of the Crisis Negotiation Team, and Civil Disturbance Unit.

Following Charleston John went on to serve as a Special Agent of the Federal Bureau of Investigation where he was a member of the Evidence Response Team. Following service with the FBI, John was a Special Agent of the Naval Criminal Investigative Service. There he served as a member of the Major Crimes Response Team and the Contingency Response Field Office where he completed multiple deployments to areas in the Middle East and the Horn of Africa.

John is a member of the International Thriller Writers Association.

He lives in Georgia with his wife, two boys, and one old lazy dogs.

Social Media:

Facebook:
@Johnstampwriter

Twitter:
@Johnstampwriter

Instagram:
@Johnstampwriter

Acknowledgement

I must acknowledge my wife for putting up with the obsession which takes up far too much of the time that should be spent with her and the kids. Thanks to the dogs, Maggie and Tiger for letting me bounce ideas off of them. Their input is always dead on. Also thank you to my select test audience for taking the time and providing the feedback I need to iron out loose ends, you know who you are. Also, big thanks to my Editor Cynthia Ley who is ever ready to clean up the mess I call a manuscript and Melissa Miller for the outstanding cover art. Could not have made this work without any of you. Looking forward to our next adventure.

Acknowledgement also must be made to the men and women of the various law enforcement and military components I have worked with over the years. Though you would do it anyway, thank you for your service. Stay safe and look out for each other.

Finally, but by no means last, I give thanks to God. I give thanks every day for every second I've had and those I still hope to still experience.

Melissa Miller, for taking my raw attempt at a book cover and making it look spectacular.

If you enjoyed this story, check out these other books by John Stamp:

Brother's Keeper

Alex and Charlie were brothers born of blood and violence during the battle of Fallujah. Then they came home and became cops. Charlie couldn't let go the adrenaline rush of the battlefield and it showed on the street. Always looking for a fight, he went dark, crossing the line one too many times until he went so far even Alex couldn't bring him back.

That's what Alex thought anyway until a terse message lead him into a gunfight and a recording Charlie left him in case the worst happened. Turns out Charlie hadn't gone dark, he'd gone deep undercover, infiltrating a massive criminal syndicate, and sacrificing his entire life to do so. The worst has happened, and now Alex has to save the life of a man he's written off. But brothers are brothers, Alex will run the gauntlet through anything and anyone to save the life of his brother. Then he'll kill Charlie himself.

Brother's Keeper details to what length a man will go to save the life of a friend. This fast-paced crime thriller also illustrates the dark, hidden reality that is human trafficking.

Shattered Circle

Jackson Cole is a newly minted homicide detective thrown head first into the grinder when he is ordered to investigate the grisly murder of three women, each adorned with seemingly occult symbols.

The press is stirring up a killer cult frenzy in the media. The mayor, the Chief of Police, and Cole's Captain want results to calm an increasingly fearful public; and Cole's supposed partner is nowhere to be found. It's just another day at the office until a stranger shows up spouting a wild theory: blood magic.

Cole won't even consider it. There is no such thing as magic, no such thing as voodoo; and there are no demons roaming the Charleston Peninsula. There's always a rational explanation for the evil humans commit upon one another.

Then a demon tries to take Cole's head off.
How do you stop a supernatural evil, something ancient and unencumbered by the laws of either physics or man? Especially when all you bring to the fight is a pistol and a pair of handcuffs.

If Jackson Cole wants this case to close he will need to open his mind to a world of the impossible. A world he never knew existed. Then he'll have to survive it.

Spoilers

What happens when a clandestine group of politicians and intelligence operatives run prototype weapons through Lieutenant Peter Bank's jurisdiction? Nothing, they're clandestine, no one knows they exist or what they do...Right?

Correct, right up until one of those weapons turn up at a drug bust, along with a congressman's son who likes to moonlight as criminal elite.

The paperwork on the arrest is still wet when an army of political and local executive pressure comes down on Banks and his narcotics unit like a thousand-year flood. Everyone wants to make the arrest of a prominent politician's son go away, even Bank's own Chief of Police. Nine times out of ten that wouldn't be a problem. Most cops follow orders, most cops have a stake in their careers.

Peter Banks has his pension locked up and has been burned before by political fixer's who seemed to think the various strata of society are not all created, or treated equally under the law. On top of that Banks has a team behind him that would follow him to hell and back if it meant getting the job done. They are the Spoilers.

From an exclusive island off the coast of South Carolina, the mountains in the upstate, to the gutters of Charleston, SC, Banks, and his team react poorly to corruption and will charge through mercenaries, government assassins, and their own hierarchy to see justice done; and they will do it at terrible cost.

Spoilers details what happens when a determined police unit puts service and doing the right thing above themselves. It is a fast paced, intricate, and explosive read that leaves the audience exhausted and begging for more even after the last page is turned.